Code Murder

by

Olive Balla

Code Murder

Cover Art by *Jennifer Greeff*

The Wild Rose Press, Inc.
PO Box 708
Adams Basin, NY 14410-0708
Visit us at www.thewildrosepress.com

Publishing History
First Crimson Rose Edition, 2020
Trade Paperback ISBN 978-1-5092-3387-8
Digital ISBN 978-1-5092-3388-5

Published in the United States of America

Dix jumped through the careening van's open passenger door and landed with an unceremonious thud, her upper torso on the seat, one knee on the floorboard, and the other leg hanging out the door.

…After several nail-biting seconds, she managed to pull herself into the vehicle…

Shots rang out, and the van's rear window shattered.

"We're going to die," Booger wailed.

"Shut up, Booger," Dix and Lil said simultaneously.

Lil floored the pedal. Stones dinged and popped against the undercarriage as the vehicle careened around the corner and onto the highway.

Dix shot a frantic look through the shattered rear window. Silhouetted by light from the warehouse door, a figure ran toward the parked Jeep. The roar of an engine was followed by headlights panning across the vast, empty desert as the Jeep sped toward the highway seconds behind them.

Praise for *CODE MURDER*

"*CODE MURDER* is more than a mystery; tinged with humor, it hustles the reader through high-action suspense, then tosses in a dollop of romance."

~*~

"A thrilling suspense novel that will grab readers' attention and keep them enthralled until the last page."

~*~

"Dix and Lil Ruiz are intriguing protagonists whose fight for survival drives the plot forward and proves they are not to be messed with."

~*~

"As she did in her first two novels, *AN ARM AND A LEG* and *JILLIE*, Olive Balla delivers a taut suspense novel that keeps the reader guessing what's going to happen next from beginning to end."

Dedication

For my exceptional daughters-in-law
and the brilliant mothers of my grandchildren
and great-grands:
Mimi, Angelika, Erin, Heather, Rachel, and Noelle.
You bless my life.

Acknowledgements

Dennis Burns - M.D.:
Professor of Pathology, University of Texas
Southwestern Medical Center
Marlon Clark: Doctor of Veterinary Medicine
Victor L. Havard: Former EMT-P and Navy Corpsman
Virginia Hutson: Beta Reader and Critiquer
Christine Munsey: Criminal Investigator for the state
        of Montana
James O'Donnell: Software Architect
Ally Robertson: Editor for The Wild Rose Press

~

Special thanks to
the Atlantic Pacific Tang Soo Do Federation -
especially Grand Master John St. James,
and Master Tom Witterholt
of Thunderbird Martial Arts
in Albuquerque, New Mexico.

Chapter One

Sixty-year-old Dix Ruiz glared across the breakfast table at her twin sister Lil in the home they shared in Los Lunas, New Mexico. A plastic, black cat-shaped clock on the kitchen wall swung its tail from side to side in sync with its green rhinestone-rimmed eyes.

"How is it possible that we sprang from the same ovum?" Dix said.

"A better question is how have you managed to stay so naïve all these years? You shouldn't be allowed out of the house alone." Lil stuffed a bite of blueberry scone into her mouth. "Who is this house-sitting gig for, anyway?"

"A nice man from my martial arts class." Dix glanced at her wristwatch. "He should be here any minute with the keys."

"Are this *nice man's* intentions honorable?"

Dix rolled her eyes at the same time the doorbell chimed, cutting off her retort. She hurried to the front door.

"Hello, Henry," she said to the distinguished-looking, seventy-ish man standing on the porch. "Got time for a cup of coffee and a blueberry scone?"

"Thanks, but I have to hustle; my flight's in a couple of hours." Henry offered Dix a handful of keys and a garage door opener. "I don't think you'll have any trouble with Lulu; she really took to you yesterday." He turned to go then snapped his fingers and turned back. "By the way, you'll notice a window in the kitchen has been boarded up. Someone broke in last night, but Lulu scared the bejeebers out of him, and he took off empty-handed." He chuckled then added, "I've scheduled someone to fix it next week. See you in a few days."

As Henry headed toward his vehicle, a car parked up the block roared to life and pulled into the street. The vehicle gained speed and bore down on Henry, who had turned toward Dix to wave a final goodbye.

"Henry, look out." Unable to believe what was happening, Dix stepped onto the porch, her hand raised as if to stop the speeding car.

A puzzled look on his face, Henry turned toward the approaching vehicle just as it smashed into him. The force of the blow catapulted him over the car's hood and sent him airborne with his arms and legs flopping like a man-sized rag doll. He landed on the asphalt with a muffled *whump*, then lay still.

The driver of the weaponized vehicle punched the gas. Its tires spinning on the asphalt, the car fishtailed a couple of times then shot up the street, leaving behind the smell of burning rubber.

Dix screamed, then ran after the vehicle until it was out of sight. "ZBD7…ZBD7…" Repeating the portion of the license she had seen, she sprinted back toward the unconscious Henry and squatted next to him.

After checking to make sure his mouth was empty and his airway clear, as she'd learned to do in a CPR training years earlier, Dix clasped one hand on top of the other and placed them on Henry's chest. Ignoring the pain shooting up her thighs from her kneecaps' contact with the hard asphalt, she pushed against the man's ribcage and counted compressions. "One, two, three, four…One, two, three, four."

Lil hurried through the still-open door of the house, stepped off the porch, and strode toward her sister.

"Call an ambulance," Dix yelled.

Lil pulled her phone from a holster attached to her belt and punched the tiny screen. When the dispatch operator came on, she repeated Dix's barked observations.

"It was an old, silver Mercury, either rusty or spattered with mud," Lil said. "The license plate starts with ZBD7, that's Zebra Bravo Delta Seven. The windows were tinted, so my sister couldn't see the driver, but the vehicle headed north on Highway Forty-Seven." Lil listened, then spoke to Dix, "Could you see how many were in the vehicle?"

"No, but the driver never even touched his brakes; this was deliberate." Dix stopped the chest compressions long enough to press her fingers against Henry's carotid artery in search of a pulse. "They'd better hurry."

As she spoke, Henry's eyelids fluttered partially open. "The honeypot," he breathed.

"What?"

"The honey—" The edges of Henry's mouth twitched downward. Within seconds, his struggle to breathe became erratic, then shallow, then stopped.

Lil peered at her sister in an unspoken question.

Dix shook her head but continued performing CPR. Grim-faced, Lil remained on the phone with the dispatch operator.

The muscles in Dix's shoulders and thighs knotted

in rebellion against the unaccustomed exercise. Her kneecaps shot bolts of pain up her legs, and her arms began to tremble.

Within minutes, a firetruck and two Los Lunas police officers on motorcycles screamed onto the scene. The officers did a quick check of the area then radioed other officers specially trained to deal with traffic fatalities.

Passing vehicles slowed as their drivers craned their necks to survey the action. Apparently drawn from their homes by the sirens, neighbors began to gather, pointing and whispering to each other.

"I'll take it from here," a kind-faced fireman said as he took Dix's place beside the fallen man. He glanced toward Dix. "Are you hurt; any injuries we can't see?"

"No, they were after Henry." Dix scooted out of the young man's way.

"Come on." Lil bent over her twin. "Let me help you up."

After a brief struggle, Dix managed to stand. She steadied herself against her sister until her legs stopped wobbling.

The paramedic attached what Dix recognized as a heart monitor to Henry and started an intravenous drip in his arm. Then, even as the fireman continued CPR, the paramedic and emergency medical technician strapped Henry onto a board, lifted him onto a gurney, then pushed the whole thing into the back of the ambulance.

Slowly, the ambulance pulled into the street. The absence of flashing lights or screaming siren announced Henry Taylor had moved beyond the need for speed.

Police officers moved the watchers back to allow the forensic crime scene van access to the area. Countless photographs were taken, and potential witnesses were questioned.

Dix turned toward her sister. "I'm going to stay at Henry's tonight."

"Why?"

"Because he hired me to, that's why."

"Can't his daughter take care of things?"

"She lives in California." Dix spoke slowly and deliberately, as if explaining String Theory to a toddler. "It'll take a day or two for her to get here. Meanwhile, Lulu's going to need to be fed and taken for walks." She squared her shoulders. "Henry paid me to look after his house and pet, and that's what I'll do."

"I still think you would be—"

"It's an act of humanity, Lil." Dix looked at her sister. "Just a small act of humanity."

Across the road, someone wearing a silver-gray designer hoodie and matching sweatpants, apparently a young man, judging by his stride, jogged down the sidewalk. Glancing neither to the left nor to the right, he pounded his arms up and down like sledgehammers with every step, as if driving tent pegs into rocky soil.

"It's awfully warm to be wearing that heavy outfit." Lil squinted at the figure. "I've never seen him before, have you?" She nodded toward the mass of lookie-loos nodding and talking animatedly to one another. "Not so much as a glance to see what all the commotion is about."

"Give it a rest," Dix said. "Not every stranger is a mass murderer."

Lil shot a sympathetic look at her sister then turned

and started toward the house.

Dix fell in line behind her twin, but after a couple of steps glanced over her shoulder.

The jogger had stopped and was looking in their direction. Although the hoodie shrouded the person's face in shadow, Dix got the feeling she was being studied.

Nonchalantly, the jogger turned away, pulled what appeared to be a phone from a pocket in the sweatpants, lifted it to one ear, spoke briefly, then moved on.

Not every stranger was a murderer…

With a determined set to her shoulders, Dix made her way to the house.

Chapter Two

Dix put her toilet articles into the already-stuffed duffel on her bed then zipped it closed. She hefted the bag and turned to her sister who stood in the doorway, arms crossed, a belligerent look on her face.

"You're being unreasonable," Lil said. "We could take the dog to a shelter. You promised to take care of it, not move in with it."

"A man's been murdered in front of our home, a man I knew and liked. It's a big deal."

"I'm not suggesting otherwise. I am, however, suggesting that all those bleeding-heart thoughts swirling around in your head are clouding your judgement. Didn't the man tell you someone broke into his house last night?"

"Nothing was taken."

"That's beside the point." Lil pointed her index finger toward her sister's nose. "He was obviously targeted."

"Not only is that an assumption," Dix said, "it's typical of your jaundiced perspective of humanity."

"*You* were the one who said he was intentionally run down."

"He was, but that's not the point. We humans need one another. You're such a fanatic for statistics; tell your accountant-brain to figure out how long the species would last if everyone ignored someone in distress."

"Distress?" Lil snorted. "Henry Taylor isn't in distress; he's dead."

"But his daughter and his furry friend are still here and they need help."

"As usual, no matter what I say, you're going to get involved."

"Only so far as I feel I must."

"Because?"

"Because, dear sister, life is not a spectator sport." Dix hefted her duffel and headed for the kitchen and its connecting door to the garage. "I'll leave my phone on."

Chapter Three

Henry's house was bathed in bright noonday sunlight when Dix pulled up the drive. Flat-roofed and made of adobe, the house was a perfect example of early twentieth century New Mexico architecture. With its pristine brown stucco exterior randomly inlaid with colorfully patterned tiles, it was a beautiful, sad house that had lost its people.

Dix pressed the garage door control, pulled into the empty garage, then pressed the control again. As the door closed behind her, she retrieved Henry's keys from her purse.

Had he sensed he was in danger when he left his house that morning? Had he intuitively felt the mists of his life beginning to evaporate?

Dix unlocked the door between the garage and utility room but stopped short of opening it immediately. Snuffling snorts coming from under the door announced that Lulu was taking stock of her.

The muscles in Dix's shoulders bunched. She had never owned a dog…had never read about or studied them. Except for her brief introduction to Lulu the day before, she had never even been around any fur-bearing creatures.

She took a deep breath and pushed the door open a couple more inches.

Please, Lord, let that animal remember me.

A mini-horse sized furry beast of unknown pedigree, Lulu shoved her tennis-ball nose against the door's opening. Huge nostrils moved in and out with each snort, while black, unblinking ping-pong-ball eyes fixed on Dix.

"Hello, Lulu. Nice to see you again. You remember me, right?" Dix spoke in her most calming voice, as much for herself as for the dog.

Opening the door just wide enough to squeeze through, Dix slipped in then gently closed it behind her. Careful to make no sudden moves, she bent at the waist and extended her arm toward the dog, her hand held in a loose fist, palm down. "Here's hoping I look friendly and not like a juicy steak or an intruder."

Several heart-stopping seconds dragged by as Lulu sniffed the proffered hand, the huge wet nose cold against Dix's flesh.

The tightness in Dix's solar plexus relaxed when the dog began to wag her tail. The metal tags on the two-inch-wide leather collar clinked with every excited twitch.

Dix bent over the behemoth and stroked her back. "I hope we're going to be friends." She stood and retrieved the leash Henry had left on the kitchen counter beside his written instructions.

The sight of the carefully handwritten notes tugged at Dix's heart. Although she had only known Henry for a few months, he seemed a genuinely nice man—soft-spoken, warm-hearted. Their frequent after-martial-arts conversations had been the highlight of Dix's week.

Why would someone kill a retired software developer? Dix's computer skills were limited to email and online shopping, so she hadn't understood Henry's description of his pre-retirement work. Algorithms, IP address, spoofing, trolling, phishing...the words might as well have been ancient Chaldean.

Maybe Henry was killed by mistake. Or maybe the driver of the Mercury had *made his bones* to get into a gang by committing a random murder—just a matter of Henry being in the wrong place at the wrong time. Or perhaps Henry had unknowingly cut too close in front of the Mercury while driving and had become a road rage statistic.

None of those scenarios, however, resonated with Dix's memory of the events. Road rage was a spur-of-the-moment thing, and the Mercury's driver had obviously been waiting for Henry.

No, there had been something desperate about that hurtling vehicle, as if the murderer didn't dare let Henry live even a few minutes longer. What else could compel someone to commit murder in such a risky and sloppy way—in broad daylight and in front of at least one witness?

At least one witness.

Something cold uncoiled in Dix's gut. She hadn't seen the driver of the murder vehicle well enough to identify him, but the murderer might not know that. Anyone who could kill another human being in such a way wouldn't hesitate to come for her...might even then be making plans—

"Stop it," she said to herself. "You're beginning to sound like Lil."

Her cellphone suddenly rang in the silence, and her heart rate spiked. It would be her sister checking up on her after mentally pulling the same thread of thought Dix had been following.

Dix and Lil had been linked emotionally and psychologically from birth…almost as if they shared a common brain. They regularly finished each other's sentences, pre-emptively answered not-yet-voiced questions, and exhibited an almost telepathic connection, regardless of the miles that separated them. They sometimes even felt each other's physical pain.

When Lil had her tonsils removed at the age of eleven, Dix's throat was sore. When Dix sprained her ankle in their high school physical education class, Lil hobbled around until her sister's ankle healed.

However, although their knee-jerk reactions to life's spitballs were similar, where Dix lived in optimistic hopefulness, Lil's default response was to blow the top off the Armageddon chart.

Dix pulled the phone from the pouch at the side of her purse and slid the pulsing dot to the green *answer* icon. "Hey, Sis."

"Where are you?" Lil's voice rang louder than usual. "You do know to be careful, right? After all, you're the only—"

"I know; I'm the only witness. Sometimes I wish we weren't on the same wavelength."

"Don't open the door to anyone before looking through the peephole," Lil said. "Don't go out alone; check the back seat before getting into your car, better yet, keep it locked; don't—"

Lulu padded toward the front door and stared pointedly over her shoulder at Dix.

"Stop it, Lil. I'll be fine. I have to take this poor animal for a walk; she's been inside all morning."

"Call me when you get back."

Dix broke the connection. She strode to Lulu,

attached the leash to her collar, and headed for the front door.

As Dix reached for the doorknob, her eyes were drawn to dozens of colored stickie notes plastered along the doorjamb—notes she hadn't noticed the day before. Some bore only single words such as *keys* or *glasses*; others were covered in blue or black ink missives.

Lulu tugged on the leash. Dix opened the door, slipped through, locked it behind them, then gave the dog its head.

"You're too young to remember this," she said to the dog's backside, "but in the sixties people didn't have to lock their doors when they left home."

Could animals sense the ending of their human's life? Had the poor creature intuited that her Alpha friend would never come home again?

The image of Henry's last moments flashed into Dix's mind, and she shuddered.

Unable to completely shut down the gloomy mutterings of her *Internal Lil*, Dix peered up and down lanes and into dark spaces between bushes and flowering shrubs. She studied every approaching vehicle. No old Mercury idled nearby, and no sketchy-looking characters either stared at or made any move toward her.

Just a typical middleclass suburb.

The tightness in Dix's stomach, however, testified that appearances often bore little resemblance to reality. During her four years as a psychologist she'd dealt with folks who appeared normal, but who were barely-human toxic waste dumps.

She once had to alert Child Protective Services about a prominent attorney who had been starving her preteen daughter because the girl *would never reach her full potential carrying around all that extra weight.* She counseled abused spouses and partners of people from every walk of life, only to learn that once the pain subsided and bruises faded, over ninety percent of them would either return to their original abusers or hook up with new ones.

Dix had considered changing careers long before the final-straw nightmare that compelled her to burn her psychologist's shingle and take on a safe position as professor of psychology at the University of New Mexico. For her first two years in private practice, she managed to maintain the objectivity required to protect her own sanity. She successfully remained detached while dealing with a stream of young victims of incest. She even managed to hang tough when faced with the grieving pregnant girlfriend of a twenty-one-year-old gangbanger who had been shot, stuffed into the trunk of his car, then set afire.

As time wore on, and her work with humanity's rotting underbelly offered an endless parade of mounting ugliness, her thoughts grew darker and darker. The final straw had come in the guise of a man named Josh Bearden—

Dix unsuccessfully tried to shut down the string of images that bubbled up in her memory at the man's name. If she had only paid attention to the clues Josh threw out, instead of being so wrapped up in her own life's angst. If she had recognized one week earlier or even one day before—

Lulu's shenanigans pulled Dix back from the dismal place where she had spent many hours over the years. In palpable exuberance at being outdoors, the dog strained at the leash, keeping it clothesline taut. Dix's tennis-shoe-shod feet slapped on the asphalt in her struggle to keep up.

Once the two arrived at the park, Lulu made a beeline for a choice patch of grass. She spun around several times, made her donation to the environment, then looked up expectantly.

Using the bag as a glove, Dix collected the dog's still-warm offering. She tied a knot in the bag's handle, headed to a city-maintained garbage can with the words *Doggie-Doo Depository* painted in neon green on its side, tossed the bag into the can, then started back the way they'd come.

As the two neared the house, movement up the street caught Dix's attention. Wearing dark blue designer sweatpants and a pulled-up hoodie, a jogger rounded the corner.

The sun briefly lit the face under the hoodie as the jogger stopped next to a fire hydrant. Unseasonably tan, the young man glanced in her direction, quickly looked away, then made a big deal of putting his right foot onto the hydrant and stretching his legs.

Joggers and runners developed a cadence—a style and rhythm. Some held their arms loose, the slightly bent elbows away from their body, hands limp, and fingers gently curled. Others carried their arms against their sides, elbows bent, and fists raised toward their shoulders. The jogger in front of Dix pumped his arms up and down, as if hammering invisible nails.

Over her years of living in the village of Los Lunas, Dix had seen the same person in more than one place on the same day. Surely seeing a jogger in front of their house in the morning then again in front of

Henry's house later wasn't necessarily…

Unable to convince herself she was overreacting, Dix tugged on the dog's leash. "Come on, Lulu, we don't have time to sniff every rock and clump of grass."

Once back inside Henry's house, she would make sure all the doors and windows were locked. She would close the drapes then feed Lulu and make herself a cup of hot tea.

Go ahead, Lil's mocking voice sounded inside Dix's head, *pretend everything is okay.*

"Go away," Dix murmured.

At the sound of Dix's voice, Lulu stopped and looked up at her, a questioning expression on her furry face.

"Don't worry." Dix patted the dog's head. "I'm not talking to you." She tugged on the leash and the two resumed their walk.

"You know I'm right," Internal Lil said. *"Just because you close your eyes doesn't mean the monster's not there; it just means you can't see it coming."*

Chapter Four

Dix locked Henry's front door and secured the deadbolt, the resulting movement of air stirring and fluttering the stickie notes affixed to the door jamb. She unfastened the dog's leash and tossed it onto a small wooden bench just inside the door then scanned the pieces of paper.

Lock the door; *Turn off porch light*; *Check Lulu's food and water dishes.*

Had Henry suffered from Obsessive Compulsive Disorder? Dix hadn't seen him perform any ritualized, repetitive behaviors or exhibit overt signs of heightened anxiety that would accompany such a diagnosis. During their many conversations after martial arts class, he seemed quite normal. Of course, people could put on a myriad of faces, depending on their audience.

"Then why all the notes?" Dix murmured.

Lulu cocked her head.

"Sorry," Dix said to the creature, "I talk to myself; you might as well get used to it."

Dix made her way toward the kitchen with Lulu galumphing happily behind her. The two large, multi-paned windows opening onto the back yard would normally have made the cozy dining area cheerful and bright. However, the plywood that covered one window bore mute testimony that all had not been right in Henry's world.

...the man was targeted...

Dix swallowed hard, shoved her uneasiness into the dark recesses of her mind, and headed to the pantry and the fifty-pound bag of kibble inside which Henry had left a large scoop. She dipped out the recommended portion and dumped it into Lulu's dish.

While the dog noisily munched her meal, Dix took the opportunity to walk through the house.

In room after room, tiny colored squares of paper had been stuck to walls and furniture. In the kitchen, reminders to check the dates of food in the refrigerator and pantry, to turn off the garbage disposal after each use, and to refill the soap dispenser fluttered in the light breeze from the open back door. A note on the wall above an electrical outlet commanded Henry to re-charge his phone before going to bed.

A calendar on the wall next to the refrigerator drew Dix's gaze. Fighting back the sense that she was invading Henry's privacy, she studied the words written in the tiny squares under each date.

Every Monday evening Henry was to call his daughter Val at six. Monthly doctor appointments, birthdays, and various social engagements were penned in blue ink. Red X's drawn through each date, up to the day of Henry's death, marked the passage of time.

A parallel line had been drawn through the squares of an upcoming four-day weekend and the words *Black Hat Conference* written above it. Stickie notes beside the date admonished Henry to *update power point*.

During one of their after-martial arts classes chats, Henry spoke animatedly about the techie conference that took place annually in Las Vegas. He had attended the conference for the past several years and was thrilled when, after generating an algorithm that drew international attention, he was asked to give the keynote speech. He had explained that the Black Hat Conference was a hacker conference attended by hundreds of tech-savvy and wannabe tech-savvy types.

Inside the calendar's square two days before his murder, Henry had scrawled a California area code and phone number followed by the words *Call Kelly.* In the margin next to the name, he'd written *Check honeypot.*

*The honeypot…*Henry's dying words echoed inside Dix's head.

As far as she knew, there were two meanings for *honeypot*—one was an old slang term referring to the onboard toilet waste receptacle on an airplane; the other was the name given to female spies used to sexually entrap and compromise other spies or government officials.

Dix's cell phone rang, jolting her out of her speculations. Ambivalent about answering when the caller ID showed an unknown number, yet incapable of *not* answering, she sighed and tapped the screen.

"Dixie Ruiz?" The feminine voice sounded young. "I'm Val Taylor, Henry Taylor's daughter."

"Oh, I'm glad you called, Val; I was going to phone you later today. I'm so sorry about your father."

"Thank you. You were there when he di…when he was hit?"

"Yes."

"Did…did he say anything?"

Something meaningless about a honeypot…

"Not anything intelligible."

"Was he in pain? Did he suffer?"

Dix flashed on Henry's struggle to breathe. "It all

took place quite fast; I don't think he knew what happened."

A heavy sigh poured across the ether and into Dix's ear. "At least that's something to be thankful for."

"I only recently met your father, but he was a genuinely nice man. I'm so very sorry."

"Thank you." Val cleared her throat. "I wanted to let you know I'll be arriving in town late this evening but would appreciate it if you could stay in the house the next couple of nights, maybe until after the memorial service. I'm not ready to be in Dad's space yet."

"Of course."

"I can't understand why anyone would want to hurt Dad. He spent his life helping people; I always thought everyone loved him."

For the next several minutes, Henry's daughter vented her frustration, anger, grief, and disbelief. Understanding the young woman's need to be heard, Dix did what her years of training had taught her—she listened until the verbal and emotional storm had run its course.

"Please don't worry about the house or Lulu," Dix said. "I'll be here."

"Oh, I forgot about the dog." Val paused, then added, "I live in an apartment; I'm not allowed to have pets. Would you be willing to take her to a shelter...someplace that adopts pets out? Dad loved her; I know he would want her to go to a good family."

"I'll do what I can," Dix said.

Don't they euthanize animals no one wants? She's too old and too big for anyone to adopt. Lil would poop a brick if I brought such a creature—

"I'm sorry," Val said, "did you say something?"

"No, just got a frog in my throat."

"I would like to talk to you, but I have to meet with Dad's attorney. There are so many things I still have to take care of…" The voice dissolved into sobs.

"Of course. If there's anything I can do to help, or if you just need to talk, please call me anytime. I'll keep my phone on."

"Dad *said* you were nice. Thank you; I'll be in touch." Val broke the connection.

Dix replaced the phone in its pouch as Lulu galloped toward her. The dog planted herself on the floor next to Dix's chair, rested one paw on top of her right foot, and stared up into her face.

Dix laughed. "Coffee first, then we'll take a nice long walk."

As if she understood every word, Lulu plopped onto the kitchen floor and went into waiting mode.

Dix stepped to the sink. She filled the drip coffee pot with water, poured it into the coffee maker that sat on the counter, then spooned grounds into the filter-lined basket. As she pulled a mug from the cabinet, a movement outside the window above the sink caught her attention.

Leaning over the sink for a better view, she scanned the back yard. Other than breeze-stirred fall flowers and grass, there was no movement. The bubbling of brewing coffee and gentle *tinkle* of a wind chime on the back porch were the only sounds.

"All's quiet on the western front." Dix filled her mug with the steaming brew then turned toward Lulu and froze.

Where the dog had been lounging on the floor, she was now standing, her head lowered, and her gaze riveted on the window beyond which lay the back yard…the window through which Dix had just been peering. The long spine fur on her neck stood stiffly in a canine mohawk, and a low rumble started from deep inside her chest.

A couple of moments later, Lulu quieted. She looked up at Dix as if nothing had happened, whipped her tail back and forth a couple of times, then dropped back onto the floor, and resumed her waiting posture.

Relief turned Dix's knees to water, and she nearly fell into one of the kitchen chairs. When her heart rate slowed, she allowed herself to breathe.

"I'm too old for this," she murmured to Lulu.

The dog raised her head and looked at Dix as if to say, *"No worries, I'm here."*

"We have a lot in common, you know." Dix patted Lulu's head. "We're both going to be in the doghouse when I bring you home, but I can't just leave you to who-knows-what fate."

Lulu *boof*-ed and wagged her tail.

Dix returned to the garage and retrieved her overnight bag. Once she'd assured herself the connecting door was locked behind her, she pulled a plastic baggie containing two granola bars and an orange from the duffel then sat at the kitchen table and ate.

Her lunch finished, she took a mystery novel from the bag and headed for a comfortable-looking loveseat and ottoman in the living room. For the next few hours, she allowed herself to get lost in the book. It wasn't until Lulu wandered in and sat at her feet that she realized how late it had grown.

"You need to go out again?"

Lulu sprinted to the back door and commenced an impatient jig. Dix slid back the door, and the dog shot outside where she meandered around, sniffing here and there. The animal peed then sauntered back inside.

Dix pulled a box of Cheerios from the pantry and milk from the fridge.

"Not the most elaborate dinner," she said to Lulu, "but it'll hold me 'til tomorrow."

After again ensuring all doors and windows were locked, Dix returned to the dining room, hefted her duffel, and carried it to the room Henry had identified as the guestroom. Under Lulu's watchful gaze, she slipped into her pajamas and climbed into the inviting bed.

"No nightmares allowed." Dix patted the dog's fuzzy, oddly comforting head.

Hopefully, her Dream-Maker would cooperate.

Chapter Five

Dix slept in fits and starts, instantly coming awake at every creak and groan the house made in its fight against the high New Mexico wind intent on blowing it down. Each time Dix woke, Lulu watchfully raised her head.

Finally, exhaustion won the skirmish, and Dix slept deeply, escorted into the rapid-eye-movement level required for dreams.

It seemed her eyes had barely closed when morning sun streaming through Henry's sheer fabric window shades awakened her. Eyes burning and throat dry, she sat up.

Lulu stood and shook herself, setting the metal tags on her collar clinking. She looked imploringly at Dix.

"I assume you need to go out?" Dix sat on the side of the bed and slid her feet into the fluffy slippers she'd brought. She tried to stand straight but froze when pain shot through her back, abdomen, and thigh muscles—the aftereffects of performing CPR on Henry for nearly twenty minutes.

Lulu cocked her head and emitted a small whimper.

"Okay, okay, just give me a second." Dix eased into a standing position then headed for the bedroom's attached bathroom, her legs stiff and complaining. Perhaps Henry's medicine cabinet would house a muscle relaxant.

Again, Dix was struck by the number of stickie notes affixed to the mirror and walls of the bathroom. Exhaustion had won out over curiosity the night before, and she hadn't taken the time to read them.

Her gaze slid over yellow, pink, blue, and green three-by-three squares of paper covered with scribblings such as *Trash on Monday*, *Meds list for doc appointment*, *Turn out the lights*, and countless other commands and reminders.

Dix opened the medicine cabinet and peered at the small plastic bottles containing headache and pain medications, each carefully labeled in black permanent marker. Two amber-colored plastic bottles containing prescription medications sat alongside the over-the-counter drugs.

She pulled out one bottle and read the name of a drug commonly prescribed for Alzheimer's disease, and something caught in her throat.

The diagnosis must have been devastating. How long had Henry known what was in store for him? A nightmare for anyone afflicted by the disease as well as for their loved ones, it would have been especially horrifying for a brilliant man who made his living by his wits.

Dix replaced the medication in the cabinet, retrieved a bottle of ibuprofen, removed two pills, then popped them into her mouth. After running water into her cupped hand, she swallowed the pills then, quickly as her complaining legs would allow, headed for the back door.

Lulu greeted her with a gotta-pee-now dance in front of the sliding door leading from the kitchen to the back yard.

"There you go." Dix unlocked then slid the door open. She left it ajar for the animal's return. "We'll walk after breakfast."

As if shot from a cannon, the dog dashed outside.

Dix prepared a bowl of raisin bran and made fresh coffee. After she finished her breakfast, she washed and put away the dishes then grabbed Lulu's leash from the countertop.

At the inaudible-to-human-ears sound of the leash's fabric rubbing against itself, the dog shot into the house, her tail wagging furiously. She skidded to a stop in front of Dix.

Chuckling, Dix attached the leash, and the two headed for the front door.

Early morning sunlight poured warmth over Dix's head and shoulders, relaxing her taut muscles.

Everything would be okay. Life would soon return to normal.

Dix repeated the words over and over, a mantra of hope aimed at dispelling the persistent uneasiness that had formed a hard ball in her stomach.

Chapter Six

Following a restless night, Lil sat in her recliner sipping coffee. She unrolled the morning paper and scanned the front page where Henry's murder had made headlines. Her brow furrowed as she read the detailed report.

The female reporter had not only identified the cross streets to their block but had described their house and neighborhood. She even included a photograph of Dix being questioned by the police.

"Great," Lil murmured.

Although Lil had enhanced their security precautions to include all sorts of pricey gizmos and gimmicks after a greedy family tried to kill them a little over a year ago, she had never quite been able to quash the fear that she was overlooking something. She believed in being prepared, but as sure as God made little green apples, things broke; electronics failed. It was the unprepared-for stuff that could get you.

Lil retrieved her phone from the table and punched in Dix's number.

"I'm having breakfast then taking Lulu for her morning walk," Dix said. "What's up?"

"Just making sure you're okay."

"So far, so good. Something spooked Lulu last night, but she's okay now, probably a bird or something. Anyway, Henry's daughter Val called; poor thing's really struggling."

"Be careful," Lil said. "The newspaper article shines a spotlight on us, and I don't like it."

"Here's the part where I tell you to stop being paranoid."

"Must I remind you it's the—"

"I know, it's the paranoid who survive."

"According to the article, Henry was a brilliant mathematician and software developer, one of the good guys."

"He made a name for himself," Dix said. "By the way, what's a honeypot?"

"As in a sexy spy or small airplane's toilet tank?"

"Any other meaning you've ever heard?"

"No, but since Henry was a tech wizard, it might have something to do with his work."

"I'll call Dillon Tartain. If anyone would know, he would. Also, Val asked me to stay here another couple of nights, so I'll be home later to pick up more clothes. I'll call when I'm on the way."

After her sister broke the phone connection, Lil closed her ancient, clamshell cellphone and resumed reading. When she finished the article, she tossed the newspaper onto the floor, headed to the office she shared with her sister, sat at the desk, and opened her laptop.

For the next hour, she browsed online professional journals, clicked on research articles, and scanned data. Finally, deep in thought, she shut down her computer.

The large *Realist* portion of Lil's brain scoffed at the possibilities thrown up by the tiny Dix-like *Dreamer* portion. No matter what her sister said, the world was filled with mean and hateful people who were willing to do unto others what they'd never tolerate being done unto them. Based on Lil's online research, Henry Taylor had more than once over the past decade put himself in the crosshairs of some very bad people—people who dealt in human trafficking, child pornography, and drugs. Unless Lil could talk Dix out of it, her twin could be stepping into some seriously deep doo-doo.

Earlier, Dix had tried to sound relaxed on the phone, but Lil knew her too well. Whatever spooked the dog the night before, had also spooked Dix.

After a short search through the pantry, Lil found an old, locally printed telephone directory and thumbed through the pages. She jotted Henry's address down on a piece of notepaper and stuck it into the breast pocket of her red flannel shirt then headed upstairs.

Once in her room, she packed a small duffel with a change of clothes then hooked the scabbard of her charged Taser onto her belt and returned downstairs.

After making sure the doors and windows were locked, she headed for the garage.

If Dix were determined to stay at the murdered man's house another night, so would Lil. Where Dix would likely feel compelled to apologize to an attacker before punching him in the chest hard enough to stop his heart, Lil had no such inclination. If anyone messed with her sister, Lil would cook him like a sausage and never bat an eye.

****

Lil pulled onto Henry's street. The normalcy of the upscale neighborhood struck her and, for the first time, she questioned the validity of her concerns. What if Dix were right, and she did have a skewed perspective of

29

humanity? What if she *had* assumed the worst about a situation and jumped to the wrong conclusion?

Lil instantly dismissed the thought. She was nearly always spot-on with her assessment of someone's character, as witnessed by her efforts to warn Dix about each of her three ex-husbands—even Dix had conceded that.

Lil had just pulled up to a four-way stop a block up the street from Henry's house, when Dix and some huge creature resembling a Star Wars Bantha without horns came out the front door. She hesitated as her sister locked the door behind herself and the dog.

Should she park in the driveway and wait for Dix to return, or would it be better for her to call and give her sibling a heads-up that she was going to stay with her?

Once Dix and the furry beast moved out of sight, Lil started her engine and pulled into Henry's drive. She opened the vehicle door then paused, mentally running through a roster of possible excuses for showing up at Henry's house.

"You're always complaining that I'm not supportive..." Lil would say. "So here I am, being supportive."

"No," Dix would respond. "You're here because you don't think I can handle myself. Admit it; you've never believed me capable of anything other than gardening."

"Not true," Lil would argue. "I know you can—"

Lil heaved a long sigh. She shook her head, closed the door, and fired up her engine.

Throughout the years, Lil had struggled with Dix's penchant for inserting herself into any human drama that moved into her orbit. Where Lil was perfectly capable of walking away from turmoil, her sister was constitutionally unable to do so. Dix found it impossible to get on with her own life when someone else's hit a snag. Put a person on hard times in front of her, and it was like saying *sic 'em* to a bulldog.

Dix prided herself on being competent, capable of dealing with anything the Cosmos threw at her. Any action on Lil's part that flew in the face of that belief would be met with a withering tirade.

Lil was too old, and life was too short to spend the next several hours arguing with her twin, who would send her back home anyway.

She started to back out of the drive when a figure suddenly appeared in her rearview mirror. A young man she hadn't seen stood mere inches from her rear bumper. Her heart rate shot up like a rocket, and she jammed on the brakes.

Scruffy, with thick black hair and a couple of days' beard growth, the man made a low, Edwardian bow, then stood to one side and motioned for her to move along. Lil backed into the street while the young man withdrew a white cloth from somewhere, blew his nose into it, then waded it up, and put it away. Peering through the windshield when she passed by, he smiled and nodded.

Lil had driven only a few yards when her gaze was drawn to the rearview mirror. Like Mickey Mouse in an old black-and-white cartoon, the man stood, hands in pockets, rocking back and forth on his heels while pretending to study the clouds.

For a nano second Lil considered backing up and asking the guy who he was and what he was doing there. However, regardless of how sketchy his appearance, he wasn't doing anything illegal. Dix would have plenty to say if she returned to find Lil interrogating a young man just for walking in front of Henry's house.

Lil gunned her engine and headed home. She would call Dix and tell her about the guy. She owed that much to her own twitching antennae, even if it meant enduring Dix's standard lecture on paranoia.

Chapter Seven

The crisp air pecked pleasantly at Dix's face and hands as she and Lulu walked to the park. She loved the autumn with its smells of burning leaves and cool weather.

Her first husband Darren had been fond of autumn as well. Dix sighed at the memory of the short marriage that taught her some of the toughest life lessons she'd been forced to learn.

Darren had been the love of her life. Although only eighteen years old, she fell hard and without reservation for the handsome newcomer. They seemed so perfectly matched that she joyfully accepted his proposal mere weeks after they first met, even though Lil and their brother Ben tried to talk her out of it.

Determined to make the marriage work, Dix took a part time job while attending the University of New Mexico. Since Darren refused to work *for less than he was worth*, the full weight of earning a living fell to Dix.

Forty years later she still remembered the utter exhaustion of getting up at five-thirty for her six-hour shift at the convenience store, going from work directly to class, then returning home to the man she thought she loved. What was that old saying—marry in haste, regret at leisure?

By the time she earned her Bachelor of Arts in

psychology, Dix finally admitted to herself that Darren was never going to change. It wasn't, however, until she came home early from work one day and found Darren in bed with their perky next-door neighbor that she decided to get a divorce.

Humans weren't built to be alone, and Dix quickly found the single life unbearable. Within less than a year, she rebounded into a second marriage.

It was during that marriage she completed her PhD in psychology and hung out her private practice shingle.

When the second marriage didn't work, she tried again. The third marriage, though, had been the worst of all. Verbally and emotionally abusive, her third husband took everything she owned and left her destitute. She was grateful when Lil allowed her to move in with her.

Dix's tense neck muscles relaxed slightly as she and Lulu neared Henry's house. The dog bounded playfully and pranced at her side as if they had known each other for years.

When the two of them stepped into the yard, however, the dog lowered her head and spiked her neck fur. With her gaze fixed on the front door, she flattened her ears as she had in the kitchen the night before.

Dix murmured gentle words and stroked the huge head. Lulu went into a crouch, lowered her tail, and focused her eyes on Dix as if awaiting some command. A low rumble started from deep in the animal's chest.

Struggling to control Lulu, Dix stepped onto the porch and prepared to identify herself to whoever was inside. Perhaps Val had changed her mind about staying in her father's house.

She unlocked and opened the front door but

stopped short of entering the house when Lulu's growl grew louder and more ominous.

A window somewhere at the rear of the house was shoved open, and something heavy was dragged across an upstairs floor. Two masculine voices bantered back and forth in amiable conversation.

Dix froze and the flesh on her arms rucked up. Dragging Lulu behind her, she stepped off the porch and behind a huge bush in Henry's front yard. She crouched, retrieved her phone from inside her bra and dialed 911.

"What is the nature of your emergency?" The feminine voice was calm, unruffled.

Dix cupped one hand around her mouth in hopes her voice wouldn't be audible to whoever was in the house. "Someone's broken into the house of a man who's just been murdered," she whispered.

From inside the house the voices rose in argument. A man shouted, "Quit complaining. The Whiz said to bring anything electronic, anything digital, even if it looks like a toaster."

Dix repeated the address then answered the dispatch operator's questions. "At least two men, and they're still here. I don't know if they have weapons; I haven't seen them, but I can hear them."

Meanwhile, the argument overhead heated up. "I said stop complaining, you got a death wish?"

"We don't even know what we're looking for," an aggrieved, second masculine voice said.

"The old guy was a geek, so grab anything that looks geeky." Again, something heavy was dragged across the floor.

"Someone will be there soon," the operator said.

"Please stay on the line with me until they arrive."

"Thank you," Dix whispered into the phone.

Lulu, her gaze riveted on the front door, strained against the leash while Dix struggled to keep hold of both it and the phone.

"What the…?" Voice One sounded as if he had moved to the landing at the top of the stairs. "You open the front door, Brainiac?"

"What?" Voice Two shouted.

"I said, did you open the front door?"

"I'm not stupid."

"Well someone did," Voice One said, quieter.

"Maybe the old lady forgot to close it, and the wind blew it open."

"There's no wind. You sure you saw the old lady leave?"

"Yeah," Voice Two yelled. "She drove away not two minutes ago."

Creaking boards telegraphed movement down the stairs and toward the front door. The sound of fabric shushing against fabric as if something was being pulled from a pocket was followed by the *schlack* of a pistol's slide being pulled back. The immediate responding *schlack* announced the guy had just chambered a round as he walked out the door and onto the porch. Through gaps in the leaves, Dix watched him scan the yard, his handgun held at the ready.

Lulu emitted a low, deep-throated growl at the same instant the phone in Dix's hand crackled to life.

"Ma'am, are you still there?"

Too late, Dix realized she had somehow engaged the speaker phone. Bile shot up her throat, and beads of perspiration popped out on her upper lip.

She held her breath, as her suddenly-sausage-like index finger wildly punched the screen. Finally, she managed to silence the phone.

The man jerked his head toward the sound, lifted his pistol, and crept toward the bush behind which Dix crouched, frozen in place and wishing she could make herself disappear. Her eyes darted around the yard in search of something, anything that might be used as a weapon.

Suddenly growling and barking furiously, Lulu lunged at the man. The move was made with such force that it pulled the leash off Dix's wrist, burning her skin in the process.

Taken by surprise, the man hollered and let loose a wild shot. Lulu yipped then growled a battle cry and rocketed after him.

Dazed by the rapidity of the attack, the man did a panicked jig and instinctively raised his pistol toward the dog. Lulu, her body a whipping, snarling blur, gnashed at the man's calves.

At that instant, two police cruisers shot around the corner a couple of blocks away. The whoop of approaching sirens gave the thug a burst of strength. He jerked his leg clear of the dog and sprinted back to the porch.

A short, thin strip of bloody denim dangling from her tightly clamped teeth, Lulu gave pursuit.

From upstairs, Voice Two yelled, "What the hell's going on?"

Voice One ran into the house and shoved the door behind him. In his panic, however, he failed to close it, and Lulu shot through the opening.

"Cops!" Voice One yelled. "Take what you got and

get out."

Sounds of Lulu's attack reached a crescendo then two shots rang out. The dog's high-pitched yelp was followed by footsteps pounding down the stairs.

Ignoring her instinct for self preservation Dix rushed out from behind the bush and toward the still-open front door.

Chapter Eight

Earlier, the man known as Razor sat slouched in his dark blue, rented SUV parked up the street from Henry Taylor's house awaiting the arrival of the anticipated break-in crew—two men called Toad and Booger. From behind windows tinted dark enough to make him nearly invisible, he lowered his high-powered binoculars, wiped the lenses with a special cloth, then lifted them to his eyes.

"A freaking babysitter, that's what I've become," he muttered.

After the stupid jerks had impulsively killed Taylor the day before, Razor had been ready to send them back to Los Angeles. However, not only had his cohort Kelly Condit argued that they could still be useful, she suggested *careful supervision* on Razor's part might help stave off any further mishaps.

So, there he sat, *carefully supervising* the second attempt to get Taylor's electronics. If Kelly Condit hadn't botched the first break-in attempt a couple of days earlier, Razor would already be home in the humid, humming city of Los Angeles. He could be sitting beside the pool watching the women who lived in the apartment complex cavort in the water or sunbathe. Or he could be enjoying a relaxing massage with his personal masseuse.

Razor grimaced and scratched his right forearm

hard enough to break the skin then used his car keys to rake his scalp. If he had to stay in the New Mexico desert much longer, he would turn into a kiln-dried mummy. Even slathering himself with expensive moisturizer that morning hadn't helped.

Worse than the weather, however, was the country lifestyle. How could anyone prefer to live where the only businesses open after nine o'clock were either bars or McDonald's? In Razor's opinion, anyone who lived in a city with less than a half million population had to be either hiding from the law or running from a vindictive spouse.

Absently, he scratched a persistent itch along his jaw and recalled his last conversation with Condit during which he suggested Toad and Booger be sent back to Los Angeles.

"They're on loan from BeeBee LeDuc," Kelly had reminded him. "Or is the real issue that you don't trust me?"

"Is there some reason I *shouldn't* trust you?" he'd responded.

"I wouldn't have invited you into this gig if I'd known how suspicious you are." Kelly had shot a rancid look at him. "Do I look stupid to you?"

"I never said you were—"

"LeDuc's a major investor in this project. I'm not dumb enough to jerk him around. Those unfortunate few who've tried have not lived long enough to regret it."

"True," Razor had said.

"And," Kelly had added, "if he hadn't talked some of his rich friends into investing, our return on investment wouldn't be nearly as much as it's ginning up to be."

When Condit had first approached Razor a little over a year earlier with the idea of investing in any of the over two hundred online cryptocurrencies on the market, he was skeptical. Although familiar with the term *digital currency*, he knew little about it. The whole thing sounded a little like smoke and mirrors.

Condit had said, however, that a couple of uber-wealthy brothers had invested in the cryptocurrency market to the tune of several million dollars, then when the currency's value shot up as a result of the infusion of money, they sold off their shares. Not only had the guys made a huge profit, the whole thing had been legal and aboveboard.

Images of piles of clean money floating around inside his head, Razor had made the proposition to LeDuc that they use online digital currencies to launder their money. Once LeDuc had done what he called *due diligence* by researching the idea, he gleefully approached a few *business associates*. Not only would all of them be able to withdraw clean money when they sold their currency shares, but they stood to make a tidy profit once the cryptocurrency's value skyrocketed as a result of being manipulated.

Several like-minded colleagues had lit up like the fourth of July at the idea. They couldn't hand their dirty money over to Condit fast enough.

The day of Taylor's hit, Razor heard the callout on his police scanner, and his stomach flipped. Toad and Booger's orders were to make Taylor give them all his electronics, do whatever necessary to ensure they had everything and anything that might incriminate the rest of the group, *then* pop the guy. Instead, when the bozos saw Taylor putting luggage in the trunk of his car, they figured he sensed he was in danger and decided to skip town. True to character, Toad opted to not only take the man out early but to do it in the messiest, most blundering way possible.

Although Toad's spur of the moment decision had effectively kept Taylor from taking his suspicions to the authorities, it also made it imperative to immediately find and destroy all the man's electronic devices. Hopefully, Taylor hadn't had time to share his concerns with anyone besides Condit.

Razor cast his mind back to the scene he witnessed upon arriving at the little old ladies' house the day before.

He'd parked a couple of blocks away to avoid getting caught in the snarl of slowing traffic, then watched through his binoculars while one old lady did CPR on Taylor, and a second old lady—a demi-clone to the first—tried to keep traffic moving.

By the time the cops and other first responders arrived, the gathering crowd was a milling mass, several of whom held phones toward the drama, no doubt hoping to record something that would result in thousands of views for their social media accounts.

Having done his early morning run and still wearing his jogging outfit, Razor made his way down the street in front of the old ladies' house, hoping that Taylor had only sustained minor injuries, and the project could be put back on track. However, Razor's worst fears were realized when the ambulance loaded up the obviously dead man and slowly drove away.

Bracing himself for what he fully expected to be a Vesuvius-like explosion, Razor had hurried back to his vehicle and called LeDuc in Los Angeles.

Rather than popping his cork, though, LeDuc calmly suggested that he and Condit generate an alternate strategy then inform Toad and Booger of the change in plans. Razor was to report back when said plan was in effect. LeDuc then obliquely reminded Razor of the chain of command.

Where LeDuc was The Uber-Boss, Condit was the Skill Set, and Razor was LeDuc's Man-on-the-ground charged with regular progress reports. Toad and Booger were muscle.

Razor's attention was pulled back to the second break-in attempt when Taylor's front door opened. He adjusted the view on his binoculars as the old lady with the black-penciled eyebrows and Taylor's dog left for a walk.

He texted the goons the all clear just as a tan coupe pulled into Taylor's drive.

Wait, Razor hurriedly texted. *Company.*

He hoisted his binoculars and studied the new arrival.

Twin to the old woman who had witnessed Taylor's hit—identical in every way except for a tightly bound bun and lack of discernible eyebrows—the woman sat in her vehicle doing who knew what.

Granny Eyebrows and Granny No-brows sitting in a tree.

One drinks coffee, the other drinks tea.

Oh, how frightened they should be;

I see them, but they can't see me.

Razor snickered at his impromptu poem. He had talent; that was for sure. If he could just find someone who properly appreciated him.

A flash of light glinting off a windshield caught his attention, and he peered up the street as Toad and Booger's van rounded the corner then eased into the alley behind Taylor's house.

Muttering every invective in his sizable repertoire, Razor again texted the men to wait. No response meant the jerks either weren't paying attention or had again decided to do things their own way.

With his lips compressed, Razor returned his gaze to the old woman in the drive, fully expecting her to notice the bozos and call the cops. However, several seconds passed during which she didn't appear to use her phone.

The old woman began backing out of the driveway, but Booger's sudden appearance in her rearview mirror compelled her to stomp on her brakes. Booger and the woman studied each other for several seconds; then, the old lady drove off.

Razor again texted the all clear and was about to put the binoculars aside when Granny Eyebrows and the dog turned the corner up the street on their way back to the house. With nightmare scenarios cascading through his mind, Razor frantically texted *abort*.

Again, no response.

Razor argued with himself about whether to take matters into his own hands. He could distract the old woman and give Toad and Booger time to get away, but that would just allow her to identify him and his vehicle to the police.

Before Razor could decide on the best course of action, something spooked the old lady.

She pulled a phone from inside her blouse and punched the screen. While speaking into the phone, she dragged the dog off the porch and ducked behind a bush, where she stooped and watched the door.

Razor grabbed his phone and texted furiously.

—*Get out the back way. Get out now.*—

Not only did Toad not respond, but he showed up on the front porch with his pistol drawn.

The screwups were about to get caught.

Although they knew very little about the project, they could identify several "investors" who would then be charged with money laundering, fraud, and racketeering. Each investor could face up to twenty years for even *conspiring* to commit money laundering, and because of the amount of money involved, that translated into very long prison sentences.

Toad and Booger, on the other hand, could cop a plea, vomit up names, and then go into Witness Protection. They would rightly figure that a life hiding out and living on the government payroll was better than being force fed fifty pounds of wet cement and then getting dumped into a lake.

If need be, Razor could take care of Toad and Booger then come up with a logical tale that would satisfy LeDuc—something to the effect that Granny Eyebrows had panicked and popped them.

Razor pulled a 9mm semiautomatic pistol from a holster stashed under the driver's seat. Unwilling to attract the airline's attention on his flight from LA by checking a bag containing his beloved Glock, he had purchased the pistol from a local estate sale the day after his arrival in Albuquerque. Although the weapon was older than dirt, it not only worked beautifully but was untraceable. He would dump it when the rest of the Taylor business was finished.

He glanced around the neighborhood for anyone who might be witnessing the goings on. No curtains moved, no faces peered from behind blinds, and no doors opened to allow for a better view.

Razor sighed and opened his door.

Suddenly, the dog jerked free from Granny Eyebrows' grasp and charged Toad. The dumbass bolted back inside the house but failed to close the door behind him, allowing the snarling animal to follow him inside.

A grim smile played on Razor's lips. A dog that size would be capable of leaving a life-altering mark.

Screaming sirens prompted Razor to re-holster his weapon. He started his engine just as the van shot out of the alley, and Toad did the first smart thing Razor had seen him do—he drove slowly down the street, stopped at the corner stop sign, then pulled onto a main thoroughfare.

As two police cruisers pulled onto Taylor's property, Razor turned up the nearest street. Careful to observe the speed limit, he headed for the motel in which he, Kelly Condit, Toad, and Booger were staying.

After Taylor's death, Condit had assured Razor and LeDuc that the project could proceed on schedule with a few minor adjustments. On the surface, LeDuc appeared to buy her story, but Razor had decided to wait and see. If things got too complicated, he'd bail.

While Razor had no reason to doubt Condit's software coding and programming skills, she was a pain to work with. Bossy as well as mouthy, she acted like she was a princess. Worst of all, she treated him like he was dumb as dirt.

More than once, he'd been tempted to print out his bank statements and shove them in her face. If he was so stupid, how had he managed to build his net worth from the few hundred dollars he earned as a gopher for LeDuc into a few hundred thousand by the time he was thirty?

A high school dropout at the age of sixteen, Razor found survival outside of home tougher than he thought it would be. To earn money for food, he mowed a few yards, but unable to abide dirty fingernails or calloused hands, he looked for other means of support.

Then he saw a nationally famous business guru on television talking about how to make a pile of dough. The man's suggestion to "work smarter, not harder" resonated with Razor. He sold his lawn and gardening equipment then took a job as a bouncer in one of LeDuc's clubs.

For three years, he enjoyed thumping troublemakers and throwing them into the street. He worked out at a local gym and soon developed not only a hard abdomen and muscled arms, but a reputation as someone not to mess with.

Word of his fighting skills and work ethic soon got back to LeDuc, and he was offered a job higher up the ladder. Over succeeding years, he single-mindedly grew his money by investing in some of LeDuc's lucrative, if illegal, enterprises. By the time he met Kelly Condit, he was hungry for bigger and better ways to increase his net worth.

Considered handsome by men and women alike, Razor never lacked for feminine companionship and he assumed that Condit would fall for him when he paid her a bit of attention. While Condit wasn't pretty, she was fit and she was single. In Razor's world, two out of three was workable.

Condit had, however, steadfastly refused his advances. In short order, his piqued interest shifted to open dislike then to roiling, barely controlled hatred. He'd often had to take himself in hand to keep from popping her. He told himself that once their business was completed, maybe he *would* pop her, just for the hell of it. No female made him feel inadequate and survived.

What could prove to be the real pee in Razor's Post Toasties, however, was the involvement of the two little old ladies. If he correctly sensed the undercurrents behind LeDuc's comments during the latest phone call, at some point Razor might be required to shove the old women through the earthly exit and into the next world. They wouldn't be the first to die because they *might have seen* or *may have heard* something that pointed to Mr. LeDuc.

BeeBee LeDuc didn't take many chances.

Chapter Nine

At the same instant Dix reached for the doorknob to check on Lulu, two police cruisers screamed up the drive. To lessen the possibility of being suspected as one of the intruders, she threw her hands in the air and froze.

Two officers exited their respective vehicles, sidearms drawn, eyes riveted on Dix. They approached her warily, barking orders as they walked.

"Hands in the air. Step off the porch, turn around, and walk backward toward us."

Dix did as commanded. "I'm the one who called," she said over her shoulder.

"Do you live here?"

"No, I'm house sitting." Dix identified herself then nodded toward the house. "There were two men but they took off when they heard your sirens. Please, I need to see to the dog inside the house."

One officer holstered his weapon and approached Dix and patted her down. The second officer held his pistol at what her nephew Davie once referred to as *the low ready*, giving the officer the ability to immediately respond if need be.

"My nephew was a detective with Los Lunas Police Department until about a year ago. Davie...I mean, David Ruiz."

One officer nodded. "I thought I recognized you. I

saw you at Ruiz's wedding. He's a good man. You said there were two men in the house; can you describe them?"

Dix shook her head. "No, but I heard them arguing. I guess it's possible there were more, but only two spoke." She glanced toward the house. "You may already know it, but the owner of this house was murdered yesterday morning, Henry Taylor?"

The officers shot a look at each other. One returned to his vehicle and put in a call requesting backup while the other stayed with Dix.

"I know you'll have to secure the area, but I'm concerned about the dog. She's wounded and might be hard to handle."

"You need to stay where you are," the first officer said. "We'll see to the dog."

Within minutes, two more cruisers arrived, lights flashing. Two more officers jumped from their vehicles. While the new arrivals headed in the front door, the other two officers moved around the back.

A few minutes later, one officer returned and spoke to Dix. "The dog was hit," he said, "but she's docile, didn't put up a fight."

"Can I go to her?" Dix said.

The officer nodded. "The house has been cleared but will be cordoned off as a crime scene. No one will be allowed inside until after forensics have finished dusting for prints." He motioned for Dix to follow him. "I'll take you to the dog."

Dix strode into the house and knelt on the floor next to Lulu, who sat trembling, her already huge eyes showing white all around. A small nick in one ear encircled with already drying blood and a long graze oozing blood along one cheek appeared to be her only injuries.

"That's my girl." Dix ran her hand in long strokes down the animal's back. "What a warrior you are." She pointed to the scrap of denim on the floor beside the dog and looked up at the officer. "That's from the man who shot Lulu."

Dix picked up the leash. "I'd like to take her to the car, but I'll also need to get her food and dishes. Oh, and I'll need Henry's instructions."

"Would you know if anything's missing?" one officer asked.

"I'm not certain, but I heard them say they were looking for anything electronic."

"Typical. That's the usual target for burglary."

The officer escorted Dix and Lulu to her car and helped load the animal into the back seat. After two more trips back and forth, during which the officer helped load two fifty-pound bags of dog food, two metal dishes, and a couple of toys, Dix climbed into the vehicle.

She buckled her seatbelt, pulled Henry's note from her vest pocket, turned her phone on, and punched in the veterinarian's number. After several rings, a young female answered.

Dix identified herself and added, "I have a dog that's been shot and am hoping you can work us in right away. I believe Henry Taylor is one of your customers…it's his dog."

"We're just getting ready to close; the doctor's leaving on vacation at noon," the young woman said. "How quickly can you get here?"

"Within ten minutes, traffic permitting."

"Hold on a minute, I'll check." The call was put on hold, and static-riffed, pan-flute music poured over the line for a couple of minutes, then the young woman returned. "The doctor will wait for you."

Dix thanked the woman and broke the connection. As the police began to affix yellow plastic tape over Henry's door, she fired up her engine, backed out of the garage and into the street. Lulu lounged in the back seat like a canine Sphinx.

During the drive to the animal hospital, Dix spoke softly to comfort the dog. She quoted poetry and repeated children's fairy tales while forcing herself to stay within the speed limit.

She pulled into the animal hospital's parking lot just as her phone rang. As usual, a tingling at the base of her neck told her it was Lil checking up on her. Debating how much to tell her twin, she sighed and answered.

"I can't talk right now," Dix said. "I'll call you back."

"Wait," Lil said. "Did you get my message? Why didn't you pick up?"

"I've been busy."

"We have to talk."

"I can't right now. I'll call—"

"What's going on?" Lil's voice had risen to fever pitch. "Are you okay?"

"*I* am."

"I knew something was up," Lil said. "Someone's been hurt?"

"I'll explain everything once I get home, but I'm okay."

Dix pulled the squawking phone away from her

ringing ear. "Calm down, Sis. You don't have to call every thirty minutes. I'll be home soon, and we'll talk." She ended the call then turned and looked at Lulu. "First we get you fixed up, after that we'll worry about how to deal with my sister."

Lulu lifted her head and looked adoringly at Dix. Her baseball bat-sized tail whumped against the seat.

****

"Thank you so much for working us in," Dix said to the young female veterinary assistant who stood holding the animal hospital's door open. "I don't know how badly she's hurt."

The young woman smiled at Dix then bent at the waist, looked into the dog's eyes, and cooed, "Hello, Lulu. Don't you worry; we're going to take good care of you." The assistant stood, nodded at Dix, and motioned. "Come on back; the doctor's ready for you."

For the next several minutes, the veterinarian's attention was focused on repairing the damage done to Lulu. After applying ointment to the wounds and bandaging them, he affixed what appeared to be a huge lampshade over the dog's head.

The vet handed a partially used tube of ointment to Dix. "Apply this to her ear and cheek twice a day to prevent infection. The cone will keep her from scratching her wounds; you'll need to leave it on until your next visit. My assistant will set up an appointment." He cocked his head, a speculative look on his face. "What happened?"

Dix recounted the main events of the last twenty-four hours.

"We heard about the hit and run," the vet said. "Do the police know who did it?"

"No, not yet."

"Henry was a nice man," the assistant said. "He was so excited when Lulu came up for adoption."

"She's fearless," Dix said. "I've never seen anything like it. I'm not sure I would be here if not for her." She reached for her purse. "Do you take credit cards?"

The doctor shook his head. "There's no charge. Henry was a good man." He smiled at Lulu and stroked her back. "Besides, this girl's a hero." He glanced up at Dix. "You might consider adopting her. She obviously trusts you."

"Animals choose their people, you know," the assistant said. "It's not the other way around."

Chapter Ten

Toad and Booger sat in the mass-produced, overstuffed loveseat in Kelly Condit's Albuquerque motel room. Razor leaned against the wall, a stormy look on his face. Condit sat at a desk staring at the screen of the laptop the men had cadged from Taylor's house.

"Is that the right—" Toad swallowed his question when Kelly jerked a hand in a shushing motion.

Condit typed furiously on the laptop for several minutes. The others in the room remained silent.

Toad, nicknamed after the bullfrog sound he made when compulsively clearing his throat, scratched his nose and stared at the ceiling. Booger, so called for his perpetually runny nose due to a myriad of plant and animal allergies, studied a fly's progress across the floor. Like a volcano preparing to blow, Razor stared at the two men.

Condit closed the laptop and leaned back in the chair. "This is the second time you've failed to do what you were told. First, you kill Taylor before getting anything from him and now you've been chased away by a little old lady and a dog."

"You also ignored my texts to get the hell out of the house," Razor said. "Why?"

Booger gulped loud enough for everyone in the room to hear.

"Booger saw the old lady drive off," Toad said. "We figured the coast was clear."

"Booger saw *one* old lady drive off," Razor said. "You still haven't answered my question. Why did you go to the house after I texted you to wait? And why didn't you answer my texts?"

"My phone went dead." Toad stared at his shoes.

"You don't keep your phone charged?" Condit said. "That's just plain—"

"Did the old woman's appearance escape your notice?" Razor said through clenched teeth.

Toad and Booger stared at Razor as if he had metamorphosed into an exotic alien life form.

"I recognized her from when we hit...you know, when we..." Booger sniffed. "She—"

"You stared at her long enough to let her memorize everything from your shoe size to the color of your nose hairs," Razor interrupted, "yet you didn't notice her appearance?"

Toad cleared his throat while Booger screwed his face up thoughtfully.

"I'm sure it was the same old lady Taylor went to see," Booger said. "She looked a little different without makeup, but it was her."

"The woman in the car," Razor said, "the one *without* makeup...she wasn't the old lady who watched you run Taylor down; she was her twin."

"Twin?" Toad and Booger said in unison.

"Twin," Condit said.

"Whoa." Booger whistled through his teeth. "Old lady twins."

"You would have known there were two of them if you bothered to watch the news or read a paper."

Condit slanted a look at the two that would fry an egg. "Let me get this straight; not only did you fail to recharge your phone, but you couldn't get the stuff because of one little old lady and a dog?"

"We didn't know about the dog..." Toad said. "That dog's a monster. He took a chunk out of my leg."

"For real," Booger said.

"Like I said, two of you against one little old lady and all you could manage to do was to scare yourselves." Condit pointed to the laptop. "That's a useless piece of crap. Henry only used it for his personal matters. There's at least one other computer in his house, the one he set up as a trap."

"We could go back late tonight after the police are gone," Toad said. "We could watch the house then hustle in right after the police pull their tape and leave."

Condit took a deep breath and grew thoughtful. "The good news is apparently no one else has an inkling of what Henry was doing; the police seem to think your bungling was just an attempted robbery." She paused, then added, "Okay, wait until the cops finish working the house and take down the tape. It should be easy enough to get in through that boarded up window. I'm going to give you one more chance."

Toad and Booger nodded energetically.

Condit pounded a fist on the desktop and smiled when the two men jumped. "You screwed up, so you're going to fix it." She pointed to a five-stick package of chewing gum on the desk. "See that? That's about the size of a memory stick. There may be several in different colors; bring them all. There should be at least one other computer or laptop."

"Same as you were told the first time." Razor

shook his head. "You worthless pieces of—"

"And don't forget the power cords," Condit said. "It would be a shame for you *and* the computer to die because you forgot the cord." She smiled as if the words were meant to be a joke.

Sweat popped out on Toad's upper lip, and he cleared his throat. Booger blinked several times and sniffed noisily.

"No more test runs and no more excuses," Condit said. "None of us is getting any older if you keep messing up."

Toad shoved Booger toward the door.

"Just so you know," Condit said. "Razor here is just dying to do some regulating on your sorry asses, so don't make me regret giving you a second chance."

As the door shushed closed behind the men, Toad put a finger to his lips and jerked his head for Booger to follow him to the elevator. It wasn't until they were alone in the enclosed space that either man spoke.

"What're we going to do?" Booger said.

"We got to find a way to get the stuff," Toad said. "We got to prove we're up to expectations."

"For real." Booger nodded his head energetically.

Wordlessly, the two men hurried to the room they shared. Once inside, Toad sat in an overstuffed chair.

"What's the plan?" Booger said.

"I figure we have a couple of hours before we can get back into the house," Toad said. "We should grab a bite then drive the van someplace near the house and wait for the police to leave."

"What if the old lady comes back while we're there?"

Toad ran his hand over his bandaged calf. "Then

we'll take care of her *and* the dog."

Chapter Eleven

Lil strode from the kitchen, through the connecting door, and into the garage as Dix pulled her car inside. She waited for her sister to turn off her red convertible Miata's engine, then strode to the driver's side and yanked the door open.

"What's going on?" Lil shouted.

"I'll tell you later." Dix waved her left hand in the air wearily. "Right now, I need to get this animal into the house."

"No, you've put me off long enough. I want to know what's happened. The truth...I'll know if you even *try* to lie to me." Lil peered into the car then pointed at the furry behemoth in the back seat. The creature's head was swathed in bandages, the whole thing surrounded by a plastic cone. "What in Goshen happened to the Bantha? She looks like she's been in a lamp factory explosion."

"This is Henry's dog Lulu."

"I figured that much, but what happened to her?"

"It's a long story, Sis, and I'm so tired I can hardly see straight; I didn't sleep a wink last night. I'll get Lulu settled, then, I have to call Dillon." Dix stepped out of the car then held the back door open for the dog.

"And what, pray tell, will *settling* that creature entail?"

"I have to take care of her for a while." Dix

avoided looking directly at her sister as the dog jumped out of the back seat and onto the garage floor.

"I must be hearing things." Lil poked an index finger into an ear canal and jiggled it up and down. "I know you aren't—"

Dix held her hand up like a crossing guard stopping traffic then described the events of the past couple of hours. As the story unfolded, the look on Lil's face grew more and more grim.

"I knew something was wrong," Lil said. "What have you gotten yourself into?"

Dix squared her shoulders defiantly. "I haven't gotten myself into anything, but evidently poor Henry did." She pointed to the bandaged places on the dog's face. "Lulu took the guy with the gun completely by surprise. The jerk shot a chunk out of her ear and grazed her cheek, but she chomped a plug out of his leg."

Seeming to understand that she'd become the topic of conversation, the dog stopped sniffing a front tire, lifted her head, and looked first at Dix then Lil. She pounded her tail against the closed car door, the sound reminiscent of a percussionist pounding a leather-headed conga drum.

Lil pursed her lips and looked down her nose at the animal. "Okay, this is not going to work for me."

"Just give me twenty-four hours to work things out."

"Twenty-four hours to work what out?"

"To figure out what to do with Lulu," Dix said.

"And where do you plan to keep the creature during that time?"

"She'll share my room tonight."

Lulu whumped her tail more vigorously than ever.

"Our yard's big enough for her to do her business in a pinch." Dix motioned toward the dog. "She's well trained." She pointed to the trunk of her car. "I brought her food and water dishes, if you would care to lend a hand."

"Wait a minute, I haven't agreed to any of this."

Ignoring her sister, Dix tugged on Lulu's lead. She held the door open, and the dog galumphed into the house as if she had lived there all her life.

"Make yourself at home, why don't you," Lil said to the animal's huge, disappearing backside. She popped Dix's trunk and retrieved two stainless steel containers, each large enough to double as a small child's bathtub.

"Nah." Lil eyed the two fifty-pound bags of food. "Not even going to try."

Once inside the house, she plopped the dishes onto the floor in the kitchen. "It's all yours," Lil said to her sister. "I don't tend animals." She sat at the kitchen table and shot stink-eye glares at Lulu.

"The vet said she's had her rabies shots and has been microchipped." Dix reached for the dog's two-inch-wide leather collar and the metal tags attached to it.

"Is that supposed to comfort me? The possibility of her going rabid is the least of my worries. If we accidentally piss her off, all she has to do is plop down on top of us...end of story."

The dog sauntered to Lil and dropped to the floor at her feet. She tried to rest her head on her front paws, but the lampshade proved awkward. The animal pawed at the cone, but it held fast.

"You know sooner or later she's going to manage to scrape that thing off," Lil said.

"I have a feeling she could do just about anything she set her mind to."

Lil frowned and crossed her arms. "Don't even think about it," she said. "We can't afford a dog, especially *that* dog."

"You've *never* allowed me to have a pet. We couldn't even afford a fish tank. When Davie brought home a stray kitten, you made him get rid of it."

"Don't bring our nephew into this. Pets are expensive. Although, if it came right down to it, I would rather have a dog than a cat. At least if we died in our sleep, a dog would stand guard and maybe mourn a little, whereas a cat would leisurely eat our soft parts."

"Why are you such a sour puss?" Dix said. "Not all cats—"

"You're in denial." Lil squinted at her sister. "By the way, you should either wear your glasses or use the magnifying mirror when you paint on your eyebrows. Either a black, furry caterpillar is nesting just above your left eye, or the eyebrow's gone rogue; it's a good half inch lower than the right."

Lulu chose that moment to look into Lil's eyes and place a small-frying-pan-sized paw on top of her right house slipper.

"Look," Dix said. "She likes you."

"Then why did she just baptize my slippers in a rope of drool?" Lil bent over and, using the thumb and forefinger of one hand, tugged her slippers off. She gingerly carried them toward the laundry room. "Not cool," she yelled over her shoulder.

The sound of the garage door opening drew Lil

back into the kitchen. Within a minute or two, Dix came back through the connecting door, carrying a small tool she used for digging in her garden.

"The food bags are too heavy for me," Dix said. "I'll have to punch a hole in one and dip the kibble out with the trowel." She carried the metal dish to the garage. "Fill her water dish, will you?" she yelled over her shoulder.

After putting her slippers into the laundry, Lil donned a pair of rubber galoshes and returned to the kitchen. She carried the dog's water dish to the sink, filled it, then carried it to the utility room. "I think she should eat out here," she hollered. "Less chance for one of us to slip on the half gallon of water she'll slosh out of her bowl every time she drinks."

"Agreed," Dix shouted in response.

Dix returned from the garage bearing the food dish, now heaped with dog food. She placed the dish on the utility room floor next to the water bowl, then sat in a chair across the table from her twin.

The animal fairly inhaled the quarter-sized chunks of kibble, licked the last crumb from the food bowl, then took a long drink. With her muzzle dripping water, she trotted back to the twins, dropped onto the floor between them, then flipped onto her back, her legs in the air.

When Dix didn't offer the requisite belly rubs, the dog looked imploringly at Lil.

"Not going to happen." Lil turned to her sister. "What are you smiling at?"

"At you," Dix said. "If you had seen the way this animal went after that gun-wielding creep—"

"Your friend Henry was murdered on our

doorstep." Lil jabbed her index finger in the air. "Then two guys carrying guns broke into his house, yet you sit here blathering on about the dead man's dog as if nothing happened?"

"I'm going to be careful," Dix said. "But you're overreacting."

"Is it even possible to overreact to that?"

"As you say, a friend has been murdered." Dix rubbed her face with the palms of her hands. "I can't just sit around the house doing nothing."

"Yes, you can. You can let the police do their thing, and we can get on with our lives."

"Spoken like the misanthrope you've been from birth." Dix shook her head.

"I prefer *realist*. And you're making your standard going-to-save-the-world noises. You can't expect other people to treat you the way you treat them. You know that, right? The Golden Rule only works if all parties concerned buy into it."

"Not true," Dix said. "The Golden Rule offers a positive way for one person to deal with another. It doesn't promise the other person will respond in kind."

"So, you're going to just keep on—" Lil began.

"Unlike you, I refuse to step aside and let nature take its course when someone I know has been hurt."

Lil rolled her eyes. "Oh no, not the *we are the world* speech."

"Every living thing is connected. Did you know that trees communicate with each other?"

"I talk to the trees—" Lil swayed back and forth, waving her arms as she intoned the lyrics to an old love song.

"Very funny. I just learned that scientists have

discovered that when they apply an electrical shock to a bunch of algae, the algae will cringe in anticipation of getting shocked again?"

"Lord have mercy," Lil said. "How many taxpayer dollars were spent on that bit of research?"

"Maybe you wouldn't be such a curmudgeon if you spent some time in the company of plants."

"Okay, okay." Lil waved a hand. "What's your plan?"

"I don't have one yet. I'm hoping Dillon will have some ideas."

"What I mean to say is you're not going to do this by yourself," Lil said in a gentler voice. "Here"—she motioned toward a kitchen chair—"have a seat and let's talk this through."

Dix looked up at her sister. "Good thing I'm familiar with your Good Twin-Bad Twin act. You think if you can delay things long enough, I'll give up."

"I'm not—"

"You may know statistics, but I know what makes people tick." *At least, some people.* "That gives me an edge to figuring this thing out. You can either help, or I'll do it on my own."

"You don't have the foggiest clue what you're getting into."

"Maybe not, but I will." Dix yawned.

"Wouldn't the police see anything you do as interfering with an investigation? You could get jail time."

"I'm not going to interfere, but the police seem to think the break-in was just a burglary. I think Henry's murder and the break-ins are linked."

"If that's the case, these are not nice people. You

can't expect any quarter from them just because you look like everyone's grandma."

"Lest you forget," Dix said, "I spent years as a therapist. I've dealt with some pretty bad actors."

"And you made excuses for every one of them." Lil shook her head. "Nothing I can say is going to change your mind?"

"Nope." Dix pulled her phone from its pouch inside her purse and began punching its screen.

Lulu cocked her head and looked at Lil.

"Don't get too comfortable." Lil eyed the dog, who eyed her in return. Like sumo wrestlers mentally gauging where to get the best hold, the two sat staring at each other. "I don't like messes," Lil finally said. "You'll be out on your ear before you can count to five if you make one."

The dog yawned.

"I don't do belly rubs and I can't abide being touched. Don't even think about licking anything, either on me or that belongs to me."

Lulu wagged her tail once then headed for the open back door.

"That's right," Lil called out, "I'm the boss."

Chapter Twelve

Dix drummed the table with the fingers of her left hand while waiting for Dillon to answer his phone. She first met the twenty-four-year-old tech genius when he was a shy twelve-year-old. An only child, he had accompanied his single mother to a local nonprofit where the then-private-practice psychologist Dix had agreed to offer free counseling to people referred by Social Services. She had been struck by the kid's loving and respectful attitude toward his mother, even though the woman was an emotional mess.

Over the succeeding decade, Dillon had developed into a single-minded mathematician and software guru. Dix had been pleased when a couple of years earlier he initiated contact.

"Hello, Dillon," she said.

"Hey, Doc, how's it going?" Dillon said.

"It's going. How's your mom?"

"She's doing great. Your magic worked...she's still sober. It's been nearly twelve years now."

"I can't believe it's been that long."

"Yep, I was just a kid. You pretty well saved us both—"

"I didn't do anything except shine a light, Dillon; your mom did the rest. Nobody gets sober until they decide to get sober."

"Humility," Dillon said. "I like that. What's up?"

"I'm not sure, but I may have stumbled onto something. Are you up for a challenge?"

"Sure. What do you need me to do?"

"Have you ever heard of a man named Henry Taylor?"

"*The* Henry Taylor?"

For the next several minutes Dix brought Dillon up to speed on the events of the past twenty-four hours.

"So, you think Henry Taylor's death might have had something to do with whatever he was working on?" Dillon said.

"I don't know, that's why I called you."

"To answer your earlier question," Dillon said, "*honeypot* is a term used in the hacking community. It refers to a computer set up on a separate server specifically for the purpose of attracting a certain kind of internet traffic. Mr. Taylor most likely used Wire Shark, a network traffic analyzer, to set it up. It's possible he found a vulnerability or exploit on Tor, that's an anonymity network with access to the Dark Web—"

"Stop, please," Dix said. "You do realize you're talking to a Luddite, right? In plain English, please."

"Sorry." Dillon chuckled. "There are bodies of sophisticated, savvy people who band together to help others. Let's just say Henry Taylor was a White Hat Hacker, a good guy whose targets of choice were sites that specialize in really bad stuff."

"And?"

"It sounds like he set up a bait computer, a honeypot, and was watching the kind of internet traffic it attracted." Dillon blew out a puff of air. "Out of over two hundred computer programming languages, it's estimated Henry Taylor was fluent in six or seven. Considering that most software developers work with maybe two or three languages, that's amazing. He generated some cool algorithms. I was fortunate enough to get into one of his presentations a couple of years ago at the Black Hat Conference in Vegas. I'm sorry to hear of his death."

"On the surface he seemed like a nice, average guy."

"He *was* nice, but he was anything *but* average. I hope you're wrong about his death being murder, but it wouldn't be the first time someone's stumbled onto malignant online activities, started to expose it, then disappeared or died in suspicious circumstances. Generally, when someone discovers malicious bots, they immediately go to the police or the news media. That's the safest thing to do, since once the public knows about it, the person who discovered it generally becomes bullet proof."

"So, the fact that Henry was murdered tells us he hadn't had time to expose the bad guys?" Dix grew thoughtful.

"That's one possibility. Or maybe he shared his suspicions with the wrong person."

"Good Lord, what kind of world are we living in?"

"Yeah, well stay tuned. You want me to do some digging?"

"I was hoping you could tell me what Henry might have been working on," Dix said.

"It would be a lot easier if I could access Mr. Taylor's honeypot. The whole point of setting one up is that it's exploitable, so I could get into it fairly easily. That would tell us what online traffic was coming in. Is it possible for me to get hold of it?"

"I don't know why not. I'll call and ask his daughter for permission."

"Super," Dillon said. "You should do that sooner rather than later."

"If you're right, we might be wading into deep water. I don't want you to put yourself in any danger, you understand?"

Dillon chuckled. "I have a fairly high-level security clearance for a reason. Give me the honeypot and twenty-four hours."

"What things shall I ask Val for permission to get?"

"All Mr. Taylor's electronics," Dillon said. "Anything we can carry."

"Okay, anything electric."

"Not electric, *electronic*. There's a difference." Dillon chuckled. "I should go with you. No offense, but you don't know what to look for."

"I can't ask you—"

"I'm asking *you*. If someone killed Mr. Taylor because of something he was working on, that means they're still out there doing whatever they were doing that attracted his attention. It would be my honor to help."

"Thank you, Dillon."

"I'll ask for the day off. I have several vacation days coming. If this *does* turn out to be a malicious situation, the bad guys will have to get hold of that honeypot and any of Mr. Taylor's notes and data. We need to let the FBI know of anything we find."

"Do whatever you think is best. I'll get back to you after I've spoken to Henry's daughter." Dix broke the connection, checked her call log, then dialed Val's number.

"Hello?" The voice sounded thick, as if the young woman had been crying.

Dix identified herself and made her request.

"I would like to get dad's laptop back at some point…but take whatever you need for now. I'll stay in the motel until I've settled Dad's affairs. I'm on hold now with a property management company; they'll take care of the house until I can sell it."

"Of course," Dix said. "I'll make sure everything is locked up before we leave."

"Dad's memorial service is Thursday; I hope you can come. I won't know anyone…" Val's voice trailed off and dissolved into sobs. "Will you let me know what you find?"

"Of course."

"Thanks," Val said.

"Do you have dinner plans?"

"I was planning to hang around the motel until Dad's memorial service."

"Why don't I pick you up this evening?" Dix said. "I'd like to talk to you."

"I would like that." Val sniffed. "What time?"

"Is seven too late?"

"No, it's good. I'll be waiting in the lobby."

After Val told Dix the name of the motel, Dix broke the connection then called Dillon. "We can take anything we need," she said when he answered his phone.

"We need to hustle," Dillon said. "If anyone shows up, we leave without the stuff, okay?"

"Agreed. I'll meet you there." Dix repeated

Henry's address then hung up.

She turned to Lil, who stood with her arms akimbo, an angry look on her face.

"You're going back into that house?" Lil said. "Don't the police have it taped off?"

"Only for a couple of hours, just long enough to look for fingerprints, that kind of thing."

"You're taking the dog, right?"

"I can't," Dix said. "It's inhumane to leave an animal inside a car."

"So, you're leaving her here…leaving me alone with that creature?"

"You'll be okay," Dix said. "She's picky about what she eats."

"Very funny."

"Open the back door; she'll go out when she needs to do her business."

"I don't want—"

"I'll collect Henry's stickie notes while Dillon gets whatever he needs…maybe we'll find something helpful." Dix snapped her fingers. "Oh yeah, I need to contact that Kelly person when I get back."

"Why don't you call every name in the phone book while you're at it?" Lil stood in the middle of the kitchen, a scowl on her face. "Just to make sure you don't miss anyone who might have known the man."

"Will your bottomless pit of sarcasm never run dry?" Dix turned and headed for the garage. "You're an antisocial old wart, you know that?" she hurled over her shoulder.

"Yup, and you're an old hippy kook," Lil shouted as the door closed behind her sister.

Chapter Thirteen

During the drive to Henry's house, Dix mulled over the things Dillon had told her. Had she been under a rock the past three decades not to recognize the enormity of change in the world, or was Lil's claim that she refused to see reality more accurate than she wanted to admit?

Although Lil would insist her twin lived in a fantasy world of fluff, Dix had studied human nature and worked with people long enough to have few illusions. While she believed in the general goodness of humanity, she also recognized that sometimes the species' survival required gentle folk to respond with strength to those who consistently chose their own interests over everyone else's.

On the other hand, maybe Dillon was mistaken about what got Henry killed. Maybe the young man's work at a local, government-operated laboratory made him overly suspicious.

Maybe...

Dillon had already arrived at Henry's house by the time Dix got there. He leaned against his late model Subaru, a welcoming smile lighting his face as Dix parked and exited her own vehicle.

"I got here just as the police were taking the tape off the door," Dillon said. He pushed a stray, ginger-colored forelock away from his eyes. "I have a feeling we need to hustle."

As Dix pulled Henry's keys from her purse, she unconsciously glanced up the street. A dark blue SUV sat parked in front of one of the neighbor's houses.

"What's up?" Dillon said.

Dix motioned with her head toward the vehicle. "I'm pretty sure I've seen that SUV before, but I can't remember where."

Suddenly, the SUV started up and pulled away.

Dillon blew a gust of breath through pursed lips. "In that case, I suggest we get a move on."

Dix unlocked Henry's front door, and the two stepped inside the house.

Strange how a few hours could change the atmosphere in what had been a man's home. The lighthearted feeling of the evening Henry introduced Dix to Lulu had evaporated into heaviness and stale air. The place felt forlorn, abandoned.

"You might want to lock that door behind us," Dillon said.

Over the next several minutes, Dillon quickly unplugged two electronic devices and collected thumb drives. He stacked everything beside the front door while Dix strode through the house collecting stickies and dropping them into a cloth tote bag. As an afterthought, she pulled Henry's calendar from the wall and stuffed it inside the bulging bag.

"I'm assuming the police took Mr. Taylor's Smart phone," Dillon said.

"They took everything he had with him at the time he was hit."

"Then I'm done."

"Same here," Dix said.

While Dillon carried his load to his vehicle and sped away, Dix locked Henry's door. She walked to her car, but instead of getting in, she stood beside it and scanned the street. A dirty white van—probably a plumber or something—was stopped a block away, but the SUV was nowhere in sight.

With a sensation that she was hurtling headlong into a black hole, Dix backed out of Henry's driveway and headed home.

Chapter Fourteen

Razor had been surprised when the old lady with the eyebrows froze in Taylor's driveway and stood staring in his direction. Although in his experience people tended not to be all that observant, the intensity of her gaze had given him the heebie-jeebies.

Those who lived in the large cities in which he worked hustled about their business without looking directly at anyone else. Eye contact could be construed as a sign of aggression, and a smile could make its recipient think you were either a nut job or planning to rob them. In the circles in which Razor ran, a smile not only meant weakness, it could get you hurt.

Razor started his engine and drove a couple of blocks up the street to a small bistro he spotted earlier. He pulled into the parking lot and shut off his engine.

Ignoring the phone resting in the dock on his dashboard, he pulled another from inside a compartment secreted under the left side of his drive column and punched in a number.

"One of the old ladies and some kid have just gone into Taylor's house," he said.

"And?" BeeBee LeDuc said.

"I'll keep an eye on them. They might be innocently going about their business, maybe getting stuff for Taylor's daughter, but I can't shake the feeling that they're up to something."

"Like what?"

"Maybe the old lady and Taylor were close friends, close enough for him to confide in her. Maybe she's in there looking for something specific."

"What could she know?"

"Probably nothing, she's an old lady. My grandma still pays her bills with a check. It's more likely she's stealing his stuff in hopes of selling it or pawning it." Razor sighed. "Old ladies and kids hitting a dead man's house before he's even been planted; what's the world coming to?"

"Do you know anything about either of them?"

"I've never seen the kid before, but Granny Eyebrows keeps popping up. I have a feeling she's the one to watch. Did Taylor's hit make the news in LA?"

"A mention this morning, but only because he had such a high profile."

"The local newspaper article said the old lady's name is Dix Ruiz," Razor said. "Do you have someone who could look into her?"

"I do," LeDuc said. "I'll be in touch."

After Razor broke the connection, he replaced the burner phone in its hiding place, reached for his other phone, and texted Toad.

—*Two cars at the house. Wait.*—

He rolled his eyes when Toad texted back a thumbs-up emoticon.

Razor put his cell into his jacket pocket. He maneuvered his arm behind his back and scratched just below his left shoulder blade then retrieved a black box roughly the size of a deck of cards from his glove compartment.

"Okay," he murmured under his breath. "Let's see

what Granny Eyebrows is up to."

He exited his vehicle, dropped the magnetic GPS tracking device into his pants pocket, and strolled toward Taylor's house.

However, when Razor was still a block or so away, Granny Eyebrows stepped out of Taylor's front door, and the kid immediately followed. Razor slowed, then stepped behind a large bush in a nearby yard, and peered through the spikey, wax-like leaves.

The old woman carried a cloth tote, but the way the bag moved when she locked the front door behind the two of them indicated the contents weighed very little.

Razor snorted. Was Granny ripping off Taylor's heirs by taking his jewelry or perhaps any cash he kept laying around?

The kid stepped out from behind Granny. Carrying what appeared to be a couple of laptops from which black power cords dangled, he strode toward a late model Subaru. The pockets of his safari-style vest bulged.

Razor had figured the old lady and kid would have to make several trips back and forth to their cars with whatever booty they could haul out...figured he had plenty of time to call LeDuc then plant the GPS.

However, instead of returning to the house, Granny Eyebrows and the kid got into their respective vehicles and took off. Cursing himself for a fool, Razor returned to his SUV.

Condit-the-witch would verbally shred him, Toad, *and* Booger when she found out they let Granny Eyebrows and the kid beat them to the stuff.

Razor's lip curled. When Kelly Condit first approached him with what she glowingly referred to as *the investment opportunity of the century*, he found her excitement infectious. Once he had made a sizeable investment in her project, it seemed a natural progression for them to become romantically involved.

However, when he suggested they spend a weekend in Vegas, Kelly had laughed in his face. By the time they had been partners a few weeks, Razor had not only grown to despise everything about her but had begun to fantasize about ways to teach her a lesson. Maybe when the project was over...

Razor fired up his engine and sped in the direction the Geek Kid had driven. Although the kid was *an unknown variable*, as Condit was fond of saying, his possession of the electronics also made him a key target.

If all went well, Razor would have the laptops and accessories in his hands within the hour. It would be his pleasure to dump the whole shebang on Condit's head.

If need be, he'd deal with Granny Eyebrows later. He knew where she lived.

Chapter Fifteen

Toad's phone pinged, announcing receipt of a text message. He pulled into the driveway of a house fronted by a for sale sign, took the fully charged phone from the van's built-in cup holder, and read the message.

"What's up?" Booger craned his neck to get a glimpse of the texted message.

"Razor says someone's at the house, and we're supposed to wait." Toad squinted and studied the van's ceiling. "Got your binoculars handy?"

"Always." Booger pulled a set of demi-binoculars from the van's console and peered through them at Taylor's house. "What if whoever's there is getting the stuff?"

"Shut up and let me think. If it was up to me, I'd storm the house and deal with whoever's there before they could get out with anything. That's Razor's problem; he's afraid of confrontation."

"Hey." Booger jerked his head toward the house. "There's somebody coming out the door."

Toad's phone pinged again. "Razor says he's following the kid, and for us to get back to the motel and wait for orders."

"The old lady's just standing in front of the house looking around." Booger sniffed. "Maybe she forgot where she is. Old people do that, you know."

"So what?"

"What if she sees us and calls the cops?"

"We're too far away for her to recognize us." Toad waited to give the old lady time to leave then backed out of the vacant house's driveway and into the street.

"Where are we going?" Booger said. "The motel's the other direction."

Toad pulled the van into the alley behind Taylor's house, turned off the engine, and turned toward Booger. "You ever wonder what could be valuable enough for Condit-the-whiz and Razor to leave Los Angeles and come to the sticks to get?"

"I figured it was some kind of high dollar computer or sunthin," Booger said.

"Gotta be more than that. They could order that online, never even have to leave the house."

"True," Booger said.

"So why come to this tiny burg?" Toad said. "What's here that they couldn't take care of from LA?"

"You got any ideas?" Booger said.

"Not sure, but whatever it is, you can bet there'll be somebody willing to pay a pile of money for it."

"You mean cut the Whiz and Razor out of the deal?" Booger scratched his chin, a thoughtful look on his face. "But what if that geek kid took the important stuff, and there's nothing left?"

"Then we got nothing to lose. If the kid's only interest was to grab a laptop to hock, the important stuff might still be in the house. I know a guy who has four laptops, a couple of tablets, and at least six smart phones."

"Neither the Whiz nor Razor said anything about a smart phone. You can do a lot with one of those."

"They're just like a laptop, only smaller." Toad tapped the side of his nose with an index finger. "We could gut that house of anything with a power cord, then hustle back to LA and offer it all to Uncle BeeBee."

Booger looked mystified. "Who's *Uncle BeeBee*?"

"BeeBee LeDuc."

"He's your uncle? You never said."

"I don't tell you everything. Uncle BeeBee's wife is my aunt."

"Cool," Booger said. "But I thought Mr. LeDuc and the Whiz was friends."

"That's what happens when you try to think. All that snot floating around inside your head plugs up your thinking valves. I happen to know Uncle BeeBee is no friend of Condit *or* Razor; he doesn't trust either of them."

"Wait a minute," Booger said. "Didn't Mr. LeDuc invest a ton of money in this deal?"

"So?"

"How's he going to feel about us going around Condit, especially when she's the tech person? She's the only one who knows what she's doing online."

"There you go again, trying to think. Condit may be smart when it comes to tech stuff, but she's not the only fish in the deep blue. Uncle BeeBee can afford to hire a top-rate techie straight out of Silicon Valley to do what Condit's doing, and he wouldn't have to split the profits."

"Then why is he using her in the first place?"

"Because it was all her idea, dufus. She's the one who came up with the plan and who knew how to make it work."

"I never understood what kind of business it is anyway. They don't have a building, no offices, no signs on the road…"

"They don't need any of that; everything happens online."

"Ahh." Booger blinked a couple of times and nodded as if the meaning of life had just been explained to him.

"Time to take charge of our own destinies," Toad said.

"For real," Booger said sagely.

Chapter Sixteen

Booger stared serenely out the windshield as Toad drove the van behind Taylor's house. Whatever Toad had in mind was fine with him; he was content just to be hanging out with his buddy.

The two had been friends for a couple of decades, ever since as, barely teenagers, they had run into each other shoplifting from the same convenience store in downtown Los Angeles. They eyed each other warily while waiting for the solitary clerk to become distracted by a customer, then loaded up. Their bulky jackets stuffed full of candy bars, gum, and Slim Jims, they hustled outside where they ran down the alleyway to a park a couple of blocks away.

Toad sat at a park table and began pulling stuff from his jacket as Booger sauntered over to him.

"You mind if I sit here?" Booger had said.

"It's a free country." Toad nodded once then selected a Baby Ruth from his pile of goodies and snarfed it down in two bites.

Booger took a seat across the park table and pulled a Milky Way out of his pocket. "You new to LA?" he asked.

Toad glanced at Booger and bit a chunk off his Slim Jim but didn't respond.

"You live around here?" Booger persisted. "I don't remember seeing you before."

"That's because I know better than to take a dump in my own front yard." Toad cut his eyes sideways at Booger. "If you live anywhere near here, you're screwing up. Sooner or later, someone will recognize you and spill their guts to the cops."

Booger nodded in recognition of the wisdom of the statement then stuck his hand out and introduced himself.

Toad had wiped the chocolate off his fingers then shaken the proffered hand. "Booger's a weird thing to name a kid."

"It's not my real name, just what people call me. I haven't heard my real name in so long I probably wouldn't answer to it."

"People call me Toad."

As the afternoon wore on, the two talked about their nonexistent home lives, girls, and their hopes for the future.

"I'm gonna open up a motorcycle repair shop someday," Booger had said. "I'm handy with tools and such."

"Cool," Toad said. "It'll cost a lot, though. Where are you going to get the cash…you got rich parents?"

"I wish." Booger grinned. "You?"

"Got a rich uncle, but he never liked me much." Toad looked Booger up and down. "You on the street?"

"What if I am?" For the first and last time Booger could remember, he bristled at the boy who would become his lifelong pal.

Toad shrugged. "Nothing to me."

The two fell silent. After they ate all their stolen stuff—*appropriated staples*, as Toad had called them—Toad stood. "You could come to my house," he said.

"You mean—"

"I mean you could come for a few days. You know, just until you get on your feet."

"What about your parents?"

"What about 'em?" Toad cocked his head toward Booger and lifted his eyebrows.

"Won't they—"

"My folks are never home." Toad snorted. "Too busy out of the country doing important stuff."

Booger had accepted the invitation, and the boys had taken a city bus to Toad's house.

A few days turned into weeks then months. While Booger understood Toad's invitation had been out of loneliness and to give the finger to his absentee parents, he developed a deep bond with his friend and would have done virtually anything for him. Through Toad's tutelage, Booger grew expert first at petty thievery then grand theft.

When the two turned sixteen, Toad finagled jobs for them with LeDuc. When they were eighteen, they moved into an apartment owned by Mr. LeDuc with the understanding they would do whatever he asked.

Eventually, LeDuc offered them a chance to make more money than they had ever seen by involving them in his protection racket and blackmail schemes. Bit by bit, the boys' consciences were whittled down until they were capable of doing just about anything without flinching.

Booger smiled inwardly at the memory of those early days. While Toad had frittered away all the money he made, Booger saved every penny he could get his hands on.

If all went according to schedule, he would have

enough within another year to open his motorcycle repair shop. He'd break free of LeDuc and set up a legitimate business. He could offer Toad a partnership, and together they would live the life Booger had always dreamed of having.

Booger touched his pistol and the smile melted off his face. First, though, they had to deal with the Whiz and the old ladies.

Chapter Seventeen

Razor sat in his vehicle across the street from the apartment where the kid took all the stuff he'd pulled from Taylor's house. He tapped his fingers against the steering wheel and watched the young man's movements through a large, curtain-less picture window. Within a couple of minutes, the kid moved to sit with his back to the window, his focus on something in front of him.

Razor mulled over his options. Should he bust in at gun point and take the stuff, or should he wait for the kid to leave with the gear then ambush him? Maybe he should wait until nightfall then break in. The problem with each of those tactics, however, was they almost guaranteed the need to shoot the kid. While he had never popped a kid, he would do whatever needed doing.

"Nothing personal," Razor murmured toward the back of the kid's head, "but you shouldn't have gotten involved."

When, after an hour, the kid's gingery hair-covered head still hadn't moved, Razor pulled his phone from its dock and punched in Condit's number.

"Got a problem," he said.

"I don't like the sound of that." Condit emitted what sounded like a heavy sigh.

"I'm at the kid's apartment, but something doesn't

feel right. He's just sitting in front of his window."

"What do you mean?"

"I mean I've been staring at the back of his head for over an hour. He hasn't moved, not a hair. Is that normal for you people?"

"If by *you people* you mean techies, then, yes, it's perfectly normal. I've been known to work on something from early morning until late evening without realizing the passage of time. What makes you think the kid is a techie?"

"I don't know for sure, but everything he grabbed from Taylor's house looked electronic."

Condit remained silent.

"Did you hear me?"

"I heard." Condit's voice had grown sharp enough to shred raw carrots. "Unless you want to spend the next twenty-five to thirty years of your life pressing license plates, I suggest you figure out a way to get in there and get the stuff, now, I mean this minute. I just hope he hasn't had time to…" She paused, then added, "If he sees your face—"

"I'll call you when I get the stuff." Razor broke the connection then dropped his phone into his shirt pocket.

Kelly had been proud of herself for striking up an acquaintance with Henry Taylor, bragging about how she befriended him then built his trust in her coding abilities by chatting about the kinds of things discussed in the geek realm. She crowed that he had asked her more than once to doublecheck his findings regarding some issue upon which he'd focused his attention. The poor schmuck had never dreamed that what he assumed to be a collegial friendship was really a means of keeping tabs on his efforts to expose cyber criminals.

Razor pulled his pistol from the glove compartment and glanced toward the kid's window. The kid had disappeared.

Cursing, Razor palmed the 9mm and slid it into the pocket of his windbreaker, taking care not to catch the hammer on the nylon jacket...the last thing he needed was to shoot his own ass off. He opened his vehicle's door just as the kid sauntered out his front door.

Emptyhanded, looking straight ahead, the young man headed to his car. Leisurely, he backed out of his driveway and drove off.

"Problem solved," Razor said. He replaced his pistol in its hidey-hole, pulled a worn, leather pouch about the size of a wallet from the SUV's console, and dropped it into his breast pocket. He'd have preferred to use the expensive set of lock picks he purchased a couple of years earlier when ordered to break into the office of one of LeDuc's enemies to retrieve incriminating files. The cheap set he'd spotted at a local pawn shop, however, would have to do. Razor had yet to find a lock he couldn't pick.

Whistling, he casually headed for the rear of the kid's apartment. If all worked to plan, he would be in his truck and headed back to the motel within a few minutes.

Hopefully, the kid wouldn't complicate matters by coming home before Razor scored the laptop.

Chapter Eighteen

After Dix left to meet Dillon at Taylor's house, Lil retreated to the kitchen and placed the plate of leftover homemade raspberry scones on the counter. She selected the pastry with the most visible berries, placed it on a small saucer, then sat at the kitchen table.

Lulu, her cone nowhere in sight, trotted in through the sliding back door Lil had left open to allow the not-too-cool autumn air into the kitchen. The dog sauntered to Lil then planted her butt on the floor and looked up expectantly.

"This—" Lil held up the uneaten portion of scone. "—Is mine. I don't eat your food, and you can't have mine."

As Lil munched the fruit-filled pastry, Lulu's attention remained focused on her like a laser beam.

"You're hoping I'll drop a crumb, is that it?" Lil snorted. "I'll make you a deal; any food I drop is yours."

When Lil carefully popped the last morsel into her mouth, Lulu grunted and lay down, her collar clinking against the floor.

Made of top grain leather, the collar had to have been nearly a quarter of an inch thick and almost two inches wide. At eighteen to twenty inches in length, the thing was large enough to hold a copy of the Magna Carta.

Lil sat bolt upright as scenes from old spy movies flashed into her memory. Hadn't someone done a scene in which an undercover operative secreted a microchip of top-secret military information inside a dog's collar? She remembered a documentary that focused on how the development of the internet had changed the world, and how surprised she'd been at the tiny size of modern microchips. The whole *Encyclopedia Britannica* could be put on a chip the size of a pinhead.

"Hold still, Bantha." Lil reached for the collar.

After several tries during which Lulu persistently wriggled away from her touch, Lil unbuckled the collar then hurried to the kitchen junk drawer from which she retrieved a small magnifying glass. A thorough examination of the collar, however, didn't bring to light any missing or loose stitches beneath which a cipher could be hidden.

Maybe Taylor had glued something tiny to the collar's back. Nowadays, some glues could not only permanently affix nylon rope to a brick but were nearly invisible.

After staring through the spyglass lens at the collar's backside long enough to gin up a headache, Lil tossed the collar onto the table. "So much for James Bond," she murmured.

She was debating about having another scone when the sound of the opening garage door signaled her sister's return from Henry Taylor's house.

Lulu trotted to the utility room door and stood whapping the clothes dryer with her tail as Dix stepped through the door, her face set in grim lines. Carrying a fabric tote bag stuffed full of something that crinkled when it moved, she smiled at Lulu's happy jig and patted the dog's head.

"Where's your cone?" Dix said.

"Somewhere in the back yard," Lil answered.

"Why's her collar on the table?"

After a brief report of her dead-end inspection of the collar, Lil said, "How about you, did you learn anything?"

Dix looked at her sister and shook her head. "Just that the world we thought we knew doesn't exist."

"It never did. Like I've always said, Norman Rockwell was either an optimist, incredibly naïve, or both."

"I refuse to believe that. There've always been kind and generous people, thank the Lord, but there's another reality, a sub-world peopled by the greedy and corrupt who've sold their souls one self-serving decision at a time. It's a shadow world where life means nothing…at least, no one else's life."

"Better watch yourself. You're starting to sound like me."

"However—" Dix drew a deep breath. "—As the saying goes, the only way evil can prosper is for good people to do nothing."

"There's always been evil in the world. As you may recall, Cain killed his own brother. That's why human beings came up with the idea of paying police officers, to protect them from their loved ones."

"And if there were only two people left in the world, one would spend all his time thinking up ways to take what the other had; I know all your arguments by memory."

"Then why are we having this conversation?" Lil said.

"Because I owe you the truth, and the truth is I may be putting us in jeopardy." Dix recounted her discussion with Dillon. "I called Val and got her permission to get the computer and Henry's notes. Dillon grabbed everything electronic while I collected the stickie notes and Henry's calendar."

"The police didn't take the electronics?"

"They had no reason to treat the break-in as anything but a run-of-the-mill burglary, and they only cordoned off the house long enough for forensics to check for fingerprints."

"Maybe you're wrong; maybe it *was* just a bungled burglary."

"Dillon doesn't think so. He's going to delve into whatever Henry was working on and take what he finds to the FBI. He said the FBI investigates things like cyber crime."

"Then that's that," Lil said. "There's nothing more we can do."

"There may be nothing *you* can do. Right now, I'm going to re-cone and collar Lulu then take her for a walk." Dix dropped the tote bag onto the table. "When we get back, I want to look through Henry's notes."

"You think it's wise to go out? Shouldn't we stay close to home until this whole thing blows over?"

"Huddle in our house, hands clenched against our chests, teeth chattering, afraid to go out into the sunlight? What a miserable existence."

"Just because you want the world to—"

"Put a cork in it, Lil. I'm in no mood." Dix picked up the dog's collar and patted a hand against her thigh. "Come on, Lulu."

At the sound of her name, the dog hopped toward

Dix, her tail wagging so hard her whole backside swung back and forth.

"What a good girl you are." Dix replaced the collar around the dog's neck, then the two headed for the back yard. When they returned, the cone was firmly in place.

"I'll see you in a few minutes." Dix motioned toward the tote. "You could always sift through the stickies...maybe categorize them while I'm gone. You're more organized than I."

After her sister and the Bantha left, Lil sat at the kitchen table and dumped out the tote bag's contents. Yellow, green, and pink stickie notes fluttered to the tabletop, followed by a spiral bound calendar that advertised computer components.

"Henry's nonessential commands in one pile," Lil murmured. "Notes with any phone numbers or that hint at his work in another."

When Dix and the dog returned, Lulu bounded to her water dish, took a long drink, then laid on the floor underneath the table.

"Almost done with Henry's stickie notes." Lil pointed to a page torn from a pad of notepaper on which she'd made notations.

"Excellent. We'll go over them when I get back." Dix retrieved her purse from its place hanging from the back of a kitchen chair and headed for the garage. "I'm taking Val to dinner." She waited until just before the door closed behind her before adding, "I'm going to invite her to stay with us."

Lil jumped up from her chair and strode toward the garage door. "Not another stray," she shouted. "No more strays."

"Sorry," Dix yelled through the closed door. "Can't

hear you."

"Not cool." Lil returned to the table, sat, and focused on the notes.

The yellow papers bore reminders for household chores, and the green for activities dealing with Lulu.

Two pink stickies caught Lil's eye. On one, Henry had written the words *tokens or coins?* On the second, he'd written a series of numbers separated by dots.

"One seven three, dot, six, six, dot..." Lil murmured. She scrolled through her memory, searching the hundreds of numbers once seen never forgotten until, like a bingo drum from which numbered balls dropped, the sequence completed itself.

"Oh, sister mine," she murmured, "you were right; we are indeed in over our heads."

Chapter Nineteen

It took Razor less than a minute to pick the lock on the kid's back door. He stepped into the apartment, closed the door behind him, then hurried through a tiny kitchenette and into a space that apparently doubled as a living room and office.

A brown leather sofa strategically placed a few feet in front of and facing a wall-mounted, large-screened television was fronted by a coffee table covered with electronic gadgets. A scrambled mass of electric cords beneath the television resembled chocolate and licorice spaghetti.

Razor's attention was drawn to a small desk atop which lay two laptops—one plugged in, the other not. He shot a glance around for any thumb drives. When nothing of the kind jumped out at him, he gathered the power cords then stuck the laptops under his arm and let himself out the back door.

Casually, he returned to his SUV, dropped the computers into the passenger's seat, and fired up his engine. He drove to a fast food restaurant, pulled into the parking lot, then retrieved his phone from its dock on the dash.

"Got them," he said when Condit answered.

"Bring them to me."

"The kid's got all kinds of electronic crap. That must be what he spends all his money on. It sure isn't furniture…the place could best be described as spartan."

"You're sure you got the right laptops?"

Had there been more than two?

"Yeah, I'm sure."

"What about thumb drives?"

"I didn't see any." Razor rubbed a hand along his jaw. "Why would you need them when you have the laptops?"

"Because, oh-brainy-one, Henry would have saved his data to at least one thumb drive. Even if we destroy the laptop, any memory sticks could sink us." Condit's usual screech had raised to a painful decibel level. As if talking to herself, she added, "It's always possible he asked another person to review his stuff; then there would be more than one thumb drive."

"I'm telling you I didn't see anything like that, just the laptops."

"Then you screwed up." Condit blew out a long breath of air. "Bring me what you have."

With the censure in Condit's voice banging around inside Razor's head like a ball bearing in a tin can, he pulled his burner phone from its hiding place. Scowling, he punched in BeeBee LeDuc's number.

Where did that witch get off talking to him like that? Just because she was a computer whiz didn't mean she knew everything. If he hadn't decided to take a chance on her startup idea, she'd be sitting behind a desk somewhere spitting in one hand and wishing on the other. He'd sunk every dime he could raise into it; the least she could do was act grateful.

"I have the laptops," he said when LeDuc answered. "You want I should take them to Condit or bring them to you?"

"It'll be faster to let her work on them. Once she's found whatever she needs to find, we'll discuss next steps." LeDuc broke the connection.

Razor felt his eyebrows lift until they felt like they were about to take off into outer space, and he chewed the inside of his lower lip.

Within his first couple of weeks of working with BeeBee LeDuc, Razor had learned the man had an uncanny knack for sensing when things were going south and was known to act on his suspicions without warning. First, there'd be a subtle shift in LeDuc's attitude when speaking to or about another soon to be ex-business associate...a slight change of inflection in his voice, a coolness when he began calling the poor sucker by his last name rather than first.

Next, his voice would move from friendly bonhomie to reserved monotone. No more pats on the back, no smile, and no offer of thirty-year-old Scotch from his in-office stash.

Finally, it would be an ice-cold stare, his eyelids at half mast, and his face like brushed chrome as the loser pleaded for more time to pay up or another chance to make things right.

For the first time, Razor wondered if it had been a mistake to fall for Condit's proposition. But his eyeballs had all but rolled back in his head when she described the opportunity, then offered him a partnership. The thought of sitting back and letting the arrogant, know-it-all bimbo do the work while he collected a thousand percent return on his investment appealed to him. All he had to do was supply the startup cash then bring LeDuc into the fold for an added infusion. He never even considered the possibility the whole thing might blow up in his face.

If, however, LeDuc was in the process of deciding to cut his losses and pull out of the partnership, he would also be considering how to deal with anyone involved. Razor, Condit, the two old ladies, and the kid could all wind up as plant food.

Razor comforted himself with the thought that he might still have time to make things right. First, he'd let Condit do her voodoo on the laptops, and if she was able to pull their collaborative fat out of the fire, all well and good.

If, however, she couldn't fix the problem, he would do whatever it took to make her return his and LeDuc's initial investment then offer the whole wad to LeDuc. Razor would be broke, but at least he might be allowed to live.

He pulled a tube of lip balm from his shirt pocket, removed the lid, and ran the waxy preparation along his sore, cracked lips. He was sick to death of the miserable New Mexico desert where everyone's yard was covered in rocks and cactus. The high altitude made it hard to breathe, and the relative humidity perpetually hovered around five percent. If he had the power, he'd be pleased to incinerate the whole area on his way out of town.

Images of his LA home paraded in front of his mind's eye—his condominium and its swimming pool around which a gaggle of lovelies could always be found lounging; his manicurist and hair stylist who could make him look like the prosperous up-and-coming businessman he was.

Razor peered at himself in the lighted mirror on the

back of the SUV's sun visor. He sighed and ran his hands over his hair. Although he had conditioned it that morning as usual, the soul-sucking dry air had dehydrated it to the point it would spontaneously combust if he got too near an open flame.

He barked an epithet, shoved the visor back up, then fired up the engine, and started back to the motel.

Chapter Twenty

By the time Kelly Condit broke off her phone conversation with Razor, she'd already started mentally kicking around her options. Should she wait to see what was on the laptops before changing her tac, or should she defer to the twinge of fear growing in her gut and disappear, even though it would be months earlier than originally planned?

The unknown variables were playing with her head. The old ladies, the kid, even Taylor's daughter were potential threats. How much did any of them know? Had they told anyone else their suspicions, and if so, whom?

Kelly surprised herself by chuckling at the mental image of *Rambo Razor* following the kid, watching from behind his SUV's tinted windows, planning his mode of attack. He'd been so self-congratulatory when handing her the laptops, like a fourth grader presenting an apple to his teacher and waiting for a pat on the head.

She sobered at a new thought. Although it seemed unlikely, the kid might be savvy enough to clone the laptops to The Cloud before taking off from his apartment. Half an hour was plenty of time to get into Taylor's honeypot trap and upload the whole shebang. The honeypot wouldn't have been password protected, since the reason for setting one up in the first place was to attract whatever killer bees were out there looking for something nasty to get into. If the kid *had* cloned the laptop, it and any memory sticks were not only worthless but gave the kid the ability to access all of Henry's files any time and from just about any place on the face of the planet. There were, after all, at least two high-level national labs in New Mexico with cutting edge tech capabilities and which no doubt paid nice salaries to their tech-savvy employees.

A shiver tightened cold fingers around Kelly's stomach. It was possible that because of the compounded mistakes that were beginning to add up, LeDuc could decide to get rid of her, if only out of spite. The fact that she was a young woman would mean nothing to him—LeDuc had ordered the disappearance of his own uncle after discovering the man was about to throw in with a primary competitor, a man named Diamond. LeDuc's conscience, if he ever had one, had long ago been seared to ashes.

Condit's timeline would have to be brought significantly forward.

Although the level of stupidity displayed by Razor and the goons was staggering, the payoff for the investment's success would still be astronomical. Kelly could retire and spend the rest of her life enjoying the benefits of her efforts. Retire at the age of thirty-five...how many people could do that?

She swallowed hard to tamp down the persistent feeling that the project was already spinning in its death throes and repeated the positive self-talk her therapist had suggested.

There was still time to make it work. All she needed was a few more hours to finalize her plans. She had worked too hard and had taken too many chances to just walk away.

Once in the clear, she'd leave. Whatever happened after that would be on Razor and LeDuc, not her.

Chapter Twenty-One

Dix stepped into the motel lobby just as a young woman with puffy red eyes came out of the elevator. Slender, with short, jet black hair, the woman looked enough like her father to leave no room for mistaking her identity.

Val Taylor looked expectantly around the lobby before her gaze landed on the approaching Dix.

"Thank you for agreeing to see me," Dix said.

"It's nice to meet someone who knew Dad."

After a brief discussion during which Dix outlined the gustatory options, the women agreed on a local eatery featuring authentic New Mexican food.

"We'll take my car," Dix said. "I hope you don't mind riding in a Miata ragtop."

During the drive to the restaurant, Dix kept the conversation focused on everything from the weather to the latest popular music, but once they were seated and their orders taken, she got down to business.

"Can you think of anything your father said or did recently that might hint at what he was working on?"

"I've been racking my brain since we last spoke but haven't come up with anything." Val shook her head. "I still can't believe Daddy's gone. He was always so strong. In my head I knew he was aging, but in my heart, I guess I thought he'd always be here." She shifted in her seat and heaved a sigh. "Were you able to get the things you needed from his house?"

"My tech friend Dillon is working on it now." Dix pushed a note across the table. "I've made a list of the things we took. Once Dillon's done, I can either bring it all to you or ship it to your home in California."

Val nodded her thanks and dropped the note into her purse. "The police seem to be treating dad's death as a random hit-and-run."

"I was there, Val, and I'm sure it was deliberate. So is Dillon."

"Did you say that to the police?"

"Yes, but Dillon says whatever your dad was working on went way beyond the kinds of things the locals deal with. What do you know about his latest work interests?"

"Not much. I do know something had him worried. The last time he called, he talked about how short life was and how humans put such value on material things. He sounded so tired." Val's eyes teared up, and she pulled a tissue from her purse and swiped at her face.

"Did you know he'd been diagnosed with Alzheimer's?" Dix said.

"Yes, he only found out a few weeks ago. I tried to talk him into moving in with me, but he was determined to maintain his independence as long as possible...said he didn't want to be a burden."

"I can certainly understand that," Dix said.

"He was growing more and more forgetful, though. Sometimes he'd get frustrated that he couldn't remember things." Val blew her nose. "He did say one thing last time we talked that sounded kind of unusual. He talked about how before money existed, people bartered things, and how the paper money we use is basically worthless. He said we accept paper and plastic as legal tender because we're conditioned to see them as valuable. *Our economy's all smoke and mirrors,* those were his exact words."

"Interesting." Dix took a bite of stacked enchilada and chewed thoughtfully. "Do you know anyone named Kelly?"

"Is that the first or last name?"

"I'm not sure, but your dad wrote the name on his calendar along with a note reminding him to call."

"I don't remember Dad talking about anyone by that name."

After that, Dix kept the conversation light, something for which Val seemed grateful. They chatted about places they visited and people they had known. Dix regaled Val with stories from her days as a professor of psychology, and Val delighted her with unexpectedly humorous stories of her days as a graduate student in computer science.

The café crowd thinned as the nine o'clock closing time neared. Dix paid the check, and the two left just ahead of an employee who locked the door behind them.

Typical of that time of year in New Mexico, the sun had long since gone down, changing the trees and shrubs surrounding the café into tall shadowy forms that swayed in a light breeze.

"Have you decided what to do with the house?" Dix said as the two walked into the darkened parking lot.

"I'm thinking of selling it. I was hoping to get Dad's car to use while I'm in town, but the police said it's being held as evidence or something." Val sighed.

"Does it ever get easier?"

"Time dulls the pain," Dix said. "For a while you'll experience what I call ambushers...things that feel like a punch in the stomach such as the fragrance of your dad's aftershave worn by a passing stranger, that kind of thing. Allow yourself to grieve. There'll always be a sense of loss, but the pain lessens as weeks and months go by."

"It's just that my dad..." Val's voice trailed off.

"Do you have any family, anyone you can talk to, someone who can help with the arrangements?"

"Dad has some cousins in Australia, but they didn't really stay in touch. Mom's people were from the Netherlands. It was just the two of us." Val's chin trembled. "Will you come to Dad's memorial?"

"I'll be there. How long do you plan to stay in town?"

Please let her leave quickly, before whoever killed Henry decides she's a threat.

"I'm not sure. When Dad wouldn't move in with me, I applied for a job with a local software developer. They called me day before yesterday and made an offer, but I haven't decided whether to take it or not. I never got the chance to tell Dad about it. He would have been over the moon."

"Why don't you stay with us for a few days?" Dix said. "We have a guestroom with its own bath, and you won't have to be alone, unless you want to be."

"I wouldn't want to impose—"

"It would be no imposition at all. We don't get much company."

And there's safety in numbers...

"That sounds lovely." Val sighed.

By the time Dix drove into the motel parking lot, however, she had mentally bludgeoned herself into a mass of uncertainty. Would Val be safer staying with Lil and her than in a lighted, peopled motel, or was Dix effectively bringing her into what might at some point, God forbid, prove to be ground zero?

At Val's direction, Dix pulled next to the young woman's rented vehicle, parked, and waited while Val gathered her belongings and checked out of the motel. Bouncing her right leg up and down on the ball of her foot, she looked around the motel parking lot, peering into the vehicles that entered and left. Over and over she looked at the clock on her dashboard, her jaws tight as the seconds seemed to grind to a halt.

How much longer could it take Val to pack? What if the gunmen had followed Dix when she picked the young woman up then lay waiting in her motel room for her to return? Val could be fighting for her life because Dix had focused on putting the young woman at ease instead of paying attention to her surroundings.

Unwelcomed, too-familiar images and sounds bulldozed their way through Dix's memory, images of an earlier time when she failed to heed what turned out to be life-and-death clues. Years old snippets of a client's counseling session rolled down from the darkened corridors of the past.

Dix: The question you need to ask yourself is would you be better off with or without her?

Josh: Sometimes I think I can't take even one more day in the same house with that woman.

Dix: Then for your homework I want you to brainstorm a list of options.

Josh: I don't see any options, that's the problem. I

can't afford a divorce.

Dix: There's always a way. Write down everything that comes to mind, no matter how farfetched, and bring it to your next session.

Standard procedure: listen to the client's concerns and fears, guide them as they generate their own list of possible solutions, then pat yourself on the back when they move on with their lives. Another life healed, another sad chapter closed.

But there hadn't been a next session, and there hadn't been a life healed.

By the time Val checked out of the motel, loaded her luggage into her rented vehicle, and started its engine, Dix was on the verge of hyperventilating. With her face set like one of those images carved on a totem pole, she pulled out of the parking lot and led the way to her house.

Chapter Twenty-Two

By the time Dix and Val walked through the garage and into the house, Dix had talked herself off an emotional ledge. Things would work out. They would find the men who killed Henry and offer their names, the honeypot, and all the little memory storage devices to the FBI. The murderers would be brought to justice, and Henry's death would be avenged. Lil and she could return to their normal lives.

As the two women stepped into the utility room, Lulu performed a joyous dance, wagging her tail and chuffing her language of welcome. Dix bent and patted the dog's head under the cone then led the way into the kitchen where Lil stood waiting, her arms crossed and a stormy look on her face.

"Why haven't you returned my—" Lil began.

"Lil," Dix interrupted, "this is Henry Taylor's daughter Val."

Val stepped out from behind Dix and extended her hand. "It's nice to meet you. I can't thank you enough for allowing me to stay here until I can get Dad's affairs settled."

Lil shot a hard look at Dix but shook Val's hand.

Lulu wagged her tail furiously while sniffing Val's feet and legs.

"Hello, Lulu." Val bent to pet the furry back. "Poor baby got hurt, didn't you?" She straightened and looked first at Dix then Lil. "Thank you for letting me stay here. Being alone through all of this has been kind of tough."

The look on Lil's face unexpectedly softened.

"I'll show you to your room." Dix motioned for Val to follow.

Lulu bounded up the stairs behind them, her cone cocked at a jaunty angle.

"Your bath's there, and you'll find extra towels in the linen closet." Dix pointed to a closed door and the built-in cabinet next to it.

"How very nice." Val turned toward Dix, and her eyes filled with tears.

Dix smiled. "If you need anything, please feel free to ask." She held the bedroom door open and stood to one side as the young woman carried her luggage past her and into the room. "There are a couple of blankets and an additional pillow on the shelf in the closet."

Val sat on the side of the bed, a forlorn look on her face.

"What time do you typically go to bed?" Dix said gently.

"Usually around eleven-thirty or so, but I have an appointment with Dad's attorney first thing tomorrow, so I should probably make it an early night." Val glanced at her watch. "I'll unpack and shower then hit the sack in a half hour or so."

"Good," Dix said. "How about I show you my Slinky collection?"

"You have a Slinky *collection*?"

"I do," Dix said.

"Dad gave me a Slinky for Christmas when I was about seven." Val smiled. "I loved playing with that thing."

"A couple of mine are so big, the sound of them coiling and uncoiling as they come down the wooden stairs is loud enough to set off the neighbor's car alarm."

"Sounds like fun." Val suddenly rushed to Dix and hugged her. "I haven't felt…I mean, after mom died Dad was—"

"Oh, my dear." Dix returned the hug. "You're most welcome."

Dix lead the way to the small room that housed her collection. After Val made a circuit of the room, she excused herself, and Dix started downstairs where experience told her Lil would be ginning herself into a furor.

However, much to her surprise, the expected storm never materialized. Instead of waving her arms and stomping around, as Dix expected, Lil stood quietly at the bottom of the stairs.

"I've finished collating Henry's stickie notes," Lil said.

"Anything come to light?"

"Maybe. Come to the kitchen."

Once the sisters were seated at the dining table, Lil nodded toward a loosely stacked pile of colored squares of paper and pushed a piece of lined notebook paper across the table toward Dix.

"Here's the list." Lil tapped an index finger on the paper. "The stickie notes are color coded. Henry had no less than forty yellow notes reminding himself to do everything from sweep the front porch every Saturday to watering his indoor plants."

"We can skip those."

"The green notes are reminders about Lulu's care, so there's no help there." Lil handed two pink stickies to her sister. "But check these out."

Dix read one note aloud, "Coins or tokens…" Her brow furrowed. "I think the squiggle at the end is a question mark."

"But what kind of token? Does anyplace in the country still use bus or subway tokens?"

"Not that I know of. There are the little player pieces called *tokens* used in table games like Monopoly or Clue."

"I think we can rule out board games," Lil said.

"Agreed. It could be a symbolic gift, as in a token of one's affection."

"Or maybe a token economy."

"I'm thinking the note refers to something associated with Henry's tech work." Dix grew thoughtful.

"The note says token *or* coin…as if it's one or the other. That tells me the two may be interchangeable in Henry's language."

Dix stuck the note onto the counter next to the landline they stubbornly refused to get rid of. "We'll work on it later."

"Look at the second pink note." Lil gestured at the paper. "Exactly where did you find it?"

"It was on the desk next to Henry's laptop, why?"

"I think it's part of something called an *IP address.*"

"What in blue blazes is an IP address?" Dix scowled. "And what does it have to do with Henry's murder?"

"Wish I knew." Lil shrugged. "It's a term from a

television documentary about cybercrime. Spoofing an IP address isn't typically done by upstanding citizens. I just wish I could remember more about it."

"Maybe you could Google it."

"By the way," Lil said, "the only names I found on any of the notes or in the calendar were *Val* and *Kelly*."

"I think I've learned everything I can from Val,'" Dix said. "I'll call the Kelly person tomorrow." She looked at her sister. "No quarrel about Val staying with us for a few days?"

"Contrary to what you may think, I'm not completely heartless. Besides, she's safer here than walking around town. It's possible her father said something to her about what he was working on, and I've got a feeling—"

"We're not the only ones who may have arrived at that conclusion," Dix said. "And it's *I have* a feeling, not *I've got*."

Lil made a rude hand gesture toward her sister. "Anyway, I've checked our security measures; everything is up to snuff."

"Thanks, Sis."

"Have you heard from Dillon yet?" Lil said as the two headed in tandem for the stairs.

"I called and left a message," Dix said. "Hopefully, he'll get back to me soon."

"How long can it take for him to figure out what Henry was working on?"

"I don't know…I keep telling myself time's gotten away from him, and he'll call when he thinks of it."

"I don't like anything about this," Lil said. "And neither do you."

"I'll go to Dillon's apartment first thing in the

morning after breakfast." Dix struggled to make her voice light. "Then we can wrap this all up."

Lil shot a sideways glance at her twin but remained silent. When the two of them reached the stair landing, she turned. "Along about now, you're praying that your young friend Dillon is safe."

Dix opened her mouth to respond, but Lil interrupted, "Don't even *try* to deny it. You're afraid he's in trouble." Lil shook her head, then headed toward her room, her unspoken words *I warned you not to get involved* hanging in the air between them.

Chapter Twenty-Three

Within twenty minutes of returning to his apartment with Taylor's laptops, Dillon knew he was being watched. Once he started working, he usually lost track of time and space, existing in a dimension of his own crafting. Eventually, however, he could no longer ignore a small but persistent tingling at the base of his skull that soon grew to a claxon-like decibel level.

He quickly backed up whatever was on the honeypot then shut off the machine.

Congratulating himself on successfully saving all of Mr. Taylor's work to a location where he could access it at any time, Dillon closed the now-unnecessary laptop. He stuffed several thumb drives in his pocket, stood, and pretended to walk toward the bathroom.

Seconds later, he was in his back yard, his body plastered against the side of the apartment, his eyes searching the street for whoever had toggled his antennae. No people strolled along the sidewalk, and no neighbors worked in their yards. The street was empty except for a dark blue SUV, the windows of which had been tinted so dark as to make it impossible to see if anyone sat inside.

I think that SUV might have followed us...I'm pretty sure I've seen it before...

Miss Dix's words exploded into incandescent relief

in Dillon's memory. His mother's frequent comments about his growing paranoia notwithstanding, he had seen enough skullduggery during his short tenure at the research lab to recognize a brewing maelstrom when he saw it.

Although he hadn't had time to fully plumb the depths of Mr. Taylor's data, he had seen enough to recognize something big was going down, something that could potentially affect the stock market and rock more than one country's financial institutions.

Dillon took a deep breath, hurried back into the apartment, grabbed his phone and car keys, then headed for the front door.

Time to go dark.

Chapter Twenty-Four

Dix arose early next morning. With Lulu padding in her wake, she hurried into the kitchen and prepared bacon, eggs, new potatoes sautéed with onions, and homemade biscuits. The sad strangeness of the past couple of days cast a pall over her spirits, and she tried to make her voice cheery as she called Lil and Val downstairs for breakfast.

Val ate in silence, while Dix and Lil chatted about the weather. Once breakfast was over and the dishes cleared, Val left for her appointment with her dad's attorney.

Dix and Lil refilled their coffee cups and returned to the table.

"When're you going to call Kelly?" Lil asked.

Dix glanced at her wristwatch. "It's only eight-thirty; I'll wait until nine."

Lil nodded, took a sip of coffee, and scrunched up her face. "You should have let me make the coffee."

"Here we go." Dix glared at her twin. "We're locked inside a veritable pressure cooker, and you're going to complain about my coffee."

"Just stating fact. You have a knack for making even the pricey stuff taste like burning rubber." Lil stuck her index finger into her coffee cup, fished something out, and shoved the finger toward Dix. "Not to mention the requisite bit of dog hair." She glared at

Lulu reclining on the floor. "How much longer are we going to keep that animal?"

"I knew your helpful attitude of last night was too good to be true." Dix drew in a deep breath and blew it out through pursed lips, her cheeks puffed.

"You look like a blowfish when you do that...a scary blowfish with fake, black eyebrows."

"I'm intrigued that you know what a scary blowfish looks like when you've never been out of the desert." Dix pointed an index finger in the air. "And you agreed to give me twenty-four hours."

"Albeit reluctantly. Your time's up this evening."

"I still have a full day." Dix shoved her chair back. "By the way, I'd be more than happy to let you do the cooking and make the coffee in the future, but I would prefer to die of natural causes." She stood and stepped to the calendar on the counter. Repeating Kelly's number over and over, she punched her phone's screen.

A cultured, prerecorded masculine voice informed the caller that the person was not available but would return the call as soon as possible if the caller would please leave a number.

Dix identified herself, apologized for the early hour, then added, "I'm a friend of Henry Taylor's. Your name and number were written on his calendar, and I was hoping to talk to you. If you would, please call me when you get a chance." She repeated her own phone number then broke the connection and looked at her sister. "Not available."

"Man or woman?"

"I couldn't tell...the voicemail greeting sounded like a British robot."

"Maybe Kelly's screening incoming calls," Lil

said. "Something you should try. Just because the thing rings doesn't mean you have to answer it."

"I can't make myself *not* answer a ringing phone…it's hardwired into my brain." Dix looked pointedly at her twin. "At least *I* get the periodic phone call. I'm surprised your inner skinflint allows you to pay for a landline *and* two phones when you never use any of them."

"It's a safety precaution." Lil shrugged. "Kind of like paying a couple extra bucks for roadside help on our car insurance. I keep my car in top running condition, but you never know when one of us might have car trouble and need a tow. The more important issue is that you answer your phone without first checking the caller identification. Between opening yourself up to political robo-calls and every scam artist in the world—"

Dix's phone suddenly rang, and both women jumped. Dix glanced at the number on her caller identification, mouthed *Kelly* to her sister, then answered.

"Dix Ruiz? This is Kelly Condit." The feminine voice was nasal, high pitched, and imperious. "I'm on the road, so couldn't answer your call until I could pull into a rest area. Your message said you had a question about Henry Taylor?"

"Yes, I wondered how well you knew him."

"He was just a casual acquaintance." Kelly paused. "I heard what happened to him on the news."

"Do you have any idea why he wrote himself a note to call you?" Dix said.

"Probably to see if I was going to either the Black Hat or DEF CON Conferences in Vegas this year. I met him at the Black Hat conference three or four years ago. Since then, we've made it a point to have dinner at least one evening during each conference to talk shop."

"Do you remember the last time you saw or talked to him?"

"Sorry," Kelly said, "but why all the questions; are you with the police?"

"No, I'm just a friend trying to find out what was going on in his life that might have led to his death."

"Aren't the police investigating?"

"They are, of course, but they seem to believe his death was random."

"You don't?" Kelly said.

After a brief pause, Dix continued, "Did he mention anything he was working on last time you saw him?"

"I don't remember his being involved in anything specific. I believe he was retired."

"Did he tell you he set up a honeypot?"

Kelly coughed then cleared her throat. "Sorry, a what?"

"A honeypot. I understand it's a kind of online trap."

"Now that you mention it, he did sound a bit preoccupied last time we talked."

Dix sat up straight. "Can you remember anything he said, anything that might hint at what he was working on?"

"Not really. He talked about some ideas for a new algorithm to help address global warming, but that's about it."

"Do you still live in California?"

"How did you know—"

"Your area code."

"Ah." Kelly chuckled. "Actually, it's a bit of a coincidence that you should call. I'll be passing through Albuquerque on my way to Chicago for a combined job interview and vacation. I was going to call Henry for lunch, but now, of course…"

"His memorial is Thursday; is there any chance you could come to that?" Dix looked up at her sister who was pounding the air with her fist, shaking her head, and mouthing *No*.

"His daughter doesn't know anyone here," Dix continued, "and it would be a comfort for her to meet one of Henry's friends."

"No," Lil stage whispered. She shoved her chair back, stood over her sister, and made chopping motions with her hands.

Kelly remained silent.

"I don't mean to be pushy," Dix said, "but it would be a nice gesture."

"Actually, my schedule *is* pretty flexible," Kelly said. "I don't have to be in Chicago until early next week."

"Marvelous, what time do you think you'll be coming through town?"

"I'm in Gallup right now, so barring any unforeseen problem, I should get to Albuquerque sometime around ten-thirty this morning. Maybe we could meet somewhere for coffee."

"We live only about half an hour south of Albuquerque via Interstate 25. How about coming to our place for coffee?" Dix pretended not to notice Lil frantically flapping her arms, shaking her head, and mouthing invectives. "I make the best banana nut bread you've ever tasted."

"Ah, now you're speaking my language."

With a resigned sigh, Lil dropped into her chair. If her eyes had been lasers, Dix would have been fried to a crisp.

Dix gave Kelly directions to the house from the interstate then broke the connection.

"Have you finally lost what little mind you had left?" Lil said.

"What?" Dix held her hands out, palms up.

"You've invited a complete stranger to our house."

"You realize how inconsistent that is? You're okay with Val staying in our house but can't abide my inviting Kelly Condit for coffee?"

"That's different, Val's the daughter of a mathematical genius."

"Here I was beginning to think your single, stunted, humanitarian neuron was beginning to show signs of firing up. You're not being generous...you're star struck at the thought of rubbing shoulders with the daughter of one of the globe's premier software engineers."

Lil snorted. "I don't get star struck."

"Besides, Kelly's not a complete stranger...she knew Henry."

"She's still a stranger. Why bring her here instead of meeting in a café or some other public place?"

"I want her to feel relaxed. She might be more inclined to remember details over a cup of coffee and slice of banana bread than while sitting in a room full of chattering people."

"She could be Lizzie Borden."

"Oh, wait." Dix lifted her index finger to her

cheek, her voice high-pitched, and her eyes opened in wide-eyed innocence. "She was polite and sounded young, therefore she must be a rogue."

"One of these days you're going to get us into something we can't walk away from."

"She lives in California, Lil. She can't have had anything to do with Henry's death."

"So?"

"It's just coffee."

Lil stood and shoved her chair under the table. "I'll be in my room."

"How about taking Lulu for her walk while I make the bread." Dix donned an apron then began pulling ingredients from the pantry and refrigerator.

Grumbling, Lil retrieved the dog's leash. "This place is becoming a menagerie. I'll be glad when things get back to normal." With Lulu prancing in joyous anticipation, Lil adjusted the cone, attached the leash, then headed for the front door. "Please, don't invite anyone else to move into our house while I'm gone."

Chapter Twenty-Five

The doorbell rang, and Dix glanced at her watch. "Right on time. Get that, will you?" she called to Lil who sat at the kitchen table, a pen and piece of lined notebook paper in front of her.

"No, I will not," Lil said. "Remember that old Dracula movie? You have to invite him in, but once he's in, you're dead meat." She folded the paper in half and sat with her arms crossed.

Dix rolled her eyes, wiped her hands on her apron, then headed toward the front door.

The blurry image on the other side of the patterned glass proved to be a petite, young woman wearing a black pantsuit and matching low heeled pumps. Her bleached blonde hair cut in an updated version of the retro style called a pixie, the woman smiled.

"Is this the Ruiz house?"

"It is," Dix said. "You must be Kelly Condit."

"Right in one," the young woman said. "Something smells marvelous."

"Please come in." Dix stood to one side as Kelly entered then closed the door behind her. She pointed to the hat rack immediately to the left of the door. "You may hang your purse there then come on back."

Kelly did as Dix suggested then followed her to the kitchen.

Lil was nowhere in sight.

"You have a lovely home," the young woman said. "Do you live alone?"

"I live with my sister." Dix motioned toward a chair. "Have a seat…it'll just be a few minutes. What can I offer you to drink, perhaps iced tea or coffee?"

"I could go for a cup of coffee, thanks."

Dix pulled a mug from the cabinet. She filled it with steaming liquid, handed it to the young woman, then pulled a bread knife from the wooden block on the counter. She sliced three generous portions of warm banana bread and placed them on saucers.

Just then Lil stepped into view outside the sliding glass door. She slid it open, and Lulu shot through the opening, her cone askew.

At the sight of Kelly, the dog lowered her head, flattened her ears, and bared her teeth.

Wild-eyed, Kelly shrieked and jumped up from her chair, dropping her coffee cup in the process. Shards of pottery skittered across the floor, and hot brown liquid made a steaming puddle on the tan tile.

Lulu took a slow step forward, her eyes fastened like a heat-seeking missile on the young woman.

"Lulu," Lil shouted. "Sit."

The animal shot a glance first at Dix then Lil but held her position for several tense seconds.

Dix hurried to the dog, grabbed her by the collar, and hauled her back outside. She stroked the animal's fur and spoke gently. "Everything's okay. I know you're just doing your job, but you'll have to stay outside until our guest leaves."

Lulu stared through the glass and barked until Dix drew the blinds. After a few more deep-throated warning barks, the dog fell silent. Again, Lil was nowhere in sight.

"I'm so sorry," Dix said to Kelly while dabbing at the young woman's blouse with a paper towel.

Kelly shot a vicious look toward the back door, her own teeth bared. Then, as if realizing Dix was watching her, she wiped the look off her face as if it were a squiggle on an etch-a-sketch. "You've got quite a guard dog there," she said.

"You *have*, not *you've got*," Dix said automatically. She felt her face heat up. "Oh, Lord, my apologies." She nodded toward the closed back door. "Lulu was Henry's pet; we're—"

"We're just keeping her until we can find her a good home," Lil said from just inside the kitchen doorway where she suddenly appeared.

Kelly looked back and forth between the sisters.

"This is my sister Lil." Dix waved her hand toward her sister then returned her attention to Kelly. "Shall I get you a fresh cup of coffee?"

"Please." Kelly sat back down.

Lil pulled a wad of paper towels from the roll on the counter and dabbed up the spilled coffee while Dix swept up the shattered coffee cup. She pulled another mug from the cabinet, filled it with coffee, then placed it on the table in front of Kelly.

"Would you mind if I use your restroom?" Kelly held her arms stiffly away from her body and glanced down at her stained blouse.

"Of course." Dix motioned for the young woman to follow her to the stairs. She pointed to a closed door beyond the landing. "Let me know if you need anything."

As Kelly started up the stairs, Dix returned to the

kitchen where Lil was finishing the spilt coffee cleanup.

After the young woman returned, the three women ate banana bread and drank coffee in an uncomfortable silence.

"That was delicious," Kelly said once she finished eating. "The coffee was superb."

Dix shot a victorious look at Lil, then said, "Will you be able to attend Henry's memorial?"

"I'm really sorry, but I got a call from my brother in Chicago a few minutes before I got here. Mom's had a fall and I need to get going." Kelly pushed her chair back and stood. "Let me help clean up." She carried her plate to the sink. Her gaze moved around the kitchen then came to rest on the notes next to the landline. She stared hard at them for a nano second then quickly looked away, but not before Dix caught the tight look on her face.

"We found those notes at Henry's house," Dix said. "Any idea what they mean?"

"Can't say I do." Kelly glanced at the note on which Henry had written the string of numbers. "What's that one about?"

"Not sure," Lil said.

"You know—" Kelly snapped her fingers as if just remembering something. "—Henry called a couple of weeks ago and said there was something he wanted me to see, some data he hoped I could verify. I never heard back, so I just assumed he worked it out for himself." She lowered her eyelids and said, "Is it possible he told *you* something, maybe mentioned what was eating at him?"

"So he offered no indication as to what kind of data he wanted you to verify?" Lil unexpectedly said.

"Sorry?" Condit looked at Lil.

"I just wondered what kind of data he hoped you could verify."

"I never got to see it, so…no idea." Kelly headed toward the front door then turned and spoke to Dix, "I have your number in my list of contacts…if I remember anything, I'll let you know."

The young woman stepped onto the porch, the muscles in her jaws working as if she were chewing her tongue. She turned back toward the sisters. "I've been thinking; you do realize that whatever Henry was working on could prove to be dangerous to anyone who might get involved." Kelly lowered her eyelids. "Regardless of how innocent they may be."

From the backyard Lulu started barking again, the sound loud and insistent.

"Henry was known for his focus on organized cyber crime," Kelly continued. She paused as if waiting for a particular response. When Dix and Lil remained silent, she added, "Thanks again for the coffee and banana bread." She turned and headed for her car.

"Safe travels," Dix said before closing the door.

For several beats after Kelly drove away, Dix stood staring at the door.

"You know she was lying, right?" Lil said.

"About?"

"Nearly everything. She said she read the newspaper article about Henry's death yet asked if you lived alone."

"She might have forgotten that detail." Dix turned to her sister.

"Maybe."

"What an inconsequential thing to lie about. What

possible reason could she have?"

"Maybe on the way here she worked herself into lying mode and just couldn't stop, kind of like our politicians."

"Not all polit—"

"Besides," Lil interrupted, "if she's taking a road trip to Chicago, why's she driving a car with New Mexico tags?"

"How do you—?"

"I checked."

Dix shook her head.

"And what about Lulu's reaction to her? If we hadn't been here, that animal would have gone for her throat."

"What a terrifying thought."

"One thing for sure," Lil said, "she hadn't just traveled a hundred fifty miles in that outfit; not a wrinkle in sight."

"She could have checked into a motel and cleaned up before coming over."

"Not possible," Lil said thoughtfully. "That would account for the absence of luggage in her car, but between your call and her arrival here she didn't have time to check into a motel then shower and dress."

Dix looked aghast. "You searched her car?"

"Just popped her trunk for a quick peek. Interesting that she didn't lock the thing."

"Maybe she's not paranoid like some people."

"Guilty as charged. However, I again refer to the way that dog acted toward her. I'd bet money they've met before. On top of that, how many people would drive an extra thirty-five miles out of their way for coffee?"

"That's small-town thinking. I once had a student from New York who said his dad commuted an hour and half to and from work. An extra thirty-five minutes is nothing to someone from a large city."

"Point taken," Lil said. "But you still haven't answered the license plate question."

"You think today's not her first time in town?"

"I sure do. Maybe she doesn't live in California at all."

"Then why does her phone number have a California area code?" Dix said.

"I didn't say she *never* lived there. Did it not strike you as odd that she didn't ask about Lulu's cone and bandages out of curiosity, even if only to make conversation?"

"I noticed."

"It was like she already knew all about it," Lil said.

Dix remained silent, a thoughtful look on her face.

"And," Lil said, "was it my imagination, or did her trip to the bathroom take a lot more time than necessary?"

"Maybe she needed to, you know, relieve herself."

"She was in there long enough to blow out a whole week's worth of leftovers."

"Don't be coarse, Lil." Dix pulled her phone from her smock pocket, punched the screen and scrolled, then looked at her twin. "There's no local phone number in her name, so her number's either unpublished, or she doesn't live here."

"Let's Google her," Lil said. "No one hides from Google."

The sisters stepped into the room designated as their office, and Lil booted up the communal laptop.

She typed the words *Kelly Condit* and *California* into the search engine then studied the screen.

"It says here a woman by the name of Kelly Condit is a resident of Los Angeles," Lil said. "Other than listing her as a software developer, there's no other detail."

"Aren't there other websites that might give more information? I heard there are over fifty social media platforms where people post all kinds of personal information."

"Don't look at me," Lil said. "I'm a card-carrying dinosaur."

"In spite of the way she came across," Dix said, "I just cannot see that young woman running Henry down."

"Maybe she didn't do it herself."

"That's possible," Dix said. "However, nearly every question you've raised has a logical explanation."

"Is that a hint of hesitation I hear in your voice?"

"There *are* some things that're bothering me. When I spoke with her on the phone, she acted like she didn't know what a honeypot was. If she's a techie, it seems she would recognize that term. Dillon knew immediately."

"Good point. And?"

"The way she acted after seeing Henry's notes," Dix said. "She tried to act nonchalant, but her eyes nearly bugged out of her head. Until then, she seemed relaxed, even hinted she might stay in town for his memorial." She paused then added, "And if Henry and Kelly had a tacit agreement to share dinner at the annual Black Hat conferences, why did she act like she hardly knew him? She said Henry wanted her to verify his data, and that tells me they knew each other a lot better than she let on."

"Maybe she felt their relationship was too shallow to categorize as friendship."

"It's more than that. The whole time she was here I felt like we were being subjected to a magician's sleight-of-hand, like smoke and mirrors." Dix snapped her fingers. "That's what has been bugging me. Val said Henry recently talked about how we accept paper and plastic as payment for goods and services because we're conditioned to see them as valuable. He talked about bartering and said our economy is *all smoke and mirrors*." Dix sighed and held her hands out, palms upward. "But that might not be pertinent."

"Maybe he was just having a bad day. I've heard people with Alzheimer's are more lucid some days than others."

"Henry's disease wasn't that advanced. He was in the early stages." Dix shook her head. "I don't know…right now my brain hurts."

"Something about that young woman felt all wrong," Lil said. "There has to be a way to…" Lil's voice faded, and her mouth clamped shut. Her head jerked up and she stared off into space.

"What?" Dix said. "There has to be a way to what?"

Lil didn't respond.

"Are you listening?" Dix said. "Hey, Sis."

"What?"

"I said—"

"Yeah, yeah." Lil lifted a hand in a shushing motion, a look of deep concentration on her face. Suddenly, she looked up toward the ceiling as if remembering something. "I'm going to run a couple of errands," she said over her shoulder as she hurried toward the garage. "Shouldn't be more than an hour or so."

"You're getting weird in your old age, you know that?" Dix shouted toward the closing door. "Weird-er," she murmured.

As the garage door ground its way down after Lil's departure, Lulu barked to be let inside. Dix stepped through the kitchen and slid the door open.

Lulu ran inside the house and went into search mode. Once apparently satisfied that Kelly Condit was gone, she returned to the kitchen, sat down in front of Dix, and whumped her tail on the floor.

"I wish you could either speak English, or I could speak Canine." Dix stroked the animal's neck. "Time for your ointment."

After tending Lulu's wounds, Dix retrieved the two stickie notes that Kelly had unsuccessfully pretended not to know anything about. She pulled her phone from its resting place in her bra, sat at the kitchen table, and punched in Dillon's number. He would know what the words and numbers meant.

When the call went to voice mail, she said, "I've found something else I need to ask you about. I have no idea how long it's going to take you to work on Henry's laptops, but I'm a bit concerned that I haven't heard from you...it's been almost twenty-four hours. Would you give me a call as soon as you can, if only to give me an update and reassure me you're okay?"

Dix ended the call and sat at the table. Perhaps Dillon hadn't called because he was too absorbed in the work on Henry's laptop...but what if he hadn't called because he couldn't? What if the person following Dix had spotted Dillon and decided he was a better target?

Dix might have handed Dillon over to the people who murdered Henry.

Chapter Twenty-Six

Lil's brain had whirred into overdrive after Kelly Condit drove away. It wasn't only that nothing the woman said rang true, or the way the Bantha reacted to her presence, although that would have been enough…it was the way she acted after spotting Henry's notes and the death glare she shot over her shoulder at Dix as she left the house.

Although Lil would never admit it to her sister, she couldn't bear the thought of anything happening to Dix. Beyond the fact they started life as *womb mates*, they had shared a house for years. They raised their nephew Davie together, and together they weathered all the emotional and financial storms and crises life had thrown at them.

Lil had never felt the need for an intimate physical relationship. She never even developed a friendship with anyone other than family. However, the thought of living alone again threw her stomach into full-nausea mode. With the passing of years, that fear had fed upon itself until it escalated into a full-blown terror of isolation. She would do just about anything to keep from returning to that solitary life.

When Dix's last husband left her high and dry, Lil had been surprised at her mixed feelings. While hated seeing her sister hurt, she'd been inwardly pleased.

Everyone except Dix knew the guy wasn't worth the powder it would take to blow him up. He hadn't looked for a job but bragged about being an entrepreneur. He came up with scheme after scheme for what he enthusiastically referred to as *surefire moneymakers*. Of course, he had excuses galore when his plans, predictably, came to nothing. He loved to remind Dix that even Abraham Lincoln failed at several startup attempts before becoming president.

Of course, when Dix's money ran out, so did the jerk.

With two underwater mortgages and empty savings and checking accounts, Dix had shown up on Lil's doorstep with little more than the clothes on her back. Her house eventually sold but had netted less than the combined mortgages, requiring her to spend the next several years digging herself out of debt.

It was some months after Dix's last marriage breakup that Lil met a man named Billy Oboe.

As an accountant, Lil had done income taxes for people from all walks of life, but none quite like Billy. Within the first five minutes of reviewing Oboe's previous year's return, receipts and handwritten notes, it became obvious the man was a cheat and a lowlife.

"I've heard you're a regular magician when it comes to taxes," Billy had said. "You must have a whole truckload of loopholes that could help me out with my humble return."

Lil remained silent and continued studying Billy's documents.

Oboe shot a pointed glance at Lil's bare ring finger. "You married?" he said.

"None of your business."

Billy chuckled. "You wanna be? We would be a great team. I'd make the money, and you could protect it from the feds." He obliquely suggested Lil might be willing to falsify some of his holdings on his tax forms. "Nothing big enough to alert the taxman," he said. "Just enough so's I can keep some of my hard-earned cash. I take pride in being a responsible taxpayer, but a few thousand would help me stay off welfare."

When Lil not only declined but offered to call the IRS right then and there, Billy backed off. She informed him of her photographic memory for numbers and said she could quote chapter and verse from his documents in case of future need.

"No need to go off half-cocked," Billy said. "You can't blame a man for trying to hold on to a few bucks."

After Billy gathered up his papers and shuffled out of her office, Lil spent a couple of hours typing out the man's tax return by memory. She then made a copy and put one in her files then mailed the other with an anonymous note to the IRS office in Albuquerque. Whether or not the feds would follow up on her letter, Lil had no idea.

A couple of days later, Billy called with a dinner invitation. "I like my women the same as I like my beef jerky...tough and well-seasoned."

When Lil unceremoniously declined, Billy chuckled and said he'd keep his sofa warm if she ever changed her mind. He optimistically called a couple more times before giving up.

During his final call, he said, "You like country western music?"

"None of your business." Lil's response sent Billy into a paroxysm of laughter.

"You ever need anything, you whistle."

And just like that, Lil had a friend in low places.

Then one day while Dix was at work and Lil had come home for lunch, one of Dix's exes showed up on their porch. With his figurative hat in his hands, he asked Lil to give Dix a message: he had matured; he hadn't known what an incredible woman Dix was; he realized what a bum he used to be and wanted to make it all up to her.

"I'm staying at the Rio de Oro Motel, room number 602," he'd said. "I'll wait to hear from her."

Lil had remained silent while the guy bared his soul. Life had been rough since he made the mistake of leaving Dix; she was the only woman to ever understand him, blah, blah, blah.

"You done yet?" she said during one of the few breaks in his tale of woe.

The guy had looked taken aback then nodded.

"Okay then." Lil closed and locked the door.

"Just tell her," the guy had yelled. "Tell her what I said."

Lil had leaned against the door until she heard the guy's receding footsteps followed by a car engine roaring to life. Then she called Billy Oboe.

Billy picked up on the first ring. "Hello, hello, hello," he purred. "Long time no talk."

"You said I could call. I need someone to decide that leaving town would be in his best interests." She told Billy the name of the motel and the room number Dix's ex had given her. "I don't want any violence, but I *do* want him to be scared enough to wet himself before hauling his sorry butt out of town."

A fee was agreed upon; the learning curve was

administered, and the ex left town without further ado.

Although the outcome had been precisely what Lil wanted, she couldn't shake an uneasy feeling that by hiring Billy she had given life to a creature that could at any time turn on her.

The guy could try to blackmail her into fiddling with his tax returns. He might even suggest she succumb to his charms in exchange for his silence. Worse than anything else, however, was her fear of what Dix would do if she ever found out.

At the time, Lil had consoled herself with the thought that if crime statistics could be believed, Mr. Oboe would stick to his *modus operandi* and restrict his lawlessness to illegal betting, tax evasion, and other nonviolent endeavors. Throughout the succeeding years, however, Lil had harbored the fear that he might show up uninvited, compelling her to explain him away to Dix.

Kelly Condit's visit had brought all those memories flooding back. That, along with the cumulative effects of forty-eight hours of snowballing fear, had prompted Lil's brain to cough up what used to be Oboe's phone number.

If she were lucky, the number still belonged to Billy. If she were doubly lucky, Oboe would prove to be more interested in making a buck than in settling an old score in the event her letter to the IRS had scored a hit.

Lil made some lame excuse to Dix about needing to run a couple of errands then hustled to her car. She drove to a fast food parking lot, parked, shut off the engine, pulled her phone from its scabbard, then punched Oboe's old number into her cell. She held her breath as the phone rang at the other end.

"Speak now or go away." The voice was older but still familiar.

"It's Lil Ruiz."

"So it is. You call to see if I'm dead yet?"

"No, but that would undoubtedly improve your personality as well as your worth to humanity."

"Same old Lil. I figured you must have forgotten my number."

"That's the trouble with having a photographic memory for numbers, I couldn't forget it even if I wanted to."

"Plumb hurt my feelings not hearing from you for so long, especially after what we went through. Not to mention the IRS audit I was subjected to by some overzealous agent a few weeks after our visit."

"That was a long time ago."

"So it was, so it was." Oboe paused. "Why *are* you calling; your sister get married again?"

"Nothing like that, but I do have a proposition for you."

"I knew you would come around; better late than never. Dinner at your place?"

"Hardly." Lil gritted her teeth. "I need your help."

"That's a start."

"You have a pencil and paper handy?"

"Always."

"I need to know everything you can find out about a woman named Kelly Condit, her background, work, contacts, anything and everything." Lil slowly spelled the name.

"Kelly Condit," Billy repeated. "Doesn't ring a bell. Is that her real name?"

"I was hoping you could find that out as well."

"That'll cost you extra," Oboe said. "Why do you want to know?"

"That's not your concern."

"Okay, when do you need it?"

"Within the next twenty-four hours," Lil said. "Think you can manage that?"

"You know me; I never could resist a challenge."

"You still have the same bank account?" Lil said.

"Yessum. I don't believe in changing something that's not broke. I read somewhere that change is stressful. You need my account information?"

"Nope. I've had your bank's name and your account and routing numbers floating around in my head for the past decade and half."

"And yet you've never tried to drain my account? Brainy, beautiful, *and* honest." Billy coughed. "Multiply what you paid last time by seven and that'll give you my fee."

"You're pretty proud of your time, aren't you?"

"Inflation. Besides, I got a kid needs the dough."

"You have until seven-thirty tonight then the deal's off," Lil said.

"You said twenty-four hours."

"That was before you tried to bankrupt me. In case you've forgotten, I have a long memory. Besides, you don't have a kid…no woman in her right mind—"

"Yeah, yeah, calm down." Billy chuckled. "Can't blame a guy for trying to make a buck. I'll see what I can do."

"You want payment via direct deposit or cash?"

"Cash is always good, taxes being what they are," Oboe said.

"I want hard copies of anything you find."

"Paper? How quaint. It would be less cumbersome to use Google Docs. Or I could put it on a thumb drive."

"I wouldn't begin to know how to get into one of those things. Paper's not only easier to read, no one can hack into it."

"It's your call," Oboe said. "Depending on how tough this Kelly Condit is to track down, I might come up with something before this evening."

"That would be great, but I'm not paying extra if you do. I prefer in-depth detail over speed."

"Frugal...one of the reasons I like you. When and where do you want to meet?"

"Tonight, at seven-thirty in the Los Lunas Walmart parking lot."

"Okie-dokie." Oboe hung up.

Lil sat for several minutes mulling over what she'd done.

Billy Oboe might have been about as welcome as a tick in a dog pound, but he was also just as predictable. He would dig into places no one else but the CIA could reach then try to extort a higher payoff before delivering whatever he'd unearthed.

Lil's internal penny-pincher started kicking up sand in the pit of her stomach. What if Condit turned out to be exactly who and what she appeared to be? What if there was nothing to uncover—no sinister, shadowy, hidden persona? What if Lil wound up spending a pile of money for what amounted to a blank sheet of paper?

Although it was her sister who had made the study of human nature her life's work, Lil hadn't lived over six decades without learning a few things herself. Having been born without the rose-colored filter through which her sister viewed the world, Lil had never felt compelled to give people the benefit of even the tiniest doubt.

As a result, when Dix admitted to feeling something *might* be off about Kelly Condit, Lil's *something's-fishy* meter shot into the stratosphere.

...whatever Henry was working on could prove to be dangerous to anyone who might get involved...

Condit's words had made Lil's chest tight. The cockroach of a woman knew a great deal more than she had let on about whatever Taylor had been working on.

Someone once said seeing a single cockroach meant hundreds more would be hiding in the walls. Dix had invited one cockroach into their lives; how many others remained unseen?

Worse, what would happen once they all decided to come out of hiding?

Chapter Twenty-Seven

After delivering the laptops to Condit, Razor had driven his pickup to an all-night diner's parking lot. He walked back to the kid's apartment and let himself in as before and made a quick circuit around the tiny space to ensure he hadn't overlooked anything.

Relieved to find the kid kept all the electronic gadgets in one place, he returned to the living room and called Condit.

"Describe everything you see," Condit said. "Try not to miss anything, please."

Bristling at the woman's tone, Razor did as commanded.

"Games and toys." Condit snorted derisively. "You don't have a clue, do you?"

"You know, you are one freaking witch. I'll be so glad when this mess is cleaned up and I don't have to deal with you anymore."

"Ditto," Condit said through clenched teeth.

His tired, sleep-deprived brain fuzzy and unable to think clearly, Razor sat on the sofa. "Before you ask, other than a digital bedside clock in the bedroom and a toaster oven in the kitchen, everything electronic is right here in front of me."

Razor leaned back and stretched his legs under the table. Something clattered when the toes of his Italian-made shoes bumped it.

"Wait a minute." Razor slid off the sofa, squatted on his haunches, and reached for the clear plastic box he'd kicked.

"What's going on?" Condit said.

"Found something." Razor described the repurposed, one gallon ice cream container then shook it next to his phone's speaker. The rattle and tick of plastic against plastic sounded loud in the silent apartment.

"What is it?"

Razor peeled back the plastic lid. "It seems I've found the kid's collection of thumb drives."

"Bring them all," Condit said. "Maybe we'll get lucky."

"What if none of them are the right ones?"

"The kid might have taken some with him. Too bad you didn't follow him." The tone of Condit's voice could have soured milk.

Touchy enough to chew boulders into gravel, Razor responded, "I've had just about all your crap I can take. If you hadn't bungled the first break-in, none of this would have happened. You're the one at fault here."

"Just bring the damned—"

Razor poked his finger on the phone's screen so hard a jolt of pain shot up his hand as he broke the connection.

What was it about Condit that picked at his guts? Just being in her presence, looking at that square jaw and sawed-off nose made him want to punch her pug-dog lights out. And that voice.

As a kid, he lived near a railroad station. At exactly one-thirty every morning, the squeal of the train's brakes yanked him out of a deep sleep. Even stuffing his fingers into his ears and wrapping his pillow around his head couldn't block out the shrieking, brain-dissolving sound.

As bad as it was, however, it would be like angels singing compared to Condit's voice.

What really ate away at him was the way she looked at him. Whenever she spoke to him, her thin upper lip curled, as if she could barely force herself to look at his face.

Once the current project was complete and secured, once they no longer needed her, maybe he would allow himself the pleasure of squeezing off the valve through which that voice piped. He could almost feel the soft flesh of her throat in his hands, almost hear her tiny little hyoid bone shatter under his grip and the gurgle that would follow. The look in her eyes would change from disgust to realization that *he* was in control, that there was finally someone she couldn't push around.

Razor let himself out of the kid's apartment, carried the plastic container of memory sticks to his SUV, and started the engine. It would be his pleasure to shove the memory sticks into Condit's face, but first he had to take care of other business.

As he pulled into the street from the parking lot, his burner phone blasted out a prearranged ring tone, and he punched the no-hands device.

"What's going on?" LeDuc's *basso profundo* voice was cultured...the diametrically opposite of Condit's blackbird caw. "Where are you now?"

"Just leaving the kid's house."

"Update?"

"I got all the memory sticks."

"At least that's progress. Got a report on the old women," LeDuc said. "From what my contacts could make out, they are exactly who and what they appear to be...two retired sisters sharing a house. Interesting note, however, they were almost solely responsible for sending several members of a family to prison a little over a year ago, so beware."

"I'm on my way to their house right now. Condit has the laptops, so the thumb drives are just backups and can be destroyed any time. She doesn't need them to trace Taylor's work."

"You're sure? There's a lot riding on this."

What if he were wrong? What if his mushy brain wasn't working right?

Razor mentally shook himself. "I'm sure."

"What's your plan?"

"It's possible the kid's hiding out at the old ladies' house," Razor said. "He's obviously close friends with Granny Eyebrows. Based on the panic in Condit's voice when she talked about him, he could turn out to be a major problem."

"And?"

"I'm going to scope out their house. If the kid's there, I'll be able to deal with all of them at the same time."

"Good. As my dear sainted mama used to say, be sure to wear your gloves and galoshes." LeDuc burped then broke the connection.

"Crap and corruption," Razor muttered.

Anyone who spent more than a few minutes in LeDuc's presence knew about his self-diagnosed acid reflux. It acted up whenever the man's stomach spewed acid up his throat, and that mostly occurred when he was riled up.

People who riled LeDuc tended to have truncated lifespans…and LeDuc had just burped.

Razor pulled around the corner a block from the old ladies' house and parked on the street. The kid's car wasn't in the driveway, but that meant nothing; he could have parked in the garage. If the kid was sharp enough to know he was being watched and then went into hiding, he was more than just your average kid…he could be dangerous.

Razor rubbed his hand along his jawline. Sandpapery spikes of dark, heavy beard pricked at his palm. He reached into his glove compartment for one of the three battery-powered shavers he had stashed in various places—the constant presence of which had earned him his nickname, even though he had explained to all concerned they were *shavers*, not razors.

Never taking his eyes off the old ladies' house, he ran the humming, battery-powered machine over his face until satisfied he'd shorn the hair down to the follicles. Two things he prided himself on—his wardrobe and being cleanshaven. No one respected a slob. Even a rich slob was still a slob.

Razor replaced his shaver in its holder just as Condit's car swung around the corner and headed for the old ladies' house.

He sucked in a lung full of air. What the hell was Condit-the-witch up to? Why would she show up at the old women's house without telling him? Could have decided to go into business with the grannies and the kid?

Razor pulled his burner phone from its hidey-hole and again punched in LeDuc's number.

"What now?" LeDuc's voice sounded like he'd been chewing on a wad of steel wool.

"Condit just pulled up to the old ladies' house. Did you tell her to—"

"You sure it's her?"

"Absolutely," Razor said.

"Any idea what she has in mind?"

"No, sir."

"Where are Toad and Booger?"

"They're supposed to be at Taylor's house gathering any electronic gear that might have been left behind."

"Just wasting time, in other words." LeDuc grunted. "Worthless… Do you think the old ladies know anything?"

"It's possible, but it could be that they're just bored and looking for something to add a little excitement to their lives."

"I see." LeDuc's voice had grown distant, cold. "It seems this thing is about to go sideways. You have twenty-four hours to fix it, capisce?"

"How much latitude do I have?"

"Whatever you need to do to get the job done." LeDuc's voice became soft as if he had turned away from the phone and addressed someone in the room. "Hand me that bottle of Rolaids."

Razor licked his lips and wiped away the sudden sheen of perspiration on his forehead. It was bad news when LeDuc needed an antacid. As Condit would say, the *hapless causative factor* might want to update his will.

LeDuc made a sound in the back of his throat and put his hand over the phone's speaker. Before he completely muffled the sound, however, he said to someone, "I may need you to—"

After a couple more muted comments, LeDuc uncovered the phone's speaker. "Twenty-four hours." He broke the connection.

Unless Razor was mistaken, LeDuc had just asked at least one of his *cleaners* to prepare to fly to New Mexico. That meant the big man was on the verge of cutting his losses and going into extermination mode.

Razor's gut did a square dance with his bladder. If he had a prayer of surviving beyond the next twenty-four hours, he had to take care of the old ladies and the kid. After that, if he was still alive, he would take care of Condit. He grabbed his phone and called Toad.

"Where are you guys?" he said.

"We're on our way to Taylor's house. Condit told us to clean the place out."

"To what purpose? She already has everything."

"Don't ask me," Toad said. "She must have decided we missed something."

"Stop whatever you're doing," Razor said. "Mr. LeDuc says for you and Booger to get back to Los Angeles."

"You mean, now?"

"That's what he said." Razor ran his fingers through his immaculately groomed hair, realized he'd mussed it, and raked it back into place.

The day before, Condit had suggested Razor return to Los Angeles and allow her to handle everything. She said the fewer people involved, the less likely they would attract unwanted attention.

"You think Toad and Booger pose less risk than I do?" Razor had laughed so hard he teared up. "That's just plain rich."

"Are you suggesting I can't handle this?"

"Not at all," Razor had responded. "What I *am* suggesting is that Toad and Booger have proven themselves capable of jacking this already-bolloxed-up situation into a full-blown crap storm, and as your partner, I would really hate to lose my investment on their account. Even worse, I'd hate to wind up dodging LeDuc and the feds for the rest of my life because of their blunders."

"Fine," Condit had said. "Then you send them back to Los Angeles. When you call BeeBee and tell him why you don't want them around, be sure he understands that you're second-guessing his decision to send them out here in the first place." She smiled, a vicious, twisted thing on her face. "But do me a favor, will you? Before you call him, either let me buy you out or make me heir to your life insurance policy."

In retrospect, perhaps Razor should have gone back to Los Angeles right then. At least Condit would be the only one LeDuc held accountable for what could be in the process of becoming a major screwup.

On the upside, Condit now had Taylor's laptops and thumb drives. The local cops hadn't caught on to what was going on, and the grannies most likely had no clue as to what they had stumbled upon.

On the debit side, however, the geek kid had been in possession of the laptops and memory sticks for nearly an hour. Other than Condit, anyone else to whom Taylor might have voiced his suspicions remained unknown, so there could be more leaks waiting to punch holes in the dam. Added to all that, Condit's and Razor's failure to stop the threat posed by Taylor in the first place hadn't been lost on LeDuc, whose modus operandi tended toward the *kill them all and let God sort them out* end of the spectrum.

Toad cleared his throat, his frog-bark breaking through Razor's ruminations. "Okay," he said. "We'll check out of the motel and catch a flight home."

Razor broke the connection and sat staring at the secondhand sprinting around the face of his wristwatch. His only hope was to run the table and take out as many players as possible, as quickly as possible. After that, he would have to find a place to hole up while the maelstrom either exploded or petered out.

If he could clean everything up, there was a chance he'd be welcomed back into LeDuc's inner circle. He might even get promoted, and that would be worth killing a few people for.

Chapter Twenty-Eight

Toad slapped his palm against the steering wheel on the drive back to their motel. "We're screwed." *Smack. Smack.* "Well and truly screwed."

"For real."

"Do you know what this means?"

"We get to go home?" Booger said.

"Blow your nose; your thinker's blocked." Toad shook his head. "Razor's sending us back to Uncle BeeBee with our tails tucked under our butts."

"At least you're related; I got no protection."

"You think I'll get a pass just because I'm his nephew?" Toad snorted. "He whacked his own uncle a couple years ago. Besides, he never liked me all that much."

"What're we—?"

"Shut up and let me think."

Toad pulled into the motel parking lot and drove to the space just outside their room. After he shut off the motor, the two men sat for several minutes in silence.

"Okay, here's what we're going to do," Toad said.

When Toad had finished speaking, Booger whistled. "What if we get caught?"

"Our options are getting pretty thin." Toad jabbed Booger's forehead with his index finger. "Think about it. You in or out?"

"I'm in, I guess." Booger shook his head. "But I

never figured on grabbing some old ladies."

"Yeah, well figure on it now. We can't take the chance they know anything."

"What'll we do with them?" Booger said.

"What do you think?"

"I told you I don't do kids or women. I didn't sign on to—"

"What else can we do? If we go back to LA with this mess still brewing, we'll prove to Uncle BeeBee that we got no chops. We could wind up pushing brooms in one of his factories, but we could just as easily wind up in the desert digging our own graves. Uncle BeeBee doesn't believe in second chances."

"For real." Booger slowly nodded his head, a sad expression on his face.

"But if we take care of business, we'll be heroes." Toad rubbed his leg. "Me? I'm going to enjoy taking care of that monster dog."

Toad pulled his phone from the van's console.

"Who're you calling?" Booger said.

"My uncle. He's the one we ultimately take orders from, not Razor, and not Condit-the-Whiz." Toad punched the screen then put the thing on speaker phone. "Hello, Uncle BeeBee. I just got off the phone with Razor, and he said you want us to come home."

"Unless you have a better idea," LeDuc said. "It sounds like things could be getting dicey."

"I'd like permission to take care of stuff before we come back."

"What do you have in mind?"

Toad repeated the plan he discussed with Booger.

"Are you familiar with Roulette?"

"You mean like the wheel with the little ball,"

Toad said. "Or you mean like as in Russian?"

"Take your pick."

"I don't—" Toad cleared his throat.

"If you're in, you're all the way in, capisce?"

"Yessir."

"Call me when it's done." LeDuc hung up.

"It's on," Toad said to Booger. "We need to fix this before Razor does. Otherwise, I'll never get promoted."

"By fixing it you mean—"

"I mean taking out the old ladies and the kid, and maybe even Razor and Condit."

Booger shook his head and sniffed. His eyes lowered to slits, and his lips puckered in a look of rare rebellion as he pulled a hanky from his pants pocket and blew into it. He wadded up the cloth and returned it to his pocket.

Toad grimaced. "Why don't you use Kleenex like everyone else? Or are you saving up all that snot for some special occasion?"

Booger tapped his temple with an index finger. "I'm not so dumb…snot has DNA in it. If I use a tissue and put it in the trash, it can be traced back to me. That's how they found some guy on a true crime television show I saw. He blew his nose into a tissue and tossed it in the trash after smacking some woman around. Might as well have left a signed confession."

The two men stepped out of the van and walked toward their motel room.

"When're we going to do it?" Booger said.

Toad inserted his plastic room key into the slot above the doorknob. When the tiny light flashed green, he pushed the door open and looked at Booger. "I figure the old ladies will be asleep by midnight. That's when we'll hit them. After that, we take care of the Whiz then the kid."

"What if Razor interferes?" Booger said.

"We have to take him out as well," Toad said. "We have Uncle BeeBee's permission to do whatever it takes."

"I never cared much for Razor."

"He thinks he's too good for the rest of us." Toad cleared his throat, the ribbit-like sound loud in the motel room. "You know he uses hair spray?"

"Nah, for real?" Booger shook his head. "Now you mention it, not a single hair moved during that windstorm yesterday." He looked pensively at Toad. "My third-grade teacher's hair never moved. It was the same style every day. Even after a year, it was still—"

"Yeah, okay, enough." Toad glanced at his watch. "I've been thinking."

"Yeah?"

"Did you see all that expensive stuff at Taylor's house?"

"I saw some silverware, things like that." Booger snuffled.

"Things like that?" Toad said. "The man's house was full of all kinds of rich-man stuff."

"I don't follow."

"The man's dead, so he doesn't need it anymore," Toad said. "And we have a few hours before show-time." He pulled his pistol from its holster and placed it on the side of the bed. "I'm going to clean my gun then you and I are going out. Time to seek our fortune."

"I always wondered what it would be like to be rich." Booger retrieved his pistol and began breaking it down for cleaning.

"It's like Uncle BeeBee always says," Toad said. "There are two kinds of people in the world...people who have stuff, and people who want the other people's stuff."

"For re—"

"Shut up and clean your gun."

Chapter Twenty-Nine

As Kelly pulled away from the Ruiz sisters' house, she reviewed the time spent with the old ladies. The one named Dix had seemed nice enough, but the one named Lil had shot suspicious looks at her the whole time she was there. She couldn't put her finger on anything specific that told her the old hags weren't the dithering grannies they appeared to be, but early in her life she had developed a refined radar when it came to menacing old women.

If Rambo-Razor and the two goons had done a better job of finding Henry's electronics in the first place, she would have declined Dix's invitation for coffee. However, fear that the old women had come into possession of Taylor's thumb drives had compelled her to accept. It also offered her the perfect way to look them over.

Dix's invitation for coffee appeared on the surface as an act of kindness to someone who knew Henry. It had, however, proven to be an underhanded means to interrogate Kelly.

The good news was Kelly had destroyed the honeypot. With her skillful application of a set of jumper cables and a car battery, she generated a lovely electric arc that fried both the hard drive and the SD card. No one was going to resurrect that puppy.

The bad news was any thumb drives Henry might

have used were still floating around out there somewhere—not to mention the Cloud possibility. If the kid had cloned Henry's honeypot to The Cloud, the jig was truly up.

Had Taylor told the old women anything about Kelly? While it was possible that they innocently got caught up in Kelly's business, it was equally possible Henry had sensed the danger building around him and given them a thumb drive as backup. Kelly certainly would have.

However, why would Henry involve two old women basically living in the stone age in something so cutting-edge tech? Even something as old school as a thumb drive was probably too technical a device for them to understand. They probably didn't know how to text and thought an *emoticon* was a child's robotic toy.

They reminded Condit of Ma Bennie—the woman she'd lived with during the final two of her twelve years spent in foster care.

Ma Bennie had been nice enough. She even encouraged Kelly to see a shrink to deal with her *attachment disorder*. However, by the time Kelly aged out of the foster care system at eighteen, the old woman had finally given up trying to help her beyond providing food, clothing, and a warm bed.

Distrusting every new device that came on the market, it was like Ma Bennie was stuck in the sixties while the world around her was throwing out exciting new information free for the taking. When Kelly had tried to talk her into buying a cell phone, Ma Bennie claimed that *when the grid went down, as everyone knew it would, a cellphone would be worthless*...the landline would be her lifeline. When Kelly asked the old woman who she figured on calling if the grid went down, since hardly anyone had landlines anymore, Ma Bennie got so angry she didn't speak for three days.

If not for the computers at school and the county library, Kelly would still be stuck in the dark ages. Her salvation had manifested itself through the in-born quirk in her brain's wiring that allowed her to understand and learn computer programming languages as easily as a toddler learns to eat with a spoon.

By the time Kelly left Ma Bennie's house, the old woman's attitude toward her had changed. Initially, she'd been kindness personified, but within a few months she grew suspicious and fearful. Perhaps the old woman had sensed how close she was to becoming a statistic.

Eventually, she stopped looking directly at Kelly when speaking to her. Instead, she'd find a spot on the wall just beyond Kelly's shoulder and stare at it while mumbling mindless drivel.

Credit where it was due—Ma Bennie's instincts had been on the mark. She was only allowed to live out her miserable existence because Kelly decided it was in her own best interests, not because she cared one bit for the miserable old bag of bones.

By the time Kelly was a teenager, she had learned what society expected of her and had acted accordingly. She was not only semi-pretty but had an IQ high enough to place her firmly in the genius ranks. In her twenties, through a series of carefully planned and executed cons, she fleeced men and women alike, all while pretending to be an innocent ingenue.

She didn't intend to hurt anyone, they each said. *She's just a kid, and she didn't know any better.*

Over a few short years, Kelly's computer skills grew exponentially. She'd been surprised at the ease with which she could hack into emails, texts, and messages. She had also been pleasantly surprised at how stupid people were to put the most personal information in places easily accessible by anyone who knew what they were doing.

While reading forbidden texts and posting embarrassing photos sent to a lover on the world wide web had been fun for a while, it quickly became apparent that there were bigger and juicier plums to be plucked. That's when she hatched the project Henry had stumbled upon—the project Dix and her sister were threatening to blow up.

During Kelly's impromptu trip to the old women's bathroom, she had taken the opportunity to do a quick search of the downstairs. The only thing even remotely electronic was an ancient desktop connected to what looked like an even older printer. To say neither of the women would know an algorithm if it bit them on the nose would have been an overstatement.

Their leaving Henry's stickie note in plain sight had been an obvious attempt to draw her out. Like two hungry birds waiting for a worm to pop its head out of its hole, they watched her staring at the note while glancing back and forth at each other as if sharing a secret.

The thing that had chilled Kelly and made her throat clamp nearly closed, however, was the scrap of notebook paper seemingly carelessly tossed onto the kitchen counter. Only two people could have possibly known what those numbers meant—herself and Henry.

In the end, however, how the notes had come into

the old women's possession didn't matter. After over two years of groundwork followed by months of setting the trap, then springing it, she would not allow them to interfere, not when she was so close to wrapping everything up.

Then, of course, there had been that unfortunate scene with Taylor's dog. Henry had told her about adopting a dog, but Kelly had envisioned something small such as a pomeranian or chihuahua. It had never occurred to her he adopted a man-eating monster. The animal had nearly torn off her arm during her failed break-in attempt. She should have killed the beast then and there.

Kelly ground her teeth at the memory of Razor's reaction to her break-in failure.

You should have let me do the job like I offered, but no, you had to be Wonder Woman.

Adding insult to injury, he had called LeDuc and complained about her bungled attempt, a call that had resulted in the two inept goons being sent *to help.* As the saying went, the rest was history.

Kelly pulled into a service station parking lot and retrieved a burner phone from her car's console. Congratulating herself on her foresight to buy a disposable, anonymous cellphone, she engaged the voice-altering app she had downloaded on a lark then opened her regular phone to find the old woman's number.

Mentally crossing her fingers that one of the old women would answer even though their caller ID's readout would show *number unavailable*, she punched in the number and was pleasantly surprised when Dix answered after the first ring.

"Stop digging into Henry Taylor's death," Kelly said.

"And this is…?"

The old woman's cool, unworried voice made Kelly's face flush hot. Had she been standing in front of the old bag, she'd have smacked her.

"This is your only warning," Kelly said. "Back off."

"Thank you, Kelly," Dix said. "It is Kelly, isn't it?"

Kelly gasped then said, "What?"

"I said thank you for the call. I was still a little uncertain whether we were making too much out of Henry's death, but you've made it clear we have not."

"You think you're so smart," Kelly said. "If you don't stop interfering, you and your nasty twin will find yourselves with nowhere to hide." She broke the connection and returned the phone to the console. For several minutes, she sat flexing her fingers and chewing on her tongue.

Even though the old woman had tried to come across as calm and in control, the underlying current of fear had sent a rush of adrenaline into Kelly's vital organs, juicing her with a feeling of power she rarely experienced. Every neuron in her body hummed.

It was she, Kelly Condit, who was in control, not the old women, not Razor, not even LeDuc and his goons. If all went according to plan, she'd soon be rich enough to buy her own island in the Caribbean where no one could touch her.

Nearly three years earlier, as a prelude to her carefully orchestrated scam, she compromised a scientist who worked in a stem cell laboratory. The jerk had been so intent on impressing her, he bragged about his research involving a 3D printer capable of literally *printing* human vital organs from harvested stem cells, offering details only someone with his high level of involvement could know.

She could still hear the excitement in his voice as he droned on and on about how while the research was in its infancy, soon people who lost kidneys to disease could receive clean ones that their bodies wouldn't reject because it would be their own DNA; victims of lung cancer could receive brand new, baby-pink lungs; burn victims could receive their own scar-free skin, yada, yada, yada.

The guy's excitement, however, had been short-lived. After a brief *honeymoon*, she treated him to recordings she'd made of their pillow talk. Once he realized he'd not only lose his job but could have legal charges brought against him for disclosing details of the research, he agreed to harvest some of her stem cells then build her a heart.

Watching the initial parade of emotions move across the man's face had been priceless. He pled with her, trying to convince her that the 3D printed tissue might prove to be microscopically different than a native heart, thereby derailing her plans.

For a fleeting moment during the stem cell extraction process, Kelly had sensed the man's internal struggle about whether he should take that opportunity to kill her. In the end, however, he did as she asked.

Kelly had been mildly disappointed when the guy's efforts resulted in a shapeless mass of tissue about half the size of the palm of her hand. The man had been quick to assure her, however, that a forensic test would prove the tissue to be cardiac muscle cells, and a standard DNA test would prove it to be hers.

"It's the best I can offer," he whined when she complained that the lump didn't even resemble a heart. "Like I said, the technology is still in the early development stage."

Holding the raw meat of her heart in the palm of her hand had turned out to be an extraordinary experience. Intrigued, and at the same time repulsed, she would never forget the chill that ran up her back as she stared at the liver-colored flesh of her flesh.

Briefly, Kelly had thought that once she had the time and unlimited funds in her hands, she might consider investing in stem cell research. She even mused about the possibility of setting up her own lab. She could name her price while the wealthy from around the world paid top dollar for replacement organs. She could decide who lived and who died.

Once she had her heart tissue wrapped in plastic wrap and stored inside her refrigerator, Kelly spent hours researching ways to best preserve the tissue. Besides the old formaldehyde standby, she studied drying and freezing methods used by American pioneers to preserve food. She hacked into an online forensic journal and was surprised to learn that cooking the tissue—something that took place during the drying process—could denature the DNA, making it unreadable. Freezing wasn't an option, since the odor of tissue putrefaction upon thawing would alert LeDuc to its presence in his office.

Finally, Kelly opted to salt the tissue in the same manner used to make mummies. If it was good enough for Egyptian royalty, it was good enough for her.

She was surprised at the emotions that surfaced as

she shopped for an appropriate container, a *casket* for her heart. She considered everything from decorated cardboard, plastic, and ceramic to hammered metal boxes before selecting a two-inch square, burgundy velvet-lined wooden jewelry box with a hand carved lid. She'd surprised herself by sobbing as she placed the shapeless mass of tissue into its coffin and covered it with sea salt.

Several days before the Bozo-Boys killed Taylor, and during her last face-to-face meeting with LeDuc, she had hidden the box in the man's office on a bookcase behind a heavy copy of Webster's Unabridged Dictionary. Without doubt, LeDuc would not stumble upon the box until the police found it in response to an anonymous tip informing them where to find a dead woman's heart that the man kept as a trophy.

Then, of course, after Taylor's precipitous and much-publicized death, Kelly had been forced to tweak her plans. As luck would have it, however, the only change necessary had been to shift where she was to be "murdered" from Los Angeles to New Mexico.

Kelly hummed a pop tune from her teen years. She would be the first person ever to have choreographed her own murder, left behind enough evidence to hang her enemies, and yet still not only be alive but have enough money to buy everything she ever wanted.

She mentally patted herself on the back for her attention to detail. She would change her name and wear platform heels when in public, thereby increasing her height by two to three inches. Facial recognition software being what it was, she would undergo plastic surgery, but only a bit...maybe a chin or cheekbone implant, or perhaps a nose job…

Before disappearing, however, she would deal with the old women.

The thought of ending the old ladies sent a pleasant shiver of anticipation through her insides—those wrinkled faces staring at her, daring her to say the wrong thing or in some way betray herself.

Then she would take care of Razor.

Even better than killing him, she'd set him up for life in prison. He would have a long time to regret disrespecting her. Kelly's face pulled into a wide smile. With his fastidiousness and fancy-pants mannerisms, he would be the most popular fresh meat on the cell block in no time.

Her *coup de gras* would be the complete destruction of BeeBee LeDuc. Although she would be hard pressed to explain exactly why she hated the man, after being in his presence and observing his absolute control over everyone in his sphere, she decided she had to ruin him. Not to mention taking the man's millions of ill-gotten dollars that were just begging to be appropriated.

The only downside was that she could never tell a living soul the details of her ingenious plan. No one else would ever know the meticulous planning, the attention to detail…

On second thought, perhaps after the drama of her "murder trial" had died down and LeDuc was sent to prison, she would send him a message—something only he would understand and recognize as coming from her. It would be fun to let him know it was she who had set him up…she who'd exercised ultimate control.

LeDuc had proven to be a dolt when it came to

online security, having never changed any of his original passwords. As a result, it was easy to hack into all the man's accounts located in the States—any second grader could have done it. While his offshore accounts were untouchable, Kelly took delight in knowing the feds would shut those down once he was arrested. In a beautiful symmetry, the man would be penniless, maybe even too broke to hire a decent attorney.

Like a female Robin Hood, she would rob the rich bastard of every bloodstained dollar he'd accrued. Then she'd vanish, after having been written off as another victim of his senseless violence.

Kelly pulled out of the gas station and headed south on Interstate 25. During an earlier excursion, she'd spotted what appeared to be an abandoned metal building just outside the small village of Belen. If appearances proved to be correct, it would not only be the perfect location for Kelly's fake murder, but an ideal place to simultaneously take care of the old hags who insisted on getting in her way. To paraphrase a line from one of those unfathomable Shakespearian plays she'd hated having to read in high school—she'd do both biddies *in one fell swoop*.

Chapter Thirty

By the time Dix hung up from the threatening phone call, her breathing was ragged. Her heart pounded and perspiration had popped out on her upper lip. On wobbly legs, she lowered herself into a chair and forced herself to breath slowly.

Voice-altering technology had been in existence for decades. Lots of old spy and mystery movies included segments in which it was used. That the caller had feared Dix would recognize the voice and resorted to such a cloak-and-dagger schtick pointed a finger straight at Kelly Condit. Besides, the call had come too soon after the young woman's furious departure to be unrelated.

As if sensing something was amiss, Lulu sat at Dix's feet and stared up into her face. Dix absently stroked the dog's head then pulled her phone from its holster and dialed her twin.

"What's up?" Lil's voice sounded taut.

"I think we're in the soup." Dix described the warning call. "I'm going to Dillon's apartment to check on him."

"He's probably out with friends and just forgot to call."

"He wouldn't do that. He was convinced something bad was going on and was determined to get to the bottom of it. Something's happened to him; I'm sure of it."

"So, you're going to ignore the death threat phone call?" Lil said. "Because that's what it was, you know."

"I know, but I'm too worried about Dillon to just sit around waiting for something to break."

"Hold off until I get there," Lil said. "I'm on my way."

"There's no time; I may already be too late."

"What's his address; I'll meet you—"

Dix broke the connection as images of Dillon, hurt, bleeding, maybe even being tortured ran in a loop through her mind. She grabbed her purse and headed for the garage.

Chapter Thirty-One

As Dix pulled out of her garage, she spotted the SUV parked up the street, and her insides quivered. Having shaken off all pretense of remaining anonymous, the driver was sending the message that it didn't matter if she saw him, that either he figured her to be a minimal threat, or he knew she'd never have the opportunity to finger him in a lineup.

"Message received," Dix muttered. She wiped sudden cold sweat from her forehead as, in a fit of indecisiveness, her mind went blank. Should she continue to search for Dillon, or should she pull back into the garage then hunker down in the house and wait for him to call? Should she immediately call the police?

Dix glanced at the kubaton she'd purchased several months earlier that hung from her keychain. Six inches in length, the metal weapon could temporarily incapacitate an enemy when forcefully applied to any one of over twenty pressure points on the human body. Although the kubaton would offer no protection from a bullet, at close quarters it might be enough to shift the scales in her favor.

Without consciously deciding to do so, Dix gripped her steering wheel, floored the gas pedal, and headed for Dillon's apartment. During the drive, she berated herself for not reporting the young man as missing when her insides told her something was up with him.

Dillon would have known Dix would be worried. He'd have called had he been able to. If he wasn't at his apartment by the time she got there, she'd drive straight to the police station.

Dix was neither surprised when the SUV followed her, nor when the driver parked across the street and sat watching her as she pulled into Dillon's driveway.

Was the guy trying to intimidate her or force her into doing something reckless? Maybe he was hoping she'd lead him to Dillon, since he was the one tech-savvy person who posed a threat to whatever operation they had going on. If so, that meant Dillon was still a free agent.

Dix's phone rang, the sudden sound loud in the enclosed space of her car. Her heart pounding, she automatically answered.

"Hey, doctor lady."

"Dillon," Dix all but squealed. "Thank God. Are you okay?"

"No worries, I'm fine. Sorry it's taken me so long to get back to you. My phone's dead, so I borrowed a friend's."

"What's happened?"

"I cloned Mr. Taylor's laptop then sent the data to the FBI along with my request they investigate. That should take some of the heat off you; at least it should once the feds get going."

"Wonderful news," Dix said.

"We should be careful though, whoever's behind this won't know the game's up for a while yet."

Dix recounted Kelly Condit's visit and the subsequent threatening phone call.

"That means if she didn't kill Mr. Taylor, she

knows who did," Dillon said.

"There's no telling how many people are involved in this, is there?"

"I suspect we've just scraped the tip of the iceberg. Thanks to the World Wide Web, there could be people from all around the globe involved." Dillon paused then added, "By the way, the numbers you called about? They're an IP address."

"That's what Lil thought," Dix said. "Is it like a phone number?"

"I guess that would be one way of looking at it. It's the key to understanding what Mr. Taylor was working on. I also wanted you to know that I discovered the exploit Mr. Taylor put on the honeypot."

"In Luddite terms?"

"Mr. Taylor set an awesome trap that basically painted a target on the bad guys' real IP address. It'll be easy for the FBI to backtrack and find out who's behind it. Kind of like following Hansel and Gretel's breadcrumbs." He paused then added, "Where are you now?"

"I'm in front of your apartment,"

"Why are you—"

"I was worried about you. You remember the SUV I told you I thought was following me? He's parked across the street as if he doesn't care if I see him."

"Yeah, the same guy followed me home." Dillon whistled softly. "That's not good. You need to go back to your house and stay until help gets there."

"What about you?"

"I'm pretty sure no one knows where I am. It's you they seem to be focused on, especially since you're the one Mr. Taylor was talking to before and after he was run over. Go home; call 911 and tell the police you're being stalked. When a couple of officers show up, give them a description of the SUV and the man driving it. That should make the creep back off."

After the call ended, Dix glanced into her rearview mirror. The guy was still there, not a worry in the world.

Images of Henry's last moments scrolled through Dix's memory. Had SUV-man been the driver of the hit-and-run car?

A red mist clouded Dix's vision at the thought, and she mentally shook herself. Martial arts philosophy held that rage was an enemy that could propel one to do something reckless or dangerous. While her next move had to be decisive, it also had to be done in accordance with her training.

Dix gunned her engine and shot backward down Dillon's drive. Smoke from burning rubber floated on the still air, and tires screamed when she shoved her gearshift first into reverse then into drive. She pulled alongside the SUV close enough to prevent the driver from opening his door then powered down her window. As she'd hoped, SUV-man automatically lowered his window.

She would tell the driver that the FBI was on the way and suggest he tell his cohorts. Hopefully, that would be enough to send the jackals packing.

The feds would hunt the villains down. Dillon and Lil would be safe, and they could all sleep peacefully again without the nagging fear that had taken over their lives.

By the time she'd finished facing the guy down, however, she realized the nightmare was not over. The look on the man's face was one of pure hatred, the kind she had chosen not to see on Josh Bearden's face all those years ago...the kind that meant someone was going to die.

Dix raced home, heedless of the speed limit.

Chapter Thirty-Two

Razor had scowled and fidgeted with the SUV's steering wheel as he sat parked up the street from the Ruiz sisters' house. Periodically, he'd scanned the neighborhood, looking for signs anyone was taking undue interest in his presence. As a man of action, sitting and waiting for something to break was contrary to his every instinct.

He rubbed the back of his neck hard enough to heat the flesh, then scratched an itch under his chin. In a fit of pique, he reached into the vehicle's console, withdrew a tube of moisturizer, squeezed a blob into his hand, and rubbed the cool gel into the dry skin of his face and neck. If he didn't get out of the desert soon, he was going to lose his freaking mind.

He studied the old ladies' house and rubbed his bottom lip. Should he break into the house and make the old ladies tell him where the kid was, then finish them off? Time was, after all, clicking on its merry way.

The old ladies' garage door suddenly opened, and a tan Chevy Cruze backed out. Razor slouched in his seat as Granny No-brows shot past, an intense look on her face.

For a nano second, he considered following her, but something held him back. For the first time in his life he couldn't decide on the best course of action, and the targets were scattering.

Although one old lady was gone, her sister must still be in the house. If the kid was in the house as well, maybe all was not lost.

Razor glanced at the clock in the SUV's dash. Time to push through the bubble and do what needed doing.

No sooner had he slipped on his gloves and pulled his pistol from its hiding place, than the old ladies' garage door opened a second time. A red convertible shot backwards into the street, and Granny Eyebrows glanced in his direction then sped away. Not, however, before a look of recognition flashed across her face.

Razor replaced his pistol in its holder. He fired up his engine and followed the old woman.

The kid's car hadn't been inside the old ladies' garage, so maybe he'd ditched it somewhere then taken an Uber to their house. Maybe he was sitting inside right then, leaning back in a recliner, drinking soda, and watching old movies.

Maybe Granny Eyebrows was going to the kid's apartment to get his stuff. Better yet, maybe she was going somewhere to pick *him* up.

Razor slowed the SUV to a crawl as the old woman pulled into Geek Kid's drive. He parked across the street and sat with his engine idling.

While the old woman kept looking back at the SUV in her rearview mirror, she made no move to leave her car. Instead, she pulled a phone from somewhere and held it to her ear.

Suspecting that Granny could be calling the cops, Razor nearly drove away. However, he held off...it would take the cops a while to show up, and he would be long gone by then. Not, however, before he'd taken a shot at figuring out what she was up to.

For a couple of minutes, granny spoke animatedly, gesticulating with her left hand, and nodding her head. She put the phone away and shot a glance into her rearview then gunned her engine. Her vehicle shot backward into the street, missing Razor's SUV by inches, then shot forward.

Granny jerked her car to a stop, parallel to and facing the opposite direction of the SUV. Her vehicle sat several inches lower than Razor's, requiring her to crane her neck upward to look at him. An expression of triumph on her face, she rolled down her window and sat waiting for him to do the same.

What the—

With a feeling he'd stepped into the Twilight Zone, Razor automatically pressed the power button, and he stared down at the old woman who was making his life miserable.

"You look like such a nice young man," Granny Eyebrows said. "What a shame you'll be spending the next several years regretting whatever it is you're doing."

"What makes you think you know what I'm doing," Razor said when he finally found his voice.

"I know Henry Taylor was on the verge of exposing something really nasty, and that's what got him killed. On top of that, I got a threatening call from someone I believe to be one of your crew...a young woman named Kelly Condit."

Would Condit have been stupid enough to—

"Oh," the old woman continued, "...and I just found out that the FBI has been given enough information to start an investigation into your shenanigans. You can't hide from the feds, you know."

Eyes blinking rapidly, Razor shook his head in disbelief. There he sat, chatting away with someone he fully intended to kill, and the two of them could have been discussing the weather or the rising real estate market.

The old woman's in-your-face attitude sent heat shooting up from the soles of Razor's feet. She was so sure of herself, so filled with self-righteousness. Blood pulsed into his face, heating it to boiling. He clenched his jaws, grinding his teeth while the old biddy schooled him like he was a misbehaving kid when she should have been trembling in terror.

Razor prided himself on being fit. At a buff six foot four, he had made good money intimidating, threatening, and pounding on anyone he chose. Within the past year or so, his reputation in LA had grown to the point where all he had to do was to growl and make a move toward someone for them to cave to his demands. Yet there sat scrawny Granny Eyebrows, unflinchingly ordering him to leave town.

The woman had pulled close enough to make it nearly impossible for Razor to open his door, so he reached for his pistol. However, in his boiling anger, his fumble-fingered hands managed to knock it off the seat and onto the floor where it landed against the passenger door.

Razor growled. Heedless of the resulting metallic *crunch*, he jerked his door open, slamming it against the old woman's red convertible. He would pull the old woman out through her window, by Judas, then choke her down, and throw her away like a busted rag doll.

Somewhere in the back of his brain he knew his actions were foolhardy. Someone might be watching, or worse, videoing him, but the old bimbo had it coming, and he was too far gone to stop himself.

Granny, however, had apparently anticipated his move and began powering her window up while he was still struggling to get through his door. By the time he positioned himself to make a grab for the woman, her window had closed to an opening of only four or five inches.

At the same time something inside Razor's head warned him of the window's upward progress, his single-minded rage demanded he keep going until he had the old lady's neck in a grip.

"I'd suggest you remove your arm before the window closes and I tromp on the gas," Granny Eyebrows said. "Or shall we find out how fast you can run before losing a couple of fingers?"

Razor managed to pull his hand out of the tightening window. He raised his fist to his mouth and sucked at the blood oozing from one especially painful knuckle.

"The game's up," Granny yelled through the now-closed window. "You might want to warn your friends."

"I'm going to make you pay for that," Razor yelled through gritted teeth.

He might as well have been screaming at the wind, because Granny Eyebrows had gunned her engine and was already halfway down the block.

For several minutes Razor sat in stunned silence. What had just happened?

Of all the ways he could have responded to the old

woman's assault, why had he just sat there letting her wind him up? She took complete control of the situation while he acted like a grade-schooler being lectured by his teacher.

...the FBI has been given enough information to start an investigation...

If Granny hadn't been bluffing, Razor didn't even have what was left of the twenty-four hours LeDuc had given him to clean things up...the FBI wasn't known for wasting time.

Razor pulled away from the curb and headed toward the motel.

Chapter Thirty-Three

Lil sat in the fast food café parking lot for several minutes after getting off the phone with Billy Oboe. Within a space of three minutes after Dix hung up on her, she tried several times to call her sister back. When the final call again went to voice mail, she clamped her jaws together so tightly her temples began to throb.

"You've reached Dix, leave a number and I'll call you back."

"Call me, Dix. Call me now, dammit," Lil said through clenched teeth. "If I haven't heard from you by the time I get home, I'm calling the police."

Lil slammed her clamshell phone closed and threw it onto the passenger seat of her car. With fearful images of what could be happening to her sister leapfrogging through her mind, she jerked her gearshift into drive and shot away from the curb and into the street.

The next thing she knew, she was pulling into her side of the otherwise empty garage. As the door powered down behind her, she sat staring at her sister's empty parking space. Dix was somewhere unknown, wading neck deep into a maelstrom, and Lil was powerless to help.

"Not quite powerless," she said as she reached for her phone. Her finger was poised to dial 911 when it rang, nearly causing her to throw the thing across her car.

Lightheaded with relief, she answered. "Where have you—"

"No time." Dix's voice sounded tense. "You need to secure the house. Do that right now."

"Why—"

"Lil," Dix said, "secure the house." She broke the connection.

As Lil let herself into the house, Lulu was standing just inside the door. The animal went into its typical gyrations of welcome then headed to its empty food dish and looked up expectantly.

"I'm busy, Bantha."

Lil spent the next half hour battening down everything she could get to. With the dog padding along in her wake, she turned on all the outside lights, engaged the security alarm, and powered up her taser. She retrieved a canister of bear repellant and placed it on the kitchen counter then sat in a chair to await Dix's arrival.

Her phone rang, startling her and making her jump.

"Hello, gorgeous," Billy Oboe said. "Just wanted you to know I have what you asked for."

"That was quick," Lil said, her heart still pounding.

"Why don't I bring it by your place and save you a trip?"

"Not necessary. Give me twenty minutes and meet me at Walmart per our agreement."

"You have the cash?" Oboe said.

"I do."

"I knew I'd eventually get you to say those two little words."

"Anything you're willing to tell me now?"

"Not to be rude," Billy said, "but first you pay, *then* I dish."

"Fair enough," Lil said. "Look for a tan, four-door Chevy Cruze."

"See you in twenty." Billy hung up.

Lil hustled to the garage and climbed into her car. The fact that Lil's heart was pounding so hard she could hear the blood pulsing in her head meant Dix was terrified.

You need to secure the house.

With her trouble's-brewing antennae whipping like prairie grass in a high wind, Lil pushed the garage door opener and backed out.

She would get whatever Oboe had for her then hustle home where she and Dix would wait for help. The bad guys would be arrested, justice would be served, and she and her sister could get on with their predictable, normal lives.

Chapter Thirty-Four

Kelly had just pulled into the motel parking lot when her phone dinged.

—*Where are you?*—Razor's text read.

—*At the motel. You?*—

—*Call me. Now.*—

Kelly punched Razor's number into her phone.

"We've got a crap storm hanging fire." Razor described his confrontation with Dix.

"I don't know how fast the FBI moves," Kelly said, "but I'm guessing in a matter of hours they'll be on us."

"What're we going to do?"

We?

"I'm going to clear out, and I suggest you do the same."

"And go where?" Razor said. "There's nowhere to run now that the feds have Taylor's data. Isn't there something you can do to cover our tracks?"

"Why is everything suddenly up to me?" Kelly said. "You're the one who screwed up."

"Oh yeah, blame this mess on me," Razor said. "You're the know-it-all, so fix it. By the way, when were you going to tell me about your visit with the grannies?"

Something cold slithered around inside Kelly's stomach. Silently, she fingered the collar of her white cotton blouse and considered her words carefully.

"They invited me to—"

"Yeah, sure. I'm not stupid," Razor said through gritted teeth. "What were you hoping to achieve?"

"As I was saying, the one named Dix called me and invited me to coffee. I figured it would be the best way to find out how much they know."

"So, what did you learn?"

"That they're basically breathing down our collective necks."

"What prompted you to make a threatening phone call after you left? That was one of the dumbest things you've done to date, and that's saying something." Razor snorted.

Kelly didn't respond.

"Hey, you still there?"

"Yeah, I'm here," Kelly said. "Other than LeDuc, you, and I, who knows about our project?"

"The grannies and the kid. Why?"

"I can clean up the online mess," she lied, "but they'll still know enough to cause trouble." *Come into to my web, said the spider to the fly...* "Not only do they know about Taylor's honeypot, they somehow got hold of the spoofed IP address I set up for the account. All the FBI has to do is pull the thread and it'll lead them back to all of us."

"Okay," Razor said. "You want to pop the grannies, or should I?"

"Tell you what, as a sign of good faith, I'll set a trap for them." *And another for you...* "You can take care of them any way you want. Might I suggest you make it look like an accident?"

"What about the kid?"

"You make the old ladies tell you where he is, then

you can take care of the kid as well." Kelly paused. "I can do it if you're too sensitive."

"Here we go again with the Wonder Woman act," Razor scoffed. "When and where is this all to take place?"

And the hungry mouse moves toward the cheese…

"There's an abandoned warehouse just south of Belen. I'll text directions." Kelly smiled to herself. "If everything goes as planned, the old women should be there by five minutes after eight."

"*If* it works as you plan…the grannies *should* be there. That's an awful lot of *maybe*." Razor clicked his tongue. "What if they don't fall for it?"

"Trust me; they'll take the bait."

"They'd better."

"You going to tell LeDuc what's going on, or shall I?" Kelly said.

"You haven't worked with LeDuc long enough to know his preferred means of problem solving." Razor blew a puff of air into Kelly's ear. "I'll tell him."

"Be sure and tell him I'll cash him out; his name won't be associated with any of this."

"What about my investment?" Razor said.

"Yeah, yeah, I'll take care of you, too." *He'll never know what hit him.*

After ending the call, Kelly drove back to the motel. Her insides shook as if liquified. There were countless ways her plan could fail, but she kept telling herself the payoff was worth the risk. Besides, she was in too deep to change trajectory.

Once in her motel room, Kelly packed her bags then carried them out through the motel's back door. She placed her luggage into the trunk of her rental, returned to her room, and pulled the white top sheet off the bed. After spreading the sheet on the floor, she placed the pillows end to end in its center, and rolled them up inside the sheet.

"Oh, look," she murmured, "I've made an old woman-shaped jelly roll."

From a paper bag on the desk in front of the television, she retrieved a roll of clear packing tape purchased earlier. Humming the soundtrack from a movie in which several teenagers were sawn to bits by a small-town nut job, she pulled a length of tape from the roll then wrapped the whole thing, pushing and punching the pillows until satisfied with the result.

Congratulating herself on having had the foresight to ask for a ground level room at the back of the motel, she carried the bundle out to her car and placed it in the back seat. While it wasn't the perfect likeness of a human body, it would be good enough to make her prey move in for a closer look.

Again, Condit returned to her room. She pulled the motel's complementary plastic clothes bag out of the closet. Using the room's plastic ice bucket liner as a glove, she retrieved a crushed pop can Razor had dropped into her trash can earlier and put it into the clothes bag along with a used tube of lip balm that had fallen from his pocket. The jerk's fingerprints *and* DNA...all but giftwrapped for the cops to find. Perfect.

Kelly pocketed three small bottles of catsup from room service dinners then doublechecked her purse for the straight razor purchased at a local beauty supply house. The idea of cutting herself didn't thrill her, but careful distribution of blood at the kill site would be the cherry on top of the evidence that would hang Razor.

Then once the scrap of her 3D printed heart had been discovered in LeDuc's office, the police would follow their noses. The rest, as the cliché went, would be history.

Condit chuckled to herself at the memory of how easy it had been to convince Razor and LeDuc that she could *erase* everything online. Their joyful reactions just highlighted how ignorant they were. Once the kid cloned Taylor's laptop to The Cloud, it would be there forever, or until either he or the FBI removed it. While Kelly took pride in her magical coding skills, no one could erase information once the feds had it.

She spent the next few hours on her laptop. She wasn't crazy about using the motel's wi-fi, but she was in a time crunch. Besides, she had generated an almost impenetrable virtual firewall; no one could hack into her laptop, and she'd spoofed her IP address through multiple redirected VPNs to make tracking her impossible.

By the time the clock on the bedside table read six, Kelly had put the finishing touches on a chain of events that would rock Razor's and LeDuc's respective worlds. She checked out of the motel and headed for her rental.

At eight, when everyone showed up at the warehouse, she would take care of business, then get on with her new life.

Chapter Thirty-Five

Razor broke the phone connection with Condit then texted Toad.

—*LeDuc told you guys to get back to Los Angeles, so where are you?*—

—*Why?*—Toad responded.

—*Looks like your services are no longer needed. I said where are you?*—

A long pause was followed by—*At the motel.*—

—*Move it.*—Razor texted. He gritted his teeth when Toad sent an answering gif in which a smiling politician tossed a thumbs-up sign into his face.

How was it a loser like Toad got a pass from LeDuc no matter how bad he messed up? All that blood thicker than water malarkey aside, the kid's IQ couldn't have been much higher than your standard ball of earwax. Toad's only saving grace had to be his complete and unwavering loyalty to his uncle.

Razor had known a couple of guys who got *retired* after only one error in judgement, one ill-advised breach of LeDuc's expectations. One of them had reportedly tried to make a side deal with the old guy's primary competitor, a man name Diamond; the other made the mistake of laughing at one of LeDuc's business decisions. One thing the boss didn't tolerate was disrespect.

LeDuc's face had been completely devoid of

expression as he listened to the men's apologies and pleas for mercy. Once the dead-men-walking had run out of steam, he merely glanced at the two soldiers who never left his side and jerked his head toward the screwups.

A grim expression flitted across Razor's face. As far as he knew, their bodies had never been found.

Since hiring on with LeDuc, Razor had made it a point to tiptoe around the old man's nephew out of respect for the bloodline. It was, however, growing tougher to do.

More than once over the years, Razor had to bite his tongue to keep from saying something he'd regret as Toad swanned around his uncle's office demanding deferential treatment. Having been raised on the assumption that he would one day take over the business, Toad made sure LeDuc's workers understood that their continued livelihoods would depend on his largesse.

LeDuc had never acted particularly fond of Toad. In fact, Razor suspected he only tolerated the kid because his wife held his financial *cojones* in a vise. An unwise prenuptial agreement would give her fifty percent of everything the man owned, and LeDuc wasn't one to willingly share.

On impulse, Razor checked the readout to the GPS tracking device he'd planted in the wheel well of Toad's rented van. As he suspected, Toad had lied about their location.

Envisioning himself punching Toad's nose into jelly, Razor made a U-turn and headed for Taylor's house. The screwups were going to get all of them caught.

****

Razor pulled into the alley behind Taylor's address and exited his vehicle in time to see Toad and Booger come through the back door of the house and head to their rented vehicle. Wearing gloves, their arms loaded with boxes and objects d'art, they placed everything in the back of the van. When the men turned to make another trip to the house, they caught sight of Razor and froze.

"Hello, boys," Razor said. "What're you doing here when you said you were at the motel? You're supposed to be headed home."

Toad cleared his throat. "We were just making sure we got everything Kelly told us to get."

"For real," Booger said.

"Is that right?" Razor stepped to the back of the van and opened the door. "She already has what she needs, so what're you really doing?" He peered inside the darkened interior.

A pricey espresso machine, a couple of antique clocks, and a pile of silver service pieces had been carefully stacked next to a large, wooden men's jewelry case. Behind the smaller items were a couple of oil paintings and a large bronze sculpture of a cowboy riding a bucking bronco.

"Care to explain?" Razor reached for the jewelry box.

"Taylor's dead," Toad said. "He doesn't need this stuff."

Razor opened the box and ran his fingers through its contents. Metal clicked and ticked as he sifted through the collection of jewelry that included a heavy gold college class ring inlaid with what looked like a genuine ruby, a woman's diamond wedding ring— probably belonging to the man's dead wife—a Rolex, a solid gold set of cufflinks, and an antique pocket watch on a chain.

"What did you think you were going to do with all this? You can't take it on the plane home."

"We thought we'd drive the van back to Los Angeles," Toad said.

"We got unlimited miles—" Booger began.

"How stupid can you be?" Razor moved his hand in a circular motion, indicating the neighboring houses.

The two men simultaneously gulped and stared down at the alley's hardpacked earth.

"I hate to be the bad parent here, but I suggest you take all this stuff back into the house then get back to LA like Mr. LeDuc ordered." Razor shook his head. "By the way, you might want to carefully consider what to include in your report…he asked for a Rolaids during our last conversation."

Toad and Booger exchanged looks. A sheen of perspiration broke out on Toad's upper lip and he cleared his throat. Booger sniffed.

Razor returned everything to the jewelry box but the Rolex.

While every genuine Rolex bore an etched serial number that could identify its purchaser, at least the watch Razor held bore no inscription on its back. The serial number would be visible only through a jeweler's monocle, while any inscription could make for an awkward explanation as to how he came to be in possession of such a costly piece of jewelry.

Razor slipped his own wristwatch off, dropped it into his pocket, then slid the Rolex onto his wrist. He turned to stare at the two buffoons, daring them to say anything.

Toad's eye's opened wide enough to show the whites all around. Booger sniffed, the sound like someone trying to breathe under water.

The two men looked at each other in unspoken agreement. They hauled the stuff back into the house then climbed into the van and took off. No sooner had they pulled onto the street at the end of the alley, than the scream of sirens split the air.

Razor sprinted back to his vehicle while pressing his key fob. He jumped inside the already-running SUV, slammed the gear shift into drive, and pulled out of the alley.

His stomach tight, he forced himself to drive the speed limit as flashing lights converged on Taylor's house in his rearview mirror. It wasn't until he'd gone several blocks that he allowed himself to take a deep breath.

He pulled into the parking lot of the motel then headed toward Condit's room. He couldn't shake the feeling that she was up to something. Although it could be his imagination, there had been something vaguely threatening about her last phone call. Then again, Razor had never managed to gain even a fingerhold into how Condit's mind worked.

Maybe she was thinking about making a break for it and leaving him in the FBI's crosshairs. Based on the information he'd dug up about her before agreeing to their partnership, she was capable of just about anything.

Why hadn't she told him about going to the old ladies' house for coffee then making the threatening phone call? It was possible she tried to make a deal with the grannies then went ballistic when they refused her offer.

While that kind of behavior was more in keeping with Toad's impulsiveness, if Condit had made such a colossal blunder, it meant she was skating on the edge of losing control, and that was very bad news for all concerned.

As Razor approached Condit's room, the feeling his old man called *all-over-ishness* gripped his body…as if someone had just walked on his grave.

Chapter Thirty-Six

Lil had been sitting in the parking lot less than five minutes when Billy Oboe pulled next to her in his late model Mercedes. She got out of her car, stepped around to the driver's side of Oboe's vehicle, and peered inside.

"You haven't changed in fifteen years," Billy said.

"You got what I asked for?"

"No nonsense, just like I remember. Yeah, I got it." Oboe grinned up at Lil. "You got the cash?"

"First, let me see what you have." Lil held her hand out.

"You didn't specify what you wanted, so I took the liberty of doing a deep dig." He lifted a black folder from the passenger seat. "I pride myself in giving more than I'm asked for."

Lil reached for the binder, but Billy's hand shot out and he gripped her wrist.

"Now, you know how I feel about you," Billy said, "but it seems only fair that you pay me *before* looking at my work, what with you having a photographic memory and all."

Lil pulled her wallet from the back pocket of her jeans, removed several bills, and held them toward Billy.

Billy ceremoniously counted the money. He lifted the folder toward Lil but jerked it back before she could take it. "What I have here is worth more than you're paying me."

"A deal's a deal, Mr. Oboe." Lil tapped her temple with an index finger. "And what I have here could cost you a lot more than you could ever get out of me."

"I can't help but wonder what you're trying your best to get into." Billy's face grew serious. "This is bad mojo, Lil, the kind of stuff that could get you killed. It's the kind of stuff that could get *me* killed just for looking at it."

"How did you find out… Where did you get…?" Lil held her hand up palm out. "On second thought, I don't want to know."

"You should be careful," Oboe said. "I suggest you let your sister see that." He nodded toward the notebook. "She might change her mind about getting any deeper into whatever's going on."

"You don't know Dix," Lil said.

Billy shrugged then handed the notebook through the window. "Pleasure doing business with you. You need anything else, just call." He started to power his window up, then paused. "Just so you know, I'm pretty sure nothing in there can be connected to me, but I'd still appreciate it if you wouldn't mention where you got it."

"You have my word."

"If you find yourself in a spot and need backup," Billy said, "I might know a guy."

"I'll keep that in mind."

Billy nodded once and drove off.

Lil returned to her car. She climbed in, buckled up, and opened the folder, then withdrew two neatly typed pages with headings in bold letters.

A scan of the first page elicited the occasional murmured *aha* and *not surprised* as Lil made her way through Condit's known associates, skills, employment record, places of residence, and business ventures. Lil had been mildly surprised that the woman was a computer whiz who had taken up with one of the most notorious organized crime syndicates headquartered in the western United States.

It was the page detailing excerpts from Condit's sealed juvenile records that caused Lil to gasp. With shaking hands, she closed the notebook and placed it on the passenger seat then sat staring out the windshield.

Waves of people of all ages, ethnicities, and socio-economic levels ebbed and flowed through the store's automatic doors and into the parking lot. Average people going about their average lives caring for their average kids—surviving the best they knew how. Moms carried babies and held onto toddlers' hands; dads pushed carts filled with groceries and household items; gaggles of teenaged girls laughed and flirted with passing teenaged boys.

What were the odds that one or more of the people walking through the parking lot had committed murder? Lil mentally sifted through the statistics from a recent Google search.

If the data could be believed, an average of about six murderers per hundred thousand population was standard in the United States. If that average held across populations, there could be as many as thirty-six murderers floating around the local area at any given time. The larger the population, the higher the likelihood of more murderers.

This is bad mojo…the kind of stuff that could get

you killed.

Billy's words ran in circles through Lil's mind, growing louder and louder with every circuit. She stared at the innocuous, black folder—the kind of thing a student would take to school, or a businessperson would fill with fiduciary reports.

Lil and Dix had been through a lot over the years. They faced down bullies in elementary school, kicked a would-be kidnapper's butt when they were twelve, and managed to survive an evil family's determined efforts to kill them a little over a year ago.

But this time felt different. This time, the bad guys were the worst of the worst. There was no red line they wouldn't cross to achieve their goals, and people of their ilk were rumored to have long memories.

At some time in the future, a goon could show up on the doorstep pretending to deliver a package or claiming his car had broken down and his cell was dead, so could he please use the phone. Dix would not only let him inside the house, she would offer him coffee and scones.

Her hands trembling, Lil pulled out of the parking lot and headed home.

Chapter Thirty-Seven

When Dix arrived home and drove into the garage, she was mildly surprised to see Lil's parking spot empty. After Dix's call commanding her sister to batten down the hatches, Lil probably decided to make a trip to Home Depot to pick up a roll of barbed wire, a case of wasp spray, and a dozen air horns.

Dix punched the black button on the wall then unlocked the connecting door as the garage door powered down behind her.

Lulu greeted her as if it had been years since they had seen each other. Suddenly, the dog froze and stared beyond Dix at the connecting door.

Dix turned and opened the door then glanced into the quiet garage. All was still.

"You're just on edge," Dix said to the dog. "You sense that Lil and I are uptight and it's making you jumpy." She patted the dog's head then pulled her phone from its scabbard and punched in Lil's number.

"Where are you?" she said when the call went to voice mail. "In case it didn't register, we're in for it. Lulu's spooked and you need to get home...now."

Dix made herself wait one minute before calling again. This time, Lil answered.

"Where have you—" Relief at hearing her sister's voice made her vision go gray, and she sat in a chair.

"I'm on my way home," Lil said. "The house is

secure; I'll see you in a few minutes." The line went dead.

Dix sighed and tried to calm down. Never one to miss an opportunity to overreact, it would be like Lil to stock up on provisions in expectation of a prolonged siege. She'd most likely stomp through the door any minute, her arms laden with milk, eggs, and bread.

Dix would have to tell Val—

Val.

She jerked her head up. Her fingers trembling, she managed to key in the young woman's number.

"Hello, Dix." Val's answering voice was light, unconcerned.

"May I ask where you are?"

"I'm just finishing up some paperwork. You remember the job offer I told you about? I've decided to take it." Val paused. "Are you okay? You sound—"

"We received a threatening phone call this morning, and someone's been following me." Dix recounted the events of the past several hours.

Val gasped. "What are you going to do?"

"I'm sorry, but it might be safer for you to move back to the motel."

"I won't just sit around while you're in danger. You and Lil are involved in this only because of your concern for my dad."

"But—"

"No buts, Dix. I'll be there in fifteen minutes."

"Be careful," Dix said, but Val had already broken the connection.

Dix breathed a sigh of relief as the garage door powered up, indicating Lil's return.

Lulu stood and ambled toward the connecting door

where she sat in obvious anticipation of Lil's arrival. Within a couple of seconds, however, the dog lowered her head and stared at the door. Her ears flattened against her head, she stood unmoving, a low growl rumbling through her chest.

"You and Lil need to agree to a truce." Dix patted the dog's head. "She's tough but not mean…not really."

Lulu shot a quick glance at Dix then returned her focus to the door.

A minute or so ticked by.

When no mechanical hum announced the garage door closing behind Lil's vehicle, Dix hurried to the door behind which her sister was most likely struggling to haul too many bags of groceries instead of making multiple trips.

As Dix reached for the knob, however, Lulu's neck hair bristled. The dog growled, bared her teeth, and began pawing at the door.

Dix's stomach knotted. She hustled to the butcherblock knife holder on the counter, grabbed the longest-bladed knife in the set, then strode back to the connecting door.

The knife held low, with its blade facing up, Dix stepped into the garage.

Chapter Thirty-Eight

Lil's mind jumped from thought to thought during the drive home from her meeting with Billy Oboe. She had no doubts as to the truth of the man's report. Oboe was a con man and a thief, but he had his own weird moral compass that wouldn't allow him to give her anything less than what she was paying for.

She would show the report to Dix then call the police. She'd have to come up with a good explanation of how she got hold of the information, but once she and Dix were safely ensconced inside their house, and the police were patrolling the area, they would be safe.

While still a block from the house, Lil pushed the garage door opener clipped to the visor. Even though the house was not yet in view, she hated having to sit in the drive while waiting for the door to open. An idling car wasted gas.

When the house came into view, Lil's insides twisted themselves into a knot, and her throat clamped nearly closed. Kelly Condit's car sat in the driveway in front of the open garage door and behind Dix's car.

Lil drove up her side of the drive and pulled her phone from its dock. She'd first call the police then she would call Dix and tell her what she'd learned about Condit, who was probably sitting in the kitchen enjoying a cup of coffee and scone. Then she'd grab the tire iron from her trunk, tiptoe into the house, and sneak up behind—

Lil shoved her gearshift into park and jumped from the still-running car. Her body shaking so badly she could barely stand, she stumbled toward Condit's car. What appeared to be a body wrapped in blood-spattered bed sheets or blankets lay half in and half out of the back seat as if someone had been interrupted while trying to lift the dead weight.

"Dix." Lil whimpered and bent over the bundle. With trembling hands, she reached toward the blankets at the same time her brain registered the faintly familiar acetic odor of catsup.

Lil groaned. It wasn't Dix who'd stepped into Condit's trap.

She started to stand, but something hit the back of her head and she fell on top of the catsup-covered blankets. The last thing she remembered was someone lifting her into the car, tossing the blankets on top of her, then slamming the door.

Chapter Thirty-Nine

Razor stood behind the counter in front of the motel's receptionist, heat pulsing in his face. "Are you sure we're talking about the same person?" he said.

"Miss Condit, right?"

Razor jerked his head in a single nod.

The young man typed furiously on the desktop computer then looked up. Something about Razor's expression must have registered because he gulped loudly then said softly, "I'm sorry, she checked out about half an hour ago."

Razor hustled to his room, pulling his phone from his pocket as he went. He punched in Kelly's number then let himself into his room while waiting for her to answer.

"What's up?" Kelly's voice, never pleasant, sounded calm and self-assured.

"I thought you were online fixing things, so why have you already checked out of the motel?"

"Because it's all done."

"My money?" Razor said.

"It's in the process of transferring to the account you had me set up. The same for Mr. LeDuc's investment." Condit paused. "You know how it works; it'll take several hours for the transfer to be completed, but the funds should show up in your account by first thing in the morning."

"Taylor's data?"

"Wiped out." Kelly added, "I suggest you check out of your room. I think we're safe, but I don't want to risk hanging around longer than necessary, especially since the old woman said the feds have been contacted. There's nothing left for them to find, but they're required to check into it anyway."

Razor sighed and a smile crept across his face. Maybe Condit wasn't such a waste of space after all. He might rethink his plans for her.

"Anything else?" Kelly was saying.

"What about our airline tickets?"

"Booked our flight for midnight tonight," Condit said. "That should give us time to finish here, if we hustle."

"Where are you now?"

"Seemed like a good time to grab a latte and take in a movie."

"Okay." Razor chuckled. "You got the grannies hooked yet?"

"Hooked and waiting. Consider them my parting gift to you."

"Excellent," Razor said. "I'll meet you at the warehouse a few minutes after eight."

After the call ended, Razor sat on the side of the bed and thought about how to spend the money he was going to make off the deal. At the twenty percent profit on his investment Kelly said he'd earned, it would be a higher yield than even the most aggressive stock investors could expect, especially in the current volatile market.

Twenty percent of five hundred thousand was one hundred thousand. Not a bad chunk of change for sitting around while someone else did all the work.

Razor glanced at his newly acquired Rolex. He had a couple of hours to kill before meeting Condit and the grannies at the warehouse. Time enough to take a shower, pack, check out, and treat himself to an early dinner. A juicy, medium rare ribeye steak and salad sounded about right.

He turned on the television and found a channel that featured music from his teen years. Bopping his head to the rhythm blasting into the room, he stepped out of his clothes and headed toward the bathroom.

Razor grinned while shampooing his hair. Soap bubbles stung his eyes and dripped into his mouth, but he didn't care.

Dinner would be a celebratory occasion. After all, since Granny Eyebrows had an identical twin, it would be like killing her twice.

Chapter Forty

Kelly sat in her rental car and reviewed her plan. There could be no hesitation, nor could she take a chance on things coming to a head before she was ready. She pulled her phone from the built-in cup holder and dialed LeDuc's number.

"Miss Condit," LeDuc purred. "To what do I owe the pleasure?"

"I just need to make sure you know what's really happening here."

"Go on."

"As you may already know, I've recommended we close down the project."

"Yes." LeDuc blew a long puff of air into his phone.

"Due to Razor's multiple mistakes, I've had to take some fairly radical steps to fix things." Condit paused. "It's fairly technical but basically like backing a car out of a garage. Because of my effective manipulation of various cryptocurrencies, however, you'll have a nice return on your investment, somewhere around twenty-five percent."

"Twenty-five percent is good." LeDuc burped. "What mistakes has Razor made?"

"I would like to give him the benefit of the doubt, but he's been acting hinky for a couple of days, ever since the mishap with Henry Taylor. Did you know he went to the old lady's house, the one who witnessed Taylor's…um…accident, and confronted her? Then he made a threatening phone call telling her to back off. Until the call, she didn't know for sure that Henry's death was, you know, not quite accidental. Now the old woman is sniffing around our project like a bloodhound."

LeDuc remained silent. Kelly's mouth went dry.

"Then I overheard him talking to someone on the phone," Kelly hurried on. "I couldn't understand everything he said, but I did clearly hear him offer someone named Mr. Diamond a cut of something."

"You're sure he said Diamond?"

"I remember because I thought it might be a code name, you know, someone's alias." Kelly stifled a nervous giggle.

It had been unexpectedly easy to learn the name of LeDuc's most formidable adversary. Diamond and LeDuc had once been partners but split the sheets when Diamond decided control of all a business was better than half of a partnership. The result had been a decades long rivalry with each man lobbing the occasional death threat at the other.

LeDuc remained silent for several beats then said, "Thank you for your call. It seems a good idea, as you say, to back out of the project. How soon can I expect my money to show up in my account?"

Kelly's shoulders relaxed. *Hook, line, and sinker…*

"I can have it done within a few hours. The funds should be in your account by tomorrow morning."

"And my involvement?"

"I'll erase anything that might even come close to pointing at you."

"Okay, Miss Condit." LeDuc cleared his throat. "Although it pains me to be so direct, you are aware of the penalty for messing me over, yes?"

"Yes, sir." Kelly felt lightheaded as her phone went dead.

No one had ever clipped LeDuc and lived to brag about it.

Kelly tried to shake off the tendrils of nausea sending tentative feelers through her stomach. Over and over, she reviewed her plan.

It had to work. Even the tiniest flaw and she would be ground into bits and fed to LeDuc's guppies.

Chapter Forty-One

BeeBee LeDuc mentally chewed on his phone call with Kelly Condit. Although it would be a mistake to take everything she said as true, he sensed she was right about the need to dump the project.

Had Razor really made the colossal mistake of trying to make a deal with Diamond, or was Condit trying to play the two men against each other? What could she hope to gain by creating enmity between them?

While LeDuc didn't trust anyone, he came closer to trusting Razor than he did Condit. Razor had been in his employ for years and had unquestioningly followed LeDuc's every order.

Condit, on the other hand, was relatively unknown. Although LeDuc carefully vetted the woman before getting involved with her startup project, he ordered Razor to stick close to her and report any suspicious behavior. She was, after all, reportedly a very bad girl.

When Razor approached him with Condit's proposition to create their own cryptocurrency, LeDuc was intrigued. Old school as he was, the idea of making money from an online scheme appealed to him. He felt like Aladdin discovering the magic lamp.

As was his habit, however, he learned all he could

about Miss Kelly Condit before agreeing to her proposal. While she had primarily done free lancing tech support in the years prior to setting up the project, she had earned a reputation as being brilliant and tough, but egotistical.

A red flag had popped up when his research assistants reported hazy feedback from a couple of people with whom she worked some years earlier, as if the interviewees had been reluctant to be too specific with their comments. Rumor had it that one guy with whom she had been intimately involved, a research scientist, committed suicide shortly after she broke up with him.

BeeBee had waved the negative vibes aside. Blinded by the possibility of feeding what his sainted mother would have called *ill-gotten gains* into the project's cryptocurrency exchange, allowing Condit to do her manipulations, then pulling clean, laundered funds out of any one of hundreds of legitimate exchanges, he ignored the tingle at the base of his neck.

Although the process smacked of hocus pocus, he learned that a couple of brothers had made a fortune by doing exactly what Condit suggested—manipulating the cryptocurrency markets. It had not only netted the guys a pile of money, it had all been legal.

As a consummate businessman, LeDuc understood that the success of any project hinged on the people working on it. While he had entrusted Condit and Razor with a great deal, he would hold them accountable if the thing blew up.

It was, however, LeDuc who would ultimately be called on the Collaborative's carpet if the thing soured. The businessmen he talked into investing would demand he repay every cent they stood to lose plus the promised profit. While BeeBee was a very wealthy man, he would be unable to completely cover all their losses.

BeeBee had always prided himself on his method of managing human resources. Careful not to micro-manage unless necessary, he made it a policy to allow his employees a smattering of autonomy. If they fulfilled their obligations to him, he left them to their own devices. Like his high school history teacher had said, "The wealthy and powerful had a responsibility to care for their underlings—*noblesse oblige*—the obligations of nobility."

While LeDuc wasn't of noble birth, he *was* a king of sorts. After the project was cashed out, he'd have enough money to buy himself a crown and jeweled scepter if he wanted...and he could do it with clean money.

The dead mouse in LeDuc's chef salad, however, was the tangible enmity between Razor and Condit. He decided his best course of action would be to allow the two of them to fight it out. Of course, only one would survive, but he preferred working with winners. Long as nothing pointed to him, he was fine with whatever the outcome might be.

Anyone who worked for LeDuc knew the price of betraying his oath of allegiance. To avoid any misunderstanding, LeDuc required new employees to sign a paper copy of the oath, at the bottom of which were printed the words: *Penalty Clause—The signer understands any breach of trust will immediately and irrevocably be met with a penalty of Mr. LeDuc's choosing.*

Over the past twenty years or so, BeeBee only had to enforce the penalty clause a couple of times. He was pleased when the *penalty of his choosing* had not only sent the intended message but had resulted in his exploding reputation as someone best not to jerk around.

BeeBee raised and lowered his left arm, telling himself the chronic ache was a result of the change in barometric pressure. He had, no doubt, inherited the weakness from someone in his lineage. He remembered an uncle complaining about his bum knee kicking up whenever it was going to rain. His own mother had a bunion that acted up every spring and fall.

Weary of the aches and pains along with recurrent heartburn, he had at one time considered seeing a doctor. The problem was he didn't trust them.

Every other mob boss owned their own personal doc, but LeDuc had steadfastly refused to entrust his body to another person. He once heard about a guy whose personal fitness coach had been paid a ton of money to give him a *food supplement* that turned out to be laced with some rare, untraceable poison that caused a heart attack. Even docs had a price, and LeDuc's enemies wouldn't hesitate to buy or threaten into submission anyone with such intimate access to him.

So, BeeBee had Googled his symptoms and diagnosed himself as having GERD and a hiatal hernia. He tried to make changes in his diet based on the information on the medical website but had failed to be consistent on that front. He switched from chocolate truffles to hard candy and ate more fish and less pasta. He had tried drinking red wine instead of Scotch but hadn't managed to stick with that. He patted himself on the back when, even with his minimal efforts, his heartburn seemed to lessen.

LeDuc's path in life hadn't always been easy. Take the current situation, for example. While he was unsure of the process by which Condit would *back out of the project*, one thing he knew—she would think twice before doing him dirt. He would be the last man standing even if he had to take out every other living human being on the planet.

LeDuc jerked his head up at a new thought. People being what they were, it was possible Condit and Razor had lied about the project's impending failure. Maybe they only pretended to hate each other to keep him from getting suspicious. Maybe they figured to deal him out and keep the proceeds for themselves.

If that were the case, of course, the two were dog food. There was nowhere they could go that he couldn't reach them.

Not for the first time since his worthless nephew took it on himself to hit Taylor, LeDuc cursed himself for getting involved with Condit. He'd always been immune to the dog and pony shows put on by guys trying to pull him into various investments, always looked upon himself as too smart. He steered clear of human trafficking, child porn, and the drug trade. To his way of thinking, anyone involved in those businesses were scum.

LeDuc's entrepreneurial efforts revolved around things like buying up businesses, cleaning out the employee retirement accounts then going bankrupt. He dabbled in blackmailing politicians. Early in his career, he made a pile of money by buying a truckload of cheap olive oil, mixing it half and half with canola oil, then rebottling it as an expensive extra-virgin product and selling it in one of the storefront businesses into which he invested. Pure genius.

LeDuc glanced at his watch. It was time to check up on Condit's promises. Since it was after five in the evening, the banks would be closed. LeDuc, however, had the home phone number of the bank's vice president, a man who owed him a great deal of money.

Even if LeDuc's funds had not yet been returned to his investment account, the banker could learn of any pending action. If Condit assumed LeDuc would wait until the morning to learn of it, she had another think coming.

A pain shot through BeeBee's chest. He reached for his Rolaids, shook out a handful, popped them into his mouth, then retrieved his phone.

Chapter Forty-Two

When Lil regained consciousness, it was to utter darkness. Her head was covered with a soft fabric that smelled faintly of hairspray; her arms were tightly bound against her body. Her legs were affixed to the legs of the chair in which she sat. Pressure against her ribcage hinted that she was bound to the chair's back. She moved her tongue around inside her mouth to work up some saliva then licked her lips. Her head pounded loud enough to be heard in the next county.

"Ah, I see you're back." The nails-raking-blackboard voice was unmistakable. "Isn't duct tape just the most marvelous invention ever?" Condit's voice echoed as if they were inside a large, hollow structure. "You weigh a ton for being such an old bag of bones, you know that? It took me half an hour to get you into that chair. I had to turn it on its side to tape you into it then hoist you and the chair upright."

Lil remained silent.

"Hey," Kelly screeched, "I'm talking to you."

"So you are," Lil said.

Where was she? Lil searched her memory for any buildings within a twenty-mile radius of Los Lunas to which Condit might have brought her. An empty barn or airplane hangar? Perhaps a county-owned building in which road and highway maintenance machinery was stored?

"Don't feel much like talking?" Condit laughed. "No questions?"

"Where am I?" Lil's dry throat made her voice sound like a gila monster's hiss.

"Oh goody," Condit said. "Let's chat."

Lil heaved a sigh but remained otherwise silent.

"Okay, so it'll be a monologue. You're being held in an old abandoned warehouse out in the middle of nowhere. We're miles from civilization, so screaming won't help." Kelly's voice grew conspiratorial. "Bet you'd like to know why I brought you here."

"I know why," Lil said as Billy Oboe's report flashed onto the screen of her photographic memory.

"Really?" Kelly's laugh echoed as it caromed off the walls of what must have been an empty, large metal building. "What do you think you know?"

"I know you fancy yourself a genius when what you really are is a spoiled brat who never thought of anyone but herself."

"I *am* a genius," Kelly said. "And haven't you heard of a man named Darwin? It's all about survival of the fittest. But please, do go on."

"I know you're involved with organized crime."

Silence.

"Two names spring to mind—BeeBee LeDuc and Reston Diamond."

"How do you know—"

"You're up to your armpits in smell-bad with the foulest of the foul. You think you're going to be allowed to do whatever you're doing then swan off into the sunset? You won't; LeDuc isn't known for profit sharing."

"If you're so smart, why did you fall into my trap?"

Kelly's voice had risen in pitch until it sounded like unoiled wheels on a truck. "Getting the drop on you was easy. Did you really think that pile of rags was your ugly sister?" She chuckled.

"I didn't *fall* into your trap. I stepped into it," Lil lied.

"Oh, please."

"I admit I was taken in initially, but I allowed you to grab me because I love my sister and would do anything to protect her." Lil tried unsuccessfully to shift her butt into a more comfortable position. Even a millimeter would relieve some of the pain from her unsupported back. "But then, you wouldn't understand that, would you?"

"Understand what?"

"You wouldn't know about loving someone more than yourself."

"Now you're pissing me off," Kelly shrieked. "You don't know squat about me."

"I know you murdered your whole family when you were fourteen." Lil finally managed to scoot her bottom a little to one side. The relief to her back was immediate. "You set fire to your house killing your mom, dad, and two siblings."

"He wasn't my dad."

"Your baby brother was only three years old."

"Step-brother." Condit mumbled something unintelligible then added, "I did try to get him out, but it was too hot."

"Not according to your neighbors," Lil said. "They said you stood outside and watched the flames, smiling as your burning family screamed for help. The only reason you haven't spent your life in prison was because you were a juvenile."

A blow to the side of Lil's head set her ears ringing.

Kelly's next comment sounded like, "Rumrum old eye parents rough—"

"Just so you know, I can't hear whatever you're trying to tell me. Left my hearing aids at home."

Kelly brought her mouth close to Lil's ear. "Someone told my mom to try *tough love* on me. Tough love after years of making me think I was important." She chuckled, but the sound was devoid of mirth. "It was just my mother and me until he came along. After he moved into the house, she didn't have time for me."

"Your mother moved on with her life, and you lost control over her." Lil *tsk*-ed. "You had everything you needed, but it wasn't enough."

"She started having kids as soon they got married. We never did anything together anymore." Kelly's voice had risen in pitch. "She was *my* mommy."

"So, your step-dad finally said no when your mother had always said yes."

"He wasn't my real—"

"Yeah, yeah, so you said." Lil snorted. "That's the lamest excuse for murder I've ever heard."

Another blow, nearly hard enough to knock Lil's chair over.

"No matter. In another couple of hours, the final cogs will slip into place and I'll be moving on. But you and your precious sister won't." In a sing-song voice, she added, "Tick-tock, the game is locked, nobody in, nobody out." High-pitched, manic laughter was followed by, "See you later."

The receding clickety-clackety of footfalls on

concrete was followed by the creak of a door opening. A loud, metallic slam was followed by silence.

Lil counted twenty steps it took for Condit to get to the door. If each step covered the usual two and a half to three feet, that meant the door was about thirty feet from where she was sitting. The thought that she could frog-hop the chair up and down until she reached the door died a miserable death. Not only did she have no way to open the door even if she managed to get to it, trussed up like she was, it might as well have been thirty miles away.

"Dix?" Lil called. "Dix, are you here, too?"

Silence.

"Dix," she shouted. "If you're here, make some noise."

Lil swallowed hard. Either her sister wasn't there, or she wasn't able to respond.

"Lord," she murmured, "please give my sister sense enough not to fall for Condit's trickery."

If Condit had told the truth, Lil had two hours to escape—two short hours to free herself and find a way to warn her sister.

Furiously, Lil struggled to move her legs. When several minutes of effort resulted in no movement at all, she focused on freeing her hands and arms. As with her legs, Condit had secured her arms to the chair's armrests from wrist to elbow.

"Like a freaking mummy," Lil murmured.

Within a short time, the tightness of the tape had restricted blood circulation to the point Lil's arms fell asleep. Again, she tried to shift her butt in the chair to ease the pressure on her back. This time, however, the tiny amount of movement she could manage served only to increase the discomfort. Because of the cocked angle at which she'd been bound to the chair, her tormented spinal column soon began shooting pains down the backs of her otherwise-numb legs. Within minutes of Condit's leaving her alone, Lil had to fight to keep from screaming in pain.

"Stay away, Dix." Imagining her words as beams of energy flowing from her laser mind to her sister's, Lil focused every cell of her being into hurling them through space and time. "Do you hear me? Stay away."

Chapter Forty-Three

By the time Kelly left the warehouse, she was grinning so broadly her lips felt like they stretched all the way around her skull to meet at the back of her head. She would have enjoyed staying in the warehouse to torment the old woman but had to make a quick trip to the open desert to dump the pillows and blankets used as a trap. Although chances were slim that anyone would figure out what the bundle had been used for, she had come too far to take even the tiniest chance.

Kelly couldn't believe how easy it had been to capture Lil. Regardless of what the old woman said, it was Kelly who set the trap and who was in control. In a short time, she'd have both old women bound up like shrink-wrapped boxes of chocolates waiting for Razor's vengeance.

As Kelly walked to her car, she hooted and pounded her chest with her fists. Within a couple of hours, the old women would be removed from the equation, and Razor would come face to face with *her* brand of vengeance.

She fought down the idea of hanging around for Razor's arrival. It would have been a special treat to see the expression on his face when the cops arrested him for murder. From the moment they met, he tried everything in his power to get her to swoon into his arms like some love-struck teenager. It had been fun to watch him move from tactic to tactic until he ran out of steam. What Kelly hadn't foreseen, however, was how soon he shifted from romantic pursuer to spurned lover.

The come-hither look in his eyes, as old people used to say, turned to sour grapes, and he grew harder and harder to work with. The last straw had been his act of betrayal in calling LeDuc to complain about her failed break-in attempt, like a fourth grader tattling on a classmate.

From the time Kelly learned how easily she could hack into other people's computers and get their personal information, she had mulled over ways to use that skill to her best advantage.

When she'd read an article in a finance magazine about the growth in the cryptocurrency markets, a virtual gong went off inside her head. Roadblocks to successful outcomes were anticipated and circumvented. Potential suckers were chosen based on their reputations as being uber-wealthy then teased with guarantees of explosive returns on their investments. As a result of her years of planning, she was so close to successful completion of her long-term strategy she could feel the warm Caribbean breezes on her face.

Razor had been first to fall for the siren call of her cryptocurrency project. When she suggested increasing the number of investors to make it easier to manipulate the cryptocurrency markets and raise the yields to as much as triple digits, he ran straight to LeDuc, as she knew he would. Once LeDuc was hooked, he pulled in several likeminded businessmen, and the investment dollars rolled in.

Kelly hugged herself.

Life was good, but it was about to get better.

Chapter Forty-Four

Dix had been alarmed when Lil didn't immediately come into the house after the garage door opened. With an unpleasant sensation in her solar plexus building in intensity, she stepped through the connecting door and into the garage.

Just outside the open garage door sat Lil's car, its engine still running and driver's side door ajar. As Dix strode toward the car, the sight of thick, red drops on the concrete drive sent a shiver through her midsection. She stooped and dragged her index finger through a glob of the drying stuff and sniffed it.

Catsup.

Why would catsup be...

She peered into the interior of her sister's car. That there was no sign of a struggle and no *real* blood in Lil's car or on the driveway was good news...at least Lil hadn't been injured.

Dix bent over, reached into the car and shut off the engine. Stretching across the driver's side, she picked up a black folder lying on the passenger's seat.

A ransom note?

Breathing in short gasps, her hands trembling, she stood and opened the folder.

Not a ransom demand, the two typed pages inside appeared to be a report.

As Dix scanned the pages, the black type began to

undulate on the white background. Her vision went gray, and her knees gave way. She dropped into the driver's seat to keep from falling to the concrete.

She understood that the people who ran Henry down had to have been devoid of humanity. She even stumbled early on to Kelly Condit's involvement. Dix hadn't, however, realized the depth of wickedness she had ushered into their lives by taking it on herself to track down Henry's murderers.

Where had Lil got the information in the folder? If even a portion of it were true, the sub-humans whose attention they managed to attract wouldn't hesitate to murder her, Dix, *and* Dillon. Val could be a target just because she was Henry's daughter.

Poor Henry. The decent, kind man with the social conscience that demanded he search out and expose those predators who gnawed like rats at the vulnerable underbelly of humanity.

Suddenly, Dix's head began to throb. Her back ached and her elbows and knees began to sting. Anyone else would have assumed the pain was a building migraine or arthritis. In Dix's world, though, it meant wherever Lil was, she was hurting.

As if a tanker of clear epoxy had been poured over her and then instantly set up, Dix sat frozen in place. Unable to move, she fought against the billows of fear for her sister that threatened to swallow her whole.

At some point, Dix sensed Val's arrival. The young woman parked beside Lil's car, jumped from the vehicle, and ran to Dix. Bending at the waist, she brought her eyes level with Dix's.

"What's happened?" Val said.

The buzzing of a million bees filled Dix's head and

packed her ears with cotton. She looked at Val's moving lips and heard the words but seemed unable to process them.

"Dix." Val placed her hand on Dix's shoulder and shook gently. "Dix, what's happened?"

"Someone has taken Lil." Dix choked back a sob. "I think Kelly Condit has kidnapped her." She handed the folder to Val. "If any of this is true—"

"Come into the house." Val tucked the folder under her arm and reached a supportive hand toward Dix. "We need to think."

On wooden legs, Dix followed Val into the garage. Wordlessly, she stood as the young woman pushed the black plastic control attached to the wall, and the garage door made its descent.

Inside the kitchen, sensing Dix's mood, a subdued Lulu sat with her ears perked up as far as the cone would allow and watched the women.

"I'm going to call the police," Val said.

"No—" Dix reached her hand out as if to stop a locomotive.

Dix's phone buzzed, and she jumped. With fumbling fingers, she pulled the instrument from her bra and looked at the caller ID.

"Mizz Condit, I presume." Dix's voice sounded robotic.

"Right in one." Kelly Condit's screech assaulted Dix's eardrum. "I'll bet you'd like to know where your sister is, wouldn't you?"

"What have you done with her?"

"Nothing yet, just a few minor scrapes and bruises. But I *will* do awful things to her if you don't do exactly what I say. Are you with me?"

"Yes," Dix said.

"There's an abandoned warehouse just south of Belen." Val repeated the directions while Dix jotted them on the notepad that stayed on the counter next to the landline. "Be there at eight tonight. Five minutes before or five minutes after gets your nasty twin shot."

Dix repeated the directions.

"That's it. Oh, and need I tell you what will happen if I even suspect you've involved the police?"

"I'll do whatever you say, just please don't hurt Lil."

Kelly laughed then broke the connection.

Dix held the dead phone to her ear for several seconds then took a deep breath and slowly blew it out. She looked at Val and repeated Condit's demands.

"Oh, Dix, I'm so very sorry—"

"Not your fault, Val." Dix suddenly threw her shoulders back, lifted her chin, and took a deep breath. "That young woman shouldn't have taken Lil."

"How can I help?"

"I think it best if you stay here with Lulu." Dix smiled. "It'll be a tremendous relief to know you're safe and your father's animal friend is being cared for." She glanced at the black cat clock. "I'll double check Google maps, but if the warehouse is located where I think it is, it'll take about twenty minutes to get there, give or take. That gives me just shy of an hour to figure out what to do." She smiled. "The coffee's in the cupboard, second shelf; mugs are above the stove."

Val made a fresh pot of coffee then filled two psychedelic-floral printed mugs with the fragrant, steaming liquid. "You do know you're walking into a trap, don't you?" She handed a mug to Dix.

"Of course, it's a trap. Kelly can't leave either of us alive to testify against her." Dix looked into Val's eyes. "I'm afraid you could be a target as well."

"Then doesn't it seem that you're just helping her get away with whatever she's planning?" Val's eyes teared up. "You're basically committing suicide."

"I won't desert my sister," Dix said. "We were born holding hands and if it's our time, we'll go to Heaven holding hands."

"Please, don't talk like that."

"Trust me," Dix said. "I won't make it easy for Kelly Condit."

The two women exchanged determined looks then clinked their mugs together.

"Here's to finding your sister and not going to Heaven for many years yet," Val said.

"And here's to sending Kelly Condit and her cronies to prison for murdering your father," Dix said.

Chapter Forty-Five

Toad and Booger sat in their van beside a gas station a few blocks from the old ladies' house. Toad sipped from a can of high-protein energy drink while Booger chewed a piece of beef jerky.

"That's raw meat you're eating; you know that, right?" Toad said.

"Naw," Booger said. "It used to be raw, now it's all dried out."

"*Dried out* doesn't mean cooked. It could still have germs and bugs in it, maybe even that salmonella stuff I've been hearing so much about. You know people have died from eating stuff covered in that?"

"I don't figure salmonella can live on dried-out meat," Booger said. "Besides, bugs are protein. People all over the world eat bugs and maggots and stuff."

"You're determined to make me hurl," Toad said. "Give me the notebook."

"Is it time?" Booger reached between the seats, withdrew a spiral bound notebook, and handed it to Toad.

"Yep." Toad opened the book to the first page. "First on our to-do list is to grab the grannies."

"Do we have to pop them?" Booger sniffed.

"Do you have to snuff up like that?" Toad scowled. "Use your hanky; I'm going to lose my dinner."

"Sorry." Booger pulled his wadded-up

handkerchief out of his pocket. He opened it in search of a relatively un-used place, the resulting sound like someone pulling Velcro apart.

Toad gagged.

"Sorry." Booger blew energetically then wadded the hanky back up and stuffed it into his pocket.

"And, yes, we have to pop them." Toad jabbed a finger against the page on which was written the plan of action he'd discussed with LeDuc. "They know too much. Besides, Uncle BeeBee likes our idea. We could get a promotion if we take care of this business for him. He said to clean house, so nothing bites him on the ass later."

"But won't all that online stuff still be floating around in the air?" Booger looked thoughtful. "What if someone finds it and, you know, tracks it or sunthin?"

"Razor told Uncle BeeBee that Condit was going to get his money back and erase everything; there won't be any tracks left."

"Then why pop the Whiz?"

"She must have done or said something to make Uncle BeeBee not trust her anymore. She knows all his account information; he can't just let her walk away." Toad cleared his throat. "Nothing personal, just taking care of business."

Booger nodded. "I don't like the idea of popping the old wom—"

"That's because you've never had to hurt anyone."

"Neither have you," Booger said. "At least, not until you hit Taylor. The only reason you did that was because you panicked."

"Yeah, but I'm in line to take over the business when Uncle BeeBee pops his cork. I might as well get used to making tough decisions." Toad patted Booger's shoulder, "I'll take care of the women, so you don't have to."

"That's just plain nice," Booger said. "Kind of brings a tear to my eye."

"We've been friends a long time; you would do the same for me."

Toad shoved the notebook into the space between the seats. He pulled the van into the street and headed for the Ruiz house while Booger pulled his pistol from the holster stashed in the console.

As the van turned a corner near the old ladies' house, Booger sat straight up and yelped. Toad jammed on the brakes.

"That's the Whiz with one of the old ladies." Booger pointed toward the house.

"What the…"

"Whoa, Condit just hit the old woman over the head and shoved her into the car." Booger grinned. "Maybe she's going to take care of the grannies, and you won't have to. That's a good thing, right?"

"Maybe, maybe not. It doesn't feel right." Toad cleared his throat. "If she's going to do both old women, where's the other one?"

"Maybe the other one's already in the car," Booger said. "But if she is, she's lying down. I don't see her."

"There's not enough room in the back seat for two people to lie down." Toad blew a puff of air out puckered lips. "The other one must still be in the house."

"Maybe you should go take care of the one that's still in the house—"

"I could do that, but what if the other one *isn't* in

the house?"

"Ah," Booger said. "So, what're we—"

"We're going to follow Condit."

"But what about our plan?" Booger sniffed.

"Flexibility is the sign of a good businessman. This is where we prove to Uncle BeeBee we can be flexible."

"For real." Booger replaced his pistol in its holster.

Chapter Forty-Six

After stuffing himself with a halfway decent ribeye steak, Razor exited the steak house and headed for the SUV. Although dry enough to suck the moisture from a rock, the mild evening air was unexpectedly pleasant.

If he had more time, he would have asked the cute steak house waitress out. She was suitably impressed when he casually pulled up his shirt sleeve and pretended to study his Rolex. Willowy blonde with dimples, she would be a fun way to pass the evening.

Razor climbed into his vehicle. With a little less than an hour to get to the warehouse, he'd be cutting it close.

If Condit delivered on her promise, though, the grannies would have fallen into the trap she devised by the time he got there. He would snip the two dangling threads and be on a flight back to LA in no time.

Inexplicably, terms from his middle school English class popped into his head.

"Hey, Mizz Winowski," Razor murmured. "Watch me turn two old dangling participles into two past participles." Razor chuckled. What was a dangling participle, anyway? It sounded like a body part.

Never a particularly good or committed student, he remembered only bits and snatches of the useless crap his teachers had tried to force him to learn. Where he grew up, survival skills were more important than book learning. Was there ever any human whose life depended on his ability to diagram a sentence?

Razor buckled up, then pulled his smart phone from its dock. Condit said his money would probably not show up in his account until the next morning. Not known for his patience, though, he couldn't resist checking on his investment account. Since everything was done online, the money could already be there.

One hundred thousand dollars over and above his original investment would be a game changer. After buying a diamond studded horseshoe ring from a Rodeo Drive jeweler in Beverly Hills, he would still have about fifty thousand to add to his principal investment capital.

Of course, he would leave the principal untouched. One of the things he learned from old man LeDuc—it took money to make money, and only dummies dipped into the principal.

Razor punched several numbers into his phone. Bouncing his left leg up and down on the ball of his foot, he glanced at his watch. If he headed toward Belen within five minutes or so, he should get to the warehouse in the ten-minute window Condit allowed.

After the expected five or six rings, a recorded female voice explained the bank's offices were closed then listed the days and times of operation as well as several options.

Razor punched in the numbers associated with his account, waited for the standard prompt, and input his password. Mentally rubbing his hands together in hopeful anticipation, he waited for the mechanized voice to say the magic words that would let him know the transaction had been completed.

"We're sorry, that account has been closed. Please check—"

Stunned, Razor poked his finger against the tiny screen and shut off the voice. Telling himself he must have misremembered the numbers of his account or perhaps inverted them, he repeated them several times under his breath then again punched the screen and waited.

As before, the automated voice informed him the account had been closed.

Razor's whole body flashed heat. He ground his teeth so hard his jaw began to ache. Visions of what he'd do to Kelly Condit billowed in a red haze through his head. He would go to the warehouse as planned, but between him and Condit, only one of them would fly back to Los Angeles.

Razor started to fire up the engine, then paused as another thought flashed through his brain. Not only had Razor entrusted Condit with his investment account information, so had LeDuc. While it had struck Razor at the time as out of keeping with LeDuc's absolute distrust of any other human being, it was possible that the boss wasn't tech savvy enough to realize how much power he had handed Condit. Razor never saw him do anything online other than text and email.

Could Condit have hacked into LeDuc's business associates' accounts as well? What if she not only cleaned out Razor's account, but had done the same with all the others? If LeDuc's associates had invested or laundered as much as BeeBee had, the profits alone could number in the millions of dollars.

"Nah," Razor told himself. Even if Condit *could* access the other investors' accounts, she couldn't be that stupid. There would be nowhere in the world she could hide, not even in an underground bunker. Millions of dollars would be worthless to a dead woman.

Like the aftershocks following an earthquake, another thought sent a shiver through Razor's body. If Condit was jerking around the most powerful men and women in the business, she wouldn't only be ensuring herself a messy and perhaps protracted final few hours but would effectively be ending Razor's existence as well. He was the one who talked LeDuc into investing in the first place.

Razor's insides turned to water, and he had to fight to keep from vomiting. He tried to focus his thinking and come up with a strategy to deal with the horror his life had become, but images of what might lie in his future drove everything else from his mind.

The part of his brain that used to believe in Santa Claus suggested that maybe he was overreacting. Maybe the feared worst-case scenario wouldn't happen. Maybe there was a way around it. He read somewhere that ninety percent of the stuff people feared never actually happened.

Until it does.

If Razor couldn't figure something out, he'd have to eat a bullet. Otherwise, LeDuc would make an example of him, and the boss was partial to chainsaws.

Chapter Forty-Seven

BeeBee LeDuc had just reached for his phone to call his bank when his phone vibrated in his hand. He glanced at the screen then answered.

"Report," LeDuc said.

"You should check your investment account." Razor's voice sounded tight. "Condit's cleaned mine out."

"What?"

"Not only did she *not* replace my investment money, she took every penny and closed out the account."

BeeBee broke the connection, cutting off whatever else Razor was saying. He punched his bank's number into his smartphone then entered his investment account number and password. When a robotic female voice said the account no longer existed, he threw the phone across the room, smashing it against a brick-faced fireplace.

Cursing, he grabbed the bottle of Rolaids off his desk, popped the lid off, and threw a handful into his mouth. Once he swallowed the chalky glob, he reached for a half-empty bottle of Evian water and took a long swig then grabbed another phone and called Razor back.

"Do whatever it takes to make her put my money back." BeeBee growled in the back of his throat. "Hurt her then pop her, but not before she puts my money back. Remember to take pictures."

"It'll be my pleas—"

"Find out if she's screwed with any of the other accounts." LeDuc's breathing came in shallow gasps. "If she has, there'll be nowhere for any of us to hide."

"Yessir," Razor said.

"Call me when it's done."

"Yessir—"

BeeBee jammed his finger on the phone's screen then tossed it onto the small table beside his easy chair. He rang the bell for his bodyguards who hurried into his room and stood awaiting his orders.

"This whole thing's turned into a mess since Taylor got hit." BeeBee burped and placed his hand against his chest. "If my money's not in my account by the time Razor gets back tomorrow, you'll meet him at the airport and take care of him."

The two men nodded simultaneously.

"I'll call you when I need you."

Silently, the men left the room.

BeeBee sat back in his easy chair, his face flaming hot with rage, and his heart beating hard enough for him to hear the blood pounding in his head. Should he wait to find out if Condit had also dinged the other investors, or should he proactively call them and give them a heads-up? He wouldn't tell them about the FBI's involvement…at least not then. Better to let them find that out later. On the other hand, maybe he should wait for Razor to take care of Condit before alerting the other investors. Razor's photos of her death would provide evidence of LeDuc's willingness to do whatever it took to make things right.

Regardless of what else happened, LeDuc would have to cover any financial losses sustained by his associates. Worse than the financial hit, though, was the damage to his reputation. After years of taking chances, decades of paying politicians to vote in ways that would work to his advantage, and building his reputation as the meanest, toughest bastard on the block, he would become a joke. He would become the example of how *not* to do business. He'd lose every shred of respect for which he'd worked so long and hard. No one wanted to do business with a loser, especially a loser who'd been taken in by a woman.

LeDuc stood from his easy chair and headed to his desk. He sat in the top-of-the-line ergonomic office chair, opened the lower right desk drawer, pulled out a zippered nylon bag, and extracted a passport.

The Maldives were calling to him. The more he thought of retiring to the islands in the Indian Ocean, the better he liked the idea. He would arrange to disappear, something not easily done in the age of cameras everywhere and DNA retrieval from just a few cells.

Along with the pile of cash he kept in a vault built into the wall in his bedroom, he had other bank accounts and investments he could cash in. If he escaped before his cohorts could decide what to do to him, money would be no problem. Best of all, the United States had no extradition agreement with the Maldives.

Even without a body to prove his demise, seven years after his disappearance, LeDuc's wife could have him declared legally dead. He would like to see the expression on her face as she anticipated inheriting all his estate, rather than the fifty percent she had coming due to that damned prenup.

A grim smile played on BeeBee's lips. If there was an upside to the current fiasco, it was that there would be little left for his never-have-enough wife to grab. A hundred percent of nothing was still nothing.

BeeBee soothed himself with visions of the Maldives' bright sun, transparent blue lagoon, and white sand beaches stretching away into nothing but miles and miles of turquoise water and blue skies. Not a bad way to live out his days.

"Gordo," LeDuc hollered.

The bodyguard stepped into the room. "Yes, Boss?"

"You both packed?" he said.

"Yes, sir."

"Get to Albuquerque. You'll hit Razor and Condit, if she's still alive by the time you get there, then take care of two meddling old women and a geek kid."

"Yes, sir…"

"I'll call my man there and let him know you're coming; he'll supply you with enough fire power to blow the whole damned place up."

"Where'll we find the geek—" Gordo said.

LeDuc shot a look at the thug that would have cauterized an amputated limb. "I'll call Razor and have him meet you at the airport. He'll lead you to Condit; you figure it out from there."

"Yes, sir."

"Make sure your phones are charged," BeeBee said. "I'll need photographic proof for my associates." He waved a dismissive hand.

As the two men left the room, LeDuc reached for a

Tylenol.

He popped a couple of the extra-strength tablets and was chewing them to mush when his phone rang. He glanced at the caller identification, muttered several choice invectives, then answered.

"What the hell's going on, LeDuc?" said the man who had his cousin ground into mulch for skimming a few hundred dollars off his crack trade. "I've just learned my investment has tanked."

"Hello, Wade," BeeBee said. "It's a glitch, that's all. I'm taking care of it as we speak."

"You better be."

"You know I'm good for any losses."

"Not to be redundant, but you better be."

After the man broke the connection, BeeBee sat staring at the opposite wall. The ache that had started in his left arm had moved up to his jaw, and his chest felt like a giant metal zip tie was being tightened around it.

BeeBee's phone buzzed again. He sighed, glanced at the caller ID, and dragged the green phone icon onto the answer target.

"Hello, Mizz Deeton," he said to the woman who owned a string of brothels, massage parlors, and beauty shops through which illegally imported girls were trafficked. "I know about it and I'm on it." LeDuc held the phone away from his ear to soften the screaming voice on the other end. He tried to take a deep breath, but the tightness in his chest blocked his airway.

Panting and with blurred vision, he reached for the bottle of Scotch in his lower drawer. He poured a couple of inches of the dark liquid into a glass and sipped it while Deeton vented her spleen.

By the time the woman broke the connection,

LeDuc's breathing was shallow and rapid. He sat back in his chair, closed his eyes, and tried to sooth himself with images of what his men would do to Razor and Condit.

Chapter Forty-Eight

Taking care to stay at least a block behind Condit's vehicle, Booger gripped the steering wheel while Toad stared at the GPS monitor anchored to the dashboard. After a few miles, a sign on the highway informed travelers of their approach to a village named Belen.

"Where's she going?" Booger said.

"The GPS says after Belen there's nothing except miles of open desert. After that it's some little burg named Mountainair."

"Looks like the Whiz is hauling the old woman to the desert to pop her for sure."

"Still doesn't feel right," Toad said. "I just wish I knew what she's up to."

"You want to drive?"

"Nope," Toad said. "It's your turn."

"Maybe she's meeting someone."

"Who's she going to meet?" Toad said. "She doesn't know anyone out here, does she?"

"Maybe she's meeting Razor." Booger sniffed.

"It's possible, but why come all the way out here when they could just meet at the motel?" Toad cleared his throat, the frog-ribbet sound loud inside the van. "Why kidnap the old woman in the first place?"

"Maybe she plans to make the old woman tell her something she needs to know then pop her," Booger said. "Or maybe she's going to hold her for ransom to make a few more bucks. I never saw anyone with eyes as hungry as the Whiz's. There's not enough money in the world to satisfy that much hunger."

"You sure we're following the right car?" Toad said. "Are those Condit's taillights?"

"I memorized her tags; that's her."

Instead of turning off the interstate and into the township of Belen as the two men expected, Condit kept driving. After another half mile or so, she pulled onto a gravel-topped road and headed up a drive toward a large warehouse beside which sat a smaller metal garage.

"Won't she see us if we follow her all the way in?" Booger sniffed.

"Duuuh," Toad said sarcastically. "Go another quarter mile or so then shoot a U-turn and park."

Booger did as commanded.

"Got your binoculars?"

"Sure do." Booger stretched across Toad, reached into the glove compartment, and extracted a smaller version of Razor's military-style binoculars. He put them to his face and studied the warehouse.

"Need to move closer?" Toad said.

"Naw, I can see pretty good. The Whiz's car is empty, so either they're both inside the building or Condit left the old woman lying in the back seat."

"Perfect. We'll park in that garage or barn, whatever it is, next to the warehouse and watch what happens."

"What if there's stuff inside the garage and the van won't fit?"

"Then we'll just have to pop Condit and the old lady here and now, then track down the other old lady and the kid on our own."

"Again, with the flexibility." Booger nodded appreciatively.

"Uncle BeeBee said Razor was supposed to clean up before leaving town, but it looks like the Whiz might have figured out what he had in mind. She's no dummy, that broad."

Booger sniffed, the sound reminiscent of a kid playfully popping bubble wrap.

"Blow your nose, doofus." Toad gagged.

"Sorry." Booger pulled his hanky from its resting place, snorted goo into it, then wadded it up. He lifted his binoculars and aimed them toward the warehouse. "Good news. Looks like the garage is empty."

"Then let's get going."

Booger pulled up the gravel road, backed the van into the garage beside the warehouse, then turned off the engine.

"We'll wait for a few minutes and see if anyone else shows up," Toad said.

"How long you think they'll be inside the warehouse?"

"No idea, but I got a funny feeling the Whiz has something up her sleeve, and it smells."

"Yeah, I never did trust her."

"Hand me that bag of fried pork rinds," Toad said.

"Aren't those things bad for you?" Booger reached behind Toad's seat and pulled an unopened bag from the box of snacks they'd purchased earlier. "They're high in fat, you know."

"What they *are* is low in carbs. I'm starting that keto diet I been hearing about. If I'm going to get promoted, I need to look the part."

"For real," Booger said.

Chapter Forty-Nine

Dix sat at the kitchen table across from Val. She kept checking her watch, but the minute hand stubbornly refused to move more than a smidge from one glance to the next.

"Are you sure you're all set?" Val said.

"Everything I need is in here." Dix tapped an index finger against her temple. "In martial arts size and strength aren't critical issues. Neither is age." She smiled at the doubtful look on the young woman's face. "My instructor is over seventy years old."

"I didn't mean to—"

"No apology necessary." Dix held a hand up, palm outward. "While I may lack speed and endurance, my training focuses on ending a fight quickly and absolutely. One of the most gratifying things about studying Tang Soo Do is watching the expressions on the faces of people who come in to observe. Probably the most fun I've had in years was breaking a one-inch thick board with my bare feet then hearing *wow* and *get 'em, granny* from the audience."

Val smiled. "I'm seriously impressed."

"Don't be. I have a long way to go before I'm where I want to be." Dix again looked at her watch. "A little over an hour to go." She stood, stepped to the pantry, and took out a small can of Boston baked beans. At the questioning look on Val's face, she smiled. "This puppy weighs about half a pound. I may not win the fight, but I'll sure as thunder let Kelly know she's been in a scrap."

Val stood from her chair, rushed to Dix, and wrapped her arms around her.

"Now then." Dix patted the young woman's shoulder. "Don't you worry." When Val burst into tears, it was all Dix could do to keep from following suit.

The doorbell rang, and Val gasped. Dix looked pointedly at the young woman, put her index finger to her lips, then went to the door. Lulu placidly padded along behind her.

Dix glanced through the peephole then opened the door to the two young police officers standing on the porch. Both officers held up their credentials and identified themselves, then one officer asked if Dix was the person who had requested help with a stalker.

"Please, come in." Dix stepped toward the living room, and the officers followed. A watchful Lulu trotted along at Dix's side.

The officers asked gentle but probing questions. Dix described the SUV and driver while taking care not to say anything that might endanger Lil. Periodically, the officers shot looks at each other as if to acknowledge their awareness that she wasn't being entirely forthcoming.

Old Trickster Time chose then to speed up, and by the time the officers had been there a half hour, Dix had to fight to keep from hyperventilating. After assuring the two women that they would patrol the block regularly, the officers stood and headed toward the door.

Dix maneuvered her lips into what she hoped was a smile and thanked them for their help. As soon as the officers left, she retrieved the can of baked beans then headed for the garage door. Val and Lulu somberly followed in her wake.

Dix reached for the doorknob then turned toward Val. "Don't let anyone in that you don't know." She paused, then added, "If you don't hear from me by midnight, please call the police and tell them to come to the warehouse; I've left the directions next to the landline."

Wondering if she would ever see Lulu and Val again, Dix patted Lulu's head, smiled at Val, then stepped into the garage.

Chapter Fifty

After Dix left, Val locked the connecting door to the garage then listened until the garage door powered down behind the exiting car. Although she had agreed not to leave the house, the feeling that she should *do* something made her shoulders tight. For several minutes she tormented herself with self-doubt.

If you don't hear from me by midnight...call the police and tell them to come to the warehouse.

Even though Dix had tried to sooth Val, her words meant she was fully aware that she and her sister might be murdered.

Was it cowardice for Val to wrap herself in the safety of what amounted to a fortress while Dix, armed only with her martial arts training, her wits, and a can of baked beans, ran headlong into a trap manufactured by the people who murdered Val's father?

Perhaps she should call the police. The Condit woman had threatened to shoot Lil if the police were called, but maybe that was a bluff. It was, however, equally possible that the woman would carry out her threat, knowing she had nothing to lose.

Val could go to the warehouse and create a diversion. Dix and Lil were bright women. They would recognize and capitalize on any chance to escape that presented itself.

Lacking training in self-protection, Val would need

a weapon. To just show up and walk in would achieve nothing other than to add to the body count. The more important question, though, was could Val live with herself if something she did resulted in Dix and Lil's deaths?

Tortured thoughts swung back and forth between doing something and waiting as Dix had commanded. Time was ticking away; whatever she decided to do, she better get on with it.

Val hurried to the kitchen and strode to the set of knives jutting from slots in a wooden block. After selecting the longest, most deadly looking butcher knife in the set, she stood staring at the blade. The feel of cold stainless steel in her hand suddenly made *real* what had, until then, felt *unreal*.

Could she without hesitation plunge the twelve-inch blade into another human's body even if doing so meant saving Dix and Lil? If she hesitated, or if the killer sensed her reluctance, he could take the knife from her and turn it against the three of them.

The synthesized Winchester chimes doorbell suddenly echoed through the house and their loud peal spiked Val's already racing pulse. Thinking the police officers must have forgotten something, she placed the knife on the counter and headed for the front door.

She'd tell the police everything. They would hurry to the warehouse with sirens blaring and frighten that Condit person into running away.

Dix and Lil would be safe, and Val could live with herself.

Chapter Fifty-One

Dillon sat on his friend's sofa and stared at his now-useless phone. Among the things he left in his apartment when he bolted, the phone's missing power cord had proven to be the most problematic.

Clothes weren't an issue. Although his friend's jeans were a tad large in the waist, they stayed up just fine. The borrowed sweatshirt bagged but was clean.

His friend's ancient phone, however, was of a different make to Dillon's state of the art phone, so its charging cord was no help.

Dillon reached for a third piece of pizza from the box on the coffee table and berated himself for hiding out while Miss Dix was in danger. If not for the doctor lady, his mother would probably be dead from cirrhosis of the liver instead of making a decent living as a teacher's aide.

Dillon's cheeks flamed heat at the memory of how he had acted when he saw the SUV parked outside his apartment. He'd just lost it…all he could think of was getting away.

"Yo, Big D," Dillon's friend said. "You in some kind of trouble?"

"Maybe, but a good friend of mine certainly is."

Dillon's friend shot a look at him then stood and left the room. When he returned, he was holding an old Blackberry phone.

"All charged and ready to go," his friend said. "It won't do much except make calls, but I keep it for emergencies. It's still on my plan, but you're welcome to keep as long as you need to."

"Thanks, man," Dillon said. "Hopefully, I won't need it very long." He accepted the eighteen-year-old phone and punched Dix's number onto the keypad. When the call went to voicemail, he hung up and dialed again.

"You've reached Dix, leave a message."

"It's Dillon. I'm using my friend's phone, so I'm hoping the reason you're not answering is because you don't recognize the number. Please call me back as soon as you can."

When five minutes passed and Dix hadn't returned his call, Dillon stood, collected a couple of the thumb drives from Mr. Taylor's house, and headed for the door.

"I'm going out," he hollered over his shoulder at his friend, who sat playing his favorite video game.

"You coming back?" his friend said without taking his eyes off the screen upon which dragons and gargoyles fought to the death.

"Dunno, but thanks for the three hots and a flop."

"Any time, Big D. Mi casa es tu casa."

"I'll be in touch." Dillon opened the front door and scanned the surroundings. He stepped outside and strode toward the eighteen-wheeler his friend, a long-haul truck driver, kept parked alongside his trailer house between trips. The space behind the tractor-trailer's sixty-odd feet of length had provided the perfect hiding place for Dillon's small vehicle.

During the drive to Miss Dix's house, Dillon

swiveled his head like an oscillating fan. The SUV could be trolling the streets looking for him, and although spread out over a sizeable area, the village of Los Lunas was still small. It would be easy enough for SUV-man to spot him if he were patient and motivated.

When Dillon hadn't seen the SUV after several blocks, he breathed easier. Although Miss Dix seemed to be the guy's primary target, he obviously knew of Dillon's involvement. Based on what Dillon knew about human nature, the guy couldn't allow any of them to live.

Dillon rounded the corner up the street from Miss Dix's house, surprised to see a late model Corolla parked in the drive next to the tan Chevy belonging to Miss Dix's sister Lil. Miss Dix's red convertible wasn't in sight, so either it was in the garage or the doctor lady had gone somewhere.

Who did the Corolla belong to? Had the SUV guy exchanged the too-noticeable sport utility vehicle for a coupe?

That the SUV guy wasn't the only thug in town was a given. The malicious activities that Mr. Taylor had unearthed could involve any number of people, every one of whom would want all perceived threats to be erased. It was always possible the Corolla belonged to a paid assassin or mob *cleaner*.

Dillon's usually facile brain seized up with indecision. Should he call the police? What if it turned out that the Corolla belonged to a visiting friend or family member…would his call be looked upon as wasting police time and resources?

The fable about the little boy who cried wolf popped into his head. A kid was given the task of guarding a flock of sheep and told to cry "wolf" if danger showed up. The boy made several test runs, and each time the armed sheep-owners came running to help. When the wolf finally did show up, the kid cried for help, but the disgusted owners ignored his call—the wolves ate the sheep *and* the kid. The moral—don't call for help until and unless necessary.

Eyeing the Corolla, Dillon pulled into the driveway behind Lil's vehicle.

He punched the number nine into the phone then stepped out of his car. In the event he encountered trouble, it would only take an instant to punch in the rest of the emergency number. With what felt like a two-ton boulder rolling around in his stomach, he scanned the street then hurried onto the porch and rang the bell.

From just beyond the door, a series of rapid-fire, deep-throated barks were interspersed with sounds of someone trying unsuccessfully to shush the animal. The door, however, remained closed.

"Miss Dix?" Dillon aimed his voice toward the crack between the door and its jamb. "Miss Dix, it's Dillon. Are you okay?"

After a short pause, the most amazing young woman Dillon had ever seen opened the door. Tall and slender, her emerald green eyes were red, the lids puffy. The look on her face could only be described as a mixture of fear and relief.

What was probably the largest dog in the world stood beside the young woman, its huge eyes focused on Dillon as if trying to determine if he were friend or foe. A cone the size of a large lamp shade lay on the floor several feet away.

"I'm Val," the young woman said. "Dix told me about you." She stood to one side and motioned him into the house. "Dix and Lil are in trouble, and I've been racking my brain about what to do."

Dillon looked at the dog then at Val. "Is your dog going to let me in?"

"It's okay, Lulu." Val patted the animal's head then looked up. "I'm really glad you're here." She closed the door behind Dillon, engaged the deadbolt, then motioned for him to follow her into the kitchen. "There's a lot you need to know, and we don't have much time."

Ten minutes later, Val stopped talking. She sighed, and her shoulders sagged.

Dillon lifted his phone and began moving his index finger over the screen.

"What are you doing?" Val said.

"Calling the police. They know how to deal with this kind of thing."

"You can't," Val almost shouted. She grabbed the phone from Dillon's hand and shut down the call. "I considered calling for help, but they said they'll kill Dix and Lil if they see any police. They murdered my dad, Dillon. They have nothing to lose."

Dillon took in a long breath and slowly released it. "Based on what you said, Miss Dix has been gone twenty minutes." He looked at the cat-clock on the wall. "It's just now eight."

"She left directions to the warehouse over there." Val motioned to a note on the counter next to the landline.

Dillon stepped over to the counter and scanned the directions. A stickie-note and a scrap of notebook paper on the counter next to the landline drew his attention.

"Where did these come from?" He pointed to the notes.

"Dix found them at Dad's house. Do they mean anything to you?"

"Oh yeah," Dillon said. "They mean this thing is exactly what your dad feared." He retrieved the directions to the warehouse, picked up the knife Val had left on the cabinet, and headed for the front door.

"What're you going to do?" Val said.

"Not sure. I'll figure something out as I drive." Dillon pulled the two thumb drives from his pants pocket and handed them to Val. "You'll want to look at these."

"What are—?"

"Your dad intended them for you." Dillon headed for the door then stopped and turned back to Val. "I think you'll be safe here, but I suggest you don't open the door to anyone else except the police. These people are capable of anything." He looked down at the animal standing next to her. "Looks like you have a good friend."

Val and Lulu followed Dillon to the front door. His breath caught when the young woman pushed a stray tendril of shiny black hair behind a cute little ear.

"I'll be...um...what I mean to say is..." Dillon's face heated up. Fluent in four coding languages, he was suddenly unable to string together a complete sentence in English.

"Just help Dix and Lil," Val was saying. "And please be careful." She closed the door and locked it.

Dillon hurried to his car and fired up his engine. With various strategies cascading through his brain, he headed for the warehouse in which Dix and her sister were either being held captive pending execution or inside already murdered.

While his arrival at the warehouse might do nothing more than help the murderers clean up the loose ends represented by Miss Dix, her sister Lil, and him, Dillon owed the doctor lady a great deal. Had she not helped his mother get sober and find a job, he might have wound up in the street doing who-knew-what to survive.

Dillon eyed the GPS into which he had typed the directions to the warehouse. He should be there within fifteen or twenty minutes.

Like a trip-hammer, his brain pounded out suggestion after suggestion as to his best course of action. Everything hinged on his arriving before Miss Dix and her sister had been hurt. If he got there too late, all was lost.

"God," Dillon whispered. "If this doesn't work, and I don't make it out, please help Mom cope."

He glanced at the butcher knife he'd placed on the passenger seat, floored the gas pedal, and sped through the darkness.

Chapter Fifty-Two

Booger and Toad sat watching the warehouse. No one had come out or gone in since Condit forced the old woman into the building and then left. As time wore on, the two men became restless.

"Do you think the Whiz has already popped the old lady?" Booger absently drummed his fingers on the steering wheel.

"I wouldn't put it past her. That girl must have been raised by wolves. She's just plain mean." Toad licked neon orange powder from his fingers then reached for the half-empty bag of cheese-flavored crisps.

"I thought you were starting on that low carb diet you been talking about." Booger nodded toward the bag.

"I'll start tomorrow. This stakeout stuff is stressful. I'm probably burning a truckload of calories just sitting here."

"For real," Booger said. "I heard about a guy who was flying a small airplane when a sudden storm hit. By the time he managed to land the plane forty-five minutes later, he'd lost nearly fifteen pounds."

"This is not some television fake-mystery where you know what's going to happen," Toad said. "Real life and death stuff is stressful to the max. I figure I've lost at least ten pounds already today." He reached for a can of soda, popped the top, and chugged the whole thing in one breath.

"I'm glad you don't drink that diet stuff." Booger glanced toward the can in his friend's hand. "Sugar's not near as bad for you as that fake sweetener. Did you know that stuff can turn to crystals in your kidneys? Or is it your liver?"

"You know a lot of stuff." Toad popped the top of a second soda and took a deep swig. "I got to keep my strength up. No telling what we're—" He plopped the can into the van's drink holder and pointed to the warehouse. "Look who's back."

"It's the Whiz." Booger sniffed.

"We'll wait until she goes inside then sneak up and listen."

Kelly stepped from her car and scanned the area. Toad and Booger held their collective breaths when her gaze seemed to linger on the garage's dark opening.

"If she sees us, we'll have to—"

"Shut up," Toad whispered.

Kelly turned back toward the warehouse, opened its huge steel door, and went in.

Toad pulled his pistol from inside the van's console then retrieved Booger's weapon from the glove box and handed it to his friend.

"Radio silence," Toad said. "There has to be a rear entrance. If we're in luck, it'll be unlocked. If not, we'll have to sneak in through a window. She might be doing our work for us by making the old woman tell her where the geek is."

Booger nodded his understanding then opened the driver's side door. Instantly, the van's internal light went on, sending a beacon of light through the garage opening and into the night air.

Toad let out a squawk. "Close the damn door," he hissed.

Still seated, Booger pulled the door closed until the light went off but just shy of latching. After a brief search, he found and flipped the light's off-switch then slowly opened the door again. He stepped out and headed around the van toward Toad, who was carefully closing the passenger door.

"What're we—?" Booger said.

"Shh." Toad put a finger to his lips then motioned for Booger to follow him. He bent over and scuttled in a serpentine pattern toward the warehouse's rear.

Pleased to find the back door unlocked, the men made their way into the building. After carefully closing the door behind them, they tip-toed into a small office enclosure beyond which lay the main warehouse.

As if synchronized, they plastered themselves against the office wall beyond which lay the main warehouse area and listened to two female voices raised in argument.

Several minutes later, when a new female voice joined in, Booger looked at Toad and held up three fingers, an unspoken question on his face. Toad raised his hands palms up and shrugged.

After a few minutes of arguing, two shots rang out, cutting off whatever one of the women was saying. Toad and Booger glanced at each other.

With pistols drawn, the two men strode out of the dark office and into the dimly lit warehouse.

Chapter Fifty-Three

Kelly returned to the warehouse at fifteen minutes before eight. The seasonal darkness coupled with an overcast sky shrouded the area in a cloak of invisibility.

She exited her vehicle, then impulsively stopped and looked around the grounds. Other than the black opening of the metal garage facing the warehouse, however, she saw nothing out of the ordinary.

Shaking off the feeling she was being watched, she entered the door and strode toward the old woman seated in the chair where she left her. She studied the duct tape bonds, not surprised to find evidence of Lil's struggle to escape.

"Naughty, naughty." Kelly *tsked*. "Not very courteous to eschew my hospitality."

Lil didn't respond.

"Don't you want to know what's going to happen to you?" Kelly said.

"Knock yourself out," Lil said. "You're dying to tell me."

"My partner Razor is going to be here in a few minutes, as will your bitch of a twin." Kelly yanked the pillowcase off the woman's head so she could enjoy the range of emotions on the wrinkled face. She bent at the waist and brought her head to within inches of the other woman's. "He's been tasked with the duty of cleaning up the mess he's made, and that includes making you and your sister disappear."

Kelly had hoped the old woman would dissolve into pleading tears, but the look on her face remained one of stony disdain.

"You *will* get caught," Lil said. "There's no statute of limitations on murder."

"No, I won't."

"You sound certain, but your face says—"

"Shut up." Kelly's jaw tightened. "Shut up or I'll throttle you with my bare hands." She glanced again at her watch.

Where was Razor? Had she accidentally said something to alert him to her plans concerning him? What if the old woman was right and he figured out she was up to something, then came up with his own strategy? Or, what if LeDuc had ordered her removal? He was perfectly capable of having any number of people killed, and she knew way too much for her own good.

Again, she looked at her watch and tried to calm herself. Razor would be there any minute. Then while he was working his revenge on the old women, she would leave. She'd use her burner phone to call the cops and report gunshots. They would find the empty soda can and lip balm Kelly had planted, and that would take care of Razor. Then she would call the Los Angeles Police Department and tell them about the tiny trophy box hidden behind LeDuc's dictionary. She'd be rid of LeDuc and his cronies, leaving herself in control of all their wealth.

Kelly pulled her phone from the back pocket of her jeans and texted Razor.

—*Where are you?*—

When a minute or so passed without a response, she punched in the man's phone number, but a mechanical voice informed her the patron was not available and admonished her to call later. Kelly was in the process of sending a blistering text when the warehouse door opened and in strode Dix.

"I hoped you wouldn't come," Lil said to her sister.

"I had to," Dix said. She stopped a few feet inside the door and studied first the warehouse interior then Kelly.

"Right on time," Kelly said. She lifted the barrel of her pistol to point at Lil's chest.

As both old women stared at her, she looked from one to the other. If not for the different hairdo's and the eyebrow thing, their body language and flinty facial expressions would have been mirror images.

Kelly shot a quick glance at her watch. If Razor didn't show in the next few minutes, she'd have to deal with the women herself. While thoughts of exacting her own revenge sent pleasant tendrils of anticipation through her, they also meant her plan to frame Razor might have to be tweaked. He might even then be generating a perfect alibi for himself and setting her up to take the fall for the old women.

It didn't matter. The warehouse was overgrown with weeds, proof that no one ever came out there. By the time the old women's bodies were found, Kelly would be sunning herself and sipping a cup of the world's most expensive coffee. Produced from coffee beans which have been digested then excreted by an Indonesian cat-like creature, the elixir would offer the perfect way to toast her new beginning.

"Show time," Kelly murmured.

Chapter Fifty-Four

Razor kicked the tires of the useless, stalled SUV for the hundredth time, then glanced at the Rolex. Eight o'clock and there he sat, still several miles from the warehouse and no other vehicle in sight.

For the third time in as many minutes his phone rang. Condit, checking to see where he was and why he wasn't at the warehouse yet.

Razor punched the red, don't-answer button. There was no way he was going to tell her he ran out of gas. His plans for her didn't involve her laughing in his face and commenting on his incompetence.

He had given Toad the keys to the SUV the night before and ordered him to fill the vehicle. Admittedly, Razor should have checked the gas gauge, especially after the sly look on Toad's face when he later returned the keys.

Razor gritted his teeth. Once he was done with the old women and Condit, he was going to impress on Toad's single-celled brain how badly he messed up by habitually choosing not to follow orders.

Cursing under his breath, Razor pulled his pistol from its hidey-hole. He exited the SUV, stuffed the weapon into the pocket of his windbreaker, then pressed the key fob to lock the doors.

Walking the couple of miles back to the seven-to-eleven gas station he passed just outside of Los Lunas should take him about twenty or thirty minutes. By the time he got gas, returned to the SUV, then took off for the warehouse, Condit might have done the old biddies herself then taken off.

Razor's planned revenge, however, would only be postponed...not canceled. Once at the warehouse, he would kill anyone who was still alive.

Chapter Fifty-Five

Earlier, when Dix arrived at the entrance leading to the warehouse, she had shut off her engine and lights then allowed the car to coast to a stop. She wasn't ready to advertise her arrival just then, and she needed to do a bit of reconnaissance before facing Kelly Condit.

Dix put her kubaton in one jacket pocket and the can of baked beans in the other then gently opened her car door and stepped out. Intensely conscious of her internal clock ticking away the seconds yet compelled to familiarize herself with the terrain, she scouted the area outside of the warehouse. If she could manage to get Lil safely away, knowledge of the area could mean the difference between escape and...

Five minutes before or five minutes after gets your nasty twin shot.

Kelly's words added fuel to Dix's racing pulse. New sweat oozed from glands, plastering her already damp hair to her brow, moistening her clothes, and chilling her in the cool late autumn weather.

As Dix's eyes adjusted to the darkness, she spotted the black, gaping doorway of a two-vehicle metal garage a few feet from the warehouse. She moved toward the building, keeping to the cover of vegetation as much as possible, then plastered her body against the corrugated metal outside wall and eased through the door.

Her breath caught in her throat. Backed against the rear wall sat the white van, almost certainly the same vehicle that had been parked up the street from Dillon's apartment after the SUV had gone.

A short-lived pulse of relief that the van proved to be empty flared then died. Its presence meant Kelly wasn't alone, and that meant Dix would have to rethink her strategy. Her martial arts training had not yet advanced to the level needed to take on more than a single assailant. She would have to watch for an opportunity to pick her adversaries off one at a time.

Dix fought down a surge of nausea. When a final glance at the lighted face of her watch indicated the time to be precisely eight, she hurried to the warehouse entrance. She took a deep breath and opened the door.

Lil sat bound in a chair. Kelly Condit stood beside her, holding a pistol loosely at her side. No one else was in sight.

"Well, color me surprised. Right on time." Kelly turned the pistol toward Dix. "Come on in."

Dix took a couple of steps then stopped and studied her sister, relieved to see no sign of injury. Lil nodded her head once.

"You know the FBI has Henry's data," Dix said. "It's just a matter of time before they come for you."

"You can't hide from the feds," Lil said.

"I already have." Kelly motioned toward Lil with the pistol while looking at Dix. "How bad do you want your sister to live?"

Dix winced. "Badly," she said. "How badly do you—"

"Shut up." Condit, her face crimson with rage, took a step toward Dix. "You have guts, I'll give you that.

After the first couple of warnings, most people wouldn't have continued to press their luck, but not you."

"You killed Henry." Dix moved her right foot forward a few inches.

Lil stared at her twin, the look on her face pleading for Dix not to do anything rash.

"You got that wrong." Condit's eyes widened in an innocent expression. "I didn't kill him."

"You might as well have." Dix slid her right foot another few inches. "I suspect the murderer was following your orders."

"While it's true that Henry would have been dealt with sooner or later, my initial orders were ignored." Condit shot a look at Dix, shook her head, and pointed her pistol at Lil's temple. "Don't move again, or I'll shoot your sister."

"Okay, okay." Dix froze in place and held up her left hand, palm outward. Her right hand gripped the can of beans in her pocket.

"I'm smarter than Henry." A sly smile twisted Kelly's face. "And he was a genius. You have no idea what you've gotten yourselves into."

"I think we get the gist," Lil said. "Henry laid a trap, and you're so smart, you stepped right into it."

For the third time since Dix's arrival, Kelly glanced at her watch.

"Are you waiting for someone?" Dix said. "We holding you up?"

"Shut up."

"Seems you've been stood up." Dix shifted her weight onto the balls of her feet.

"I said shut up." Condit looked back and forth

between the twins. "When was the last time you went sightseeing in a fully loaded Jeep with leather seats?" She smiled, as if she were about to tell a child that Santa Claus was waiting outside.

Two seconds…that was all Dix needed to reset the young woman's thoughts.

"Why's your nose purple?" As Dix said the last word, she threw the can of baked beans at Condit's face and strode toward the woman.

During the instant required for Kelly's brain to process Dix's bizarre question, the young woman was completely vulnerable. She instinctively raised her hands to protect her face from the missile, but by the time she batted the flying can aside, Dix had closed the distance between them.

Reflexively, Kelly pulled the pistol's trigger and fired two shots toward the floor. The bullets ricocheted up from the concrete and smashed into the insulated metal wall, the blast echoing through the building's metal interior.

Kelly regrouped and was in the process of lifting the pistol when Dix brought her kubaton down onto the young woman's wrist. Condit screamed and dropped her pistol then grabbed the numbed wrist with her other hand.

Muscle memory from Dix's martial arts training kicked in. She twisted Kelly's arm around behind her back then delivered a side kick to her knee. Kelly dropped to the floor and Dix picked up the pistol.

"I'm going to—" Kelly began.

"Right." Dix jerked the pistol's barrel upward. "But first you're going to unwrap my sister. Start with her arms."

After a couple of tries, Kelly managed to stand. She stumbled toward Lil and pretended to wrestle with the tape on Lil's arms. Suddenly, she stepped behind the chair, putting Lil between herself and Dix. She barked a laugh and grabbed Lil's neck.

"Put the gun down or I choke her," Condit said.

"Poorly thought out," Dix said as she moved the pistol's barrel to point at Kelly's head. "You'll be trying to explain yourself to Saint Peter long before you've done any long-term damage to my sister. Now finish unwrapping her then step back with your hands raised or I *will* shoot you."

Kelly did as commanded.

"I need a minute," Lil said, "my legs are asleep and my back's on fire." She bent at the waist and massaged her legs vigorously. Using the chair back as leverage, she stood then stamped her feet and did a couple of mini squats. "When was the last time I expressed the appropriate amount of gratitude to you for spending all that money on martial arts classes?"

"Glad to be of service." Dix looked at Kelly. "How did you get mixed up in such a dreadful business? Do you have no remorse at all?"

"Spare me the old-time religion." Kelly rolled her eyes.

Suddenly, a door somewhere was shoved open so violently it ricocheted off the wall behind it. In unison, the three women jerked their heads toward the unexpected sound.

"Drop the pistol, Annie Oakley." The man Dix had dubbed Voice One at Henry's house stepped into the room, a 9mm semi-automatic pistol in his left hand.

Dix bent slightly at the waist and dropped Condit's

pistol onto the chair into which Lil had been tied.

"Well, well, if it isn't Toad and Booger." Kelly smiled. "I never thought I'd be so glad to see you boys."

Toad snorted. "You may not be so glad in a couple minutes."

"For re—"

"Shut up, Booger." Toad turned his attention to Dix and Lil. "You old broads have just shot past your use-by date."

"No old ladies—" Booger started to say.

"No worries," Toad said. "A promise is a promise."

"You're going to pay for that." Kelly rubbed her arm. She stood, strode to Dix, and yanked the kubaton out of her hands. "Nasty little old thing, aren't you?" She grabbed the old woman's arm and brought the weapon down onto her wrist. She smiled when the old woman grimaced, then stuffed the kubaton and keys into her pants pocket. She turned toward the two men. "Kill them and let's get out of here."

"Oh, I'll kill them all right," Toad said. "But *we're* not going anywhere. I don't work for you…I work for Uncle BeeBee. Did you really think he would just sit back and let you walk away?"

"LeDuc and I had a deal."

"You *had* a deal." Toad jerked the pistol's barrel upward. "I believe that's what's called the past tense in educated circles. Get up; we have an appointment at a landfill." He glanced at Booger. "Get the old ladies into the van."

Holding his pistol on Dix and Lil, Booger motioned them toward the door.

Dix headed toward the exit with Lil following

close behind.

"Careful not to get within ten feet of the one with the eyebrows," Toad said. "She's got a bite."

Her brain working furiously through a litany of options, Dix made eye contact with her sister, who nodded her head in response.

"Stop that," Booger said. "They're plotting sunthin'," he yelled over his shoulder.

"So what?" Toad said. "You're the one with the gun. Get a move on."

In single file, Dix and Lil moved toward the door. As soon as Dix stepped through the door and into the darkness, however, she stepped to the right then plastered herself against the side of the building.

Lil continued toward the garage without glancing toward her sister.

Booger stepped through the door pistol first, his eyes focused straight ahead.

Dix grabbed his wrist with one hand and the pistol barrel with the other. By the time the man realized what had happened, the barrel was pointing back at his stomach, and his wrist was bent inward at a painful angle. The subsequent *crack* announced his index finger had been broken by the trigger guard.

Dix kicked the outside of the man's knee, and Booger crumpled to the ground.

"Booger?" Toad yelled. "What's going on?"

"I'm hurt." Booger whimpered. "The old lady busted my finger and maybe my leg."

From inside the building Toad loudly commanded Kelly to stand in front of him. "Hey, old lady," he shouted, "I'm going to shoot the Whiz if you don't step back in here with your hands raised high. That would be a life-altering pity, me being the nonviolent type and all."

Dix's mind roiled. *Keep him talking and gain time to think.* "What's in it for me?" she shouted back.

"What's in it for you?" Toad chuckled. "And here I figured you to be some useless old broad. What's in it for you is that you'll be able to live with yourself. If you don't get back in here, I'm going to deal some serious damage to your conscience; you want to finish out your years knowing you got someone killed?"

If Dix did as commanded, she, Lil, *and* Kelly would be killed…of that, she had no doubt. She and Lil knew too much about LeDuc's business, and Kelly was in the process of being made redundant.

The decision was abruptly taken out of Dix's hands when sounds of scuffling from inside the building were followed by a masculine yelp followed by a gunshot then silence.

"Toad?" Booger's voice sounded like he already knew the answer to his unspoken question.

"Wrong in one." Kelly's laughter poured through the open warehouse door.

Booger's shoulders sagged. In a mournful voice he said, "The Whiz shot Toad."

Dix motioned to Lil, who strode over to her.

"See if the keys are in the van," Dix whispered. "If they are, come back outside and wave twice; if not, wave once."

"Oh, Dix." Kelly's sing song voice sounded like she was calling a neighborhood kid outside to play. "I'm getting antsy in here." The voice sounded nearer, as if Condit had moved to stand just inside the door.

Lil hurried to the garage. Within a couple of beats,

she stepped back outside and waved one time.

"I don't know what you're hoping to gain by stalling. This place is in the middle of nowhere, you and your sister are alone, I have your car keys, and you're too old to run far." Chuckle. "Quite a fix, no?"

Dix remained silent.

"Okay, let's negotiate." Kelly's voice lowered to a conversational tone. "You and your sister come back in, and I won't kill you. I'll tie you up, then you'll have to fend for yourselves, but at least you'll be alive."

A groan from inside the building was followed by a loud thump which was followed by silence.

"Booger, you still with us, or did Dix take you out?" Kelly shouted.

Dix turned toward Booger. She held her index finger to her lips then pointed the pistol into the air and squeezed off two shots.

Booger's eyes grew round, but he remained silent.

"So, Booger's out of the game." Kelly chuckled. "What do you say, ladies?"

Cradling his hurt hand, Booger looked up at Dix. "Don't trust her," he whispered. "She can't afford to let us go." With his free hand, he pulled keys from his pocket and held them out to Dix. "I'm good as dead anyway."

"How do I know you'll let us go?" Dix shouted toward the open doorway at the same time Lil moved to her side. She handed the keys to Lil and pointed to Booger. "Frisk him," she whispered. "If he's clean, haul him to the van. Give me two seconds, then come get me."

"I can hear you whispering, you know," Kelly said. "But that's okay; go ahead and talk it over with your sister. You have exactly one minute before I come out blasting. I can run faster and longer than either of you."

Lil stooped and moved her hands over Booger's body. She looked at Dix and shook her head then helped the fallen man to his feet.

Booger grimaced as he put weight on the hurt leg. Staggering, he headed toward the van with Lil a couple of steps behind.

"I said," Dix shouted toward the open door, "how can I be sure you'll let us go?"

"I guess you'll have to take my word for it. Your options are pretty limited at this point."

"You're forgetting I have Booger's pistol."

"Yes, but how many shots are left?" Kelly snorted. "The guy's famous for forgetting to reload."

Just then, Lil powered up the van.

The vehicle shot through the garage door and over to Dix, who jumped through the open passenger door. She landed with an unceremonious thud, her upper torso on the seat, one knee on the floorboard, and the other leg hanging out the door, her toes dragging the ground.

Lil grabbed her sister's extended hand and tried to haul her inside the vehicle. After several nail-biting seconds, Dix managed to pull herself all the way into the van then slam the door behind her.

Shots rang out, and the van's rear window shattered.

"We're going to die," Booger wailed.

"Shut up, Booger," Dix and Lil said simultaneously.

Lil floored the pedal. Stones dinged and popped against the undercarriage as the vehicle careened around the corner and onto the highway.

Breathing hard from the exertion of jumping into the running van, Dix turned and shot a frantic look through the shattered rear window.

A figure, silhouetted by light from the warehouse door, ran toward the Jeep. The roar of an engine was followed by the vehicle's headlights panning across the vast, empty desert as Kelly performed a U-turn on the gravel drive. She sped toward the highway seconds behind Dix, Lil, and Booger.

"Where to?" Lil said.

"Anywhere there are lights and lots of people." Dix turned and looked at Booger. "Where's your phone?"

"Should be in the cupholder."

"It's not there," Dix said.

"It must be on the floor," Booger said. "You got to get me to a doctor; my finger's hurting something awful."

After a few seconds of running her hand over the van floor, Dix's fingers encountered the phone. She lifted it victoriously and started to tap its screen, but Lil suddenly swerved the van, throwing Dix off balance and smacking her head into the window at her side.

"Another car," Lil said through clenched teeth.

"That's Dillon." Dix rolled her window down. She stuck her arm out, waved furiously and shouted at the young man who shot past them toward the warehouse. "Turn around, Lil. Kelly will kill him."

Lil jammed on the brakes and turned the vehicle in a tight U-turn.

Another shot rang out, and Dillon's vehicle swerved, ploughing up a row of dead weeds alongside the road. Dix fully expected Dillon to crash into the deep culvert beside the road, but the young man righted his vehicle at the last instant and headed straight for Kelly's Jeep. In less time than it took for Dix to realize what the young man had in mind, he had T-boned Condit's vehicle.

The force of the impact sent Dillon's car shooting backward while Condit's car went into a spin before coming to shuddering stop. Dust and tiny pebbles rained onto the vehicles for a couple of seconds then everything went silent.

"Dillon!" Dix tossed Booger's phone into Lil's lap. "Call an ambulance." She jumped from the van and ran to Dillon's car.

Dillon sat slumped over the steering wheel, his face resting against the deployed airbag. Blood ran from his nose and onto the bag.

Dix pressed her fingers to his neck, relieved to feel a strong pulse. Once convinced Dillon wasn't seriously injured, she strode to Kelly Condit's vehicle.

The force of the impact had crushed the driver's side of Condit's car and thrown her un-seat-belted-body across the front seat and into the passenger side. She sagged against the passenger's door, her bloodied head propped against the window, and her eyes rolled back in her head.

Dix limped back to Dillon's vehicle. She reached inside and touched the young man's shoulder. "I'm so sorry I dragged you into this mess, Dillon. So very sorry."

Lil pulled the keys from the van's ignition, stepped out of the vehicle, and walked to her sister. "An ambulance and the police are on the way," Lil said. "You need to sit down. You're shaking."

Chapter Fifty-Six

After leaving Miss Dix's house, Dillon had followed his GPS's audio directions to the warehouse. Within fifteen minutes, the black silhouette of the warehouse loomed in the darkness at the same time the GPS's female voice ordered him to make a right turn.

No sooner had Dillon made the prescribed turn, however, than a light-colored van shot away from the warehouse and down the dirt road directly in his path. Dix's surprised face peered at him from inside the vehicle as the van's driver swerved hard to avoid a collision.

Someone ran from the warehouse, stopped, raised an arm, and pointed something at the retreating van. Dillon's outside mirror exploded into pieces at the same instant he heard the *pop* of gunfire.

Adrenaline kicked in, and he reflexively jerked his wheel to the right, very nearly running off the dirt road. As he righted his car, a Jeep parked in front of the warehouse roared to life. The driver apparently floored the gas pedal, since it spun out then made a beeline for the van.

The van skidded to a stop. Miss Dix waved her arm and shouted something through her open window, but Dillon clamped his jaws, lowered his head, and aimed the nose of his car straight for the oncoming headlights.

At the last instant, the Jeep swerved to avoid

Dillon's vehicle, but Dillon's aim was true. The driver, her mouth open in a silent scream, stomped on her brakes. The Jeep's wheels locked, sending the vehicle into a spin that brought the driver's side directly into Dillon's path.

Without a second thought, the young man gritted his teeth and gunned his engine.

Dillon's vehicle shot forward.

Metal screamed and crunched against metal. The explosive impact threw Dillon's body against his seatbelt. The airbag in his steering wheel deployed, hitting him in the face. Wetness poured from his nose, smearing itself on the airbag. It flowed down his cheeks and the back of his throat, making him cough.

Miss Dix's anxious face peered at him through his broken window. She said something, but her words were muffled by a loud humming in Dillon's head.

Then everything went dark.

Chapter Fifty-Seven

BeeBee LeDuc was nestled deep in his easy chair when his phone rang. He looked at the clock on the fireplace mantel—ten o'clock. Though he thought he had managed to pacify all his business associates, a call that late could only be more bad news.

After a glance at the phone's screen, he answered. "What's up, nephew?"

"It's trouble, Uncle BeeBee."

BeeBee sat up straight as his Scotch-generated lethargy suddenly evaporated. "What's going on?"

Toad recounted what had taken place from the time he and Booger entered the warehouse until the geek kid rammed Condit's car.

Shockwaves of what LeDuc assumed to be heartburn sent pain radiating through his chest. He reached for a bottle of Rolaids and popped a couple into his mouth. When the pain didn't lessen, he grabbed another antacid and returned his attention to his phone conversation.

"Where are you?" LeDuc said.

"I'm in Razor's rental car," Toad said. "He spotted me on the road and picked me up."

"What's your location?"

"We're on our way back to town. I would have called earlier, but I was out cold for a while, and there's no signal at the warehouse. Condit got hold of my pistol and knocked me out with it."

"Of course, she did," LeDuc murmured.

"What?"

"Nothing, continue."

"When I came to, I heard sirens, so I hauled ass out the back way."

"So, Condit's in the hospital." LeDuc *tsk*-ed. "What about the old women?"

"I don't think they were hurt," Toad said. "When I was a good way off, I turned and saw them milling around."

"We have to assume they told the cops about Condit and Razor." LeDuc sighed. "As long as Condit's in the hospital, you won't be able to get to her, at least not for a while. There'll be one, maybe two cops sitting outside the room until she recovers enough to be taken to jail."

"What about Boog—"

"If everything went down as you've said, Booger's *already* sitting in jail." LeDuc coughed. "You still good for the cleanup?"

"Yes, sir."

"Good. You and Razor figure a way to pop the old women and the kid, then you do Razor. Understood?"

It would be a shame to lose Razor, but business was business.

"Yes, sir."

"You have a decent camera on your phone?" LeDuc said.

"Top of the line."

"Good. Get lots of closeups so there won't be any questions about the outcome." LeDuc sighed. "I'll need proof for the Collaboration."

"Yes, sir," Toad said.

"If I'm not here when you get back, talk to Gordo. He'll know what to do next." LeDuc grabbed his abdomen. "Damned acid reflux."

"What?"

"Nothing. Let me know when it's done." BeeBee jabbed an index finger onto his phone's tiny screen then threw the thing across the room.

The thought that he needed to buy more pay-as-you-go phones slanted through the gray haze that had begun to press in on him.

It occurred to LeDuc that by leaving the bombed-out business to his nephew, he was putting the kid at risk. However, if Toad survived the first six weeks after BeeBee skipped the country, he would prove himself worthy of rebuilding the business. BeeBee's conscience would be clear, since the kid would have a chance to make good. On the other hand, if the Collaborative decided to make his nephew a scapegoat, it would be no great loss to the world.

BeeBee envisioned the photos his nephew would offer the Collaborative as proof of good faith. He would have loved to see the pictures, especially the ones in which Condit starred.

LeDuc had heard of *cryptocurrency* even before he met Condit. The word was impossible to ignore; news blogs and financial magazines carried articles and opinions about the future of the growing number of cryptocurrencies popping up all over the world. There were even websites offering instructions on how to create your own cryptocurrency.

Of course, laundering money was the dicey bit, but it was well within his risk parameters. What with the feds's enhanced scrutiny of banks and other financial institutions, the process of finding ways to disguise the proceeds from selling stolen goods, then working that money into the legitimate financial system was getting tougher by the day.

From the get-go, Condit's attitude had set up an unpleasant tickle at the base of his skull. The promise of clean money with a nice bit of profit to match had sung its siren song, however, and he not only allowed Razor to talk him into investing heavily, he also pulled several likeminded *businessmen and women* in as well. So after his initial due diligence, and when things had hummed along as Condit said they would, he let down his guard.

BeeBee swallowed two more Rolaids. That many antacids would turn to marbles in his bowel, making a double dose of laxative necessary, but it was a small price to pay for the smidgen of pain relief.

He pushed a buzzer on the table beside his chair, summoning his bodyguards. Both men rushed into his room.

"Yes, Boss?" Gordo said.

"Good, you haven't left yet. Change of plans. My nephew will see to the cleanup, but you should stand by in case he meets with undue resistance."

"Yes, sir."

"I may have to leave town for a while," LeDuc said. "If I'm not back within, say, three weeks, my nephew will take over the business."

"Yes, sir."

"I'm depending on you to be his Segundo." LeDuc looked at Gordo. "He'll need all the help he can get."

"Yes, Boss." Gordo nodded. "What about Razor?"

"If he survives my nephew's efforts, it'll be up to you to take him out."

"Condit?" Gordo said.

"She's in the hospital so is untouchable for now," LeDuc said. "However, I have a premonition that she'll meet with an in-jail accident once she's out of the hospital and taken into custody." He cocked his head and grew thoughtful. "Maybe she'll end up as collateral damage in an attempted jail break or even an inmate riot."

"You want I should start the process?"

"Yeah. Condit will spend a short time in the local lockup during an investigation and before a trial date's been set; that'll be the best time to get to her. Either then or if she gets out on bail." BeeBee looked at his watch. "It's too late tonight to call our Albuquerque contacts, but you'll reach out first thing in the morning; they'll help with whatever you need." LeDuc rooted around in his top desk drawer, extracted a three-by-five index card, and handed it to his bodyguard. "Call the second name on this list. He owes me big time."

Gordo nodded then the two bodyguards left the room.

BeeBee smiled to himself as he reached for his bottle of Rolaids. The process of taking care of business always gave him a sense of accomplishment, and cleaning house of a few pesky troublemakers was especially satisfying.

Chapter Fifty-Eight

After getting off the call with his uncle, Toad sat staring out through the SUV's windshield. Razor drummed his fingers on the steering wheel keeping time to some weird music pumping from the radio.

"You going to tell me what that call was about?" Razor finally said.

"Uncle BeeBee says we need to find a way to take care of the old women and the kid." Toad cleared his throat. "Then we're supposed to head back to Los Angeles."

"What about Condit?"

"She's in the hospital," Toad said. "Uncle BeeBee will take care of her later."

"Did he offer any other details?"

"What about?" Toad cleared his throat.

"The grannies and the kid."

"Just that we're to make it messy and take pictures."

Razor nodded.

"Once we have all the photos we need, we're supposed to make their bodies disappear." Never good at hiding his intentions, Toad couldn't keep a hint of threat out of his voice.

"The cops will be looking for the SUV." Razor glanced at Toad. "We'll have to ditch it."

"Yeah, you're right." Toad's eyebrows lifted at a

sudden flash of inspiration. "We could use the Merc."

"Not a good idea." Razor paused then added, "Where did you stash it?"

"In long term parking at the Airport," Toad said.

"You're kidding, right?"

"Why—"

"Every vehicle that goes through the parking lot gate gets videoed," Razor said. "A record of the Merc's tags will be waiting for the cops to find. In no time, they'll figure out it was used in Taylor's hit."

"I didn't know they took pict—"

"Yeah, well, they do." With raised eyebrows, Razor glanced at Toad. "There'll be a clear photo of the driver as well. Don't suppose you wiped the Merc's interior down before you dumped it?"

Toad gulped loudly then cleared his throat.

"You don't know much about forensics, do you? There'll be blood, hair, who-knows-what other stuff from Taylor's body plastered to the Merc's bumper and maybe windshield."

Razor's know-it-all smile worked on Toad's nerves. Too bad he had to wait to pop the smart-ass until after they dealt with the others. He couldn't afford to go off half-cocked like he'd done by running Taylor down; otherwise it would be his pleasure to wipe that smile off the man's face

The words his uncle had bellowed during the minutes-long chewing-out after he ran over Taylor still stung—*You better grow a heavy dose of impulse control, numb nuts, otherwise I'll sure as hell leave this business to Razor.*

What had bugged Toad more than his uncle's words, though, were the smirks on the faces of the others in the room. They nodded at each other and grinned as if Toad weren't standing right there watching them. Gordo-the-goon had even elbowed his buddy in the ribs and made a face.

First thing Toad would do when he was boss was to fire everyone and hire his own people. He and Booger would show the rest of the Collaborative how business was supposed to be run. The other business owners would soon speak to him with respect. They would seek his advice and ask him to give them counsel on investments. He would become a legend, ten times better than his hateful, greedy, antique of an uncle.

"Sounds to me like you and your buddy have handed the cops enough evidence to get you convicted for Taylor's murder," Razor was saying.

"So, now you're the one with all the answers," Toad said through clenched teeth.

"Apparently," Razor said.

"What do you suggest?" Toad asked.

"We'll have to find another mode of transportation. We'll dump the SUV then rent something else." Razor patted his pants pocket. "I keep a fake ID and prepaid Visa for just such emergencies. It'll cost me plenty, but it's worth every cent. Once the job's done, I'll...we'll drive the rental back to Los Angeles and dump it."

"Why can't we fly?"

"Because every cop in the country will be looking for us," Razor said. "By now, the grannies will have given the locals our descriptions. There's probably an ATL out for the SUV."

"An AT...what?" Toad said.

"An Attempt to Locate." Razor pulled the SUV into the rear parking lot of an all-night convenience store located a few blocks from a car rental agency. "The rental place opens at eight. I suggest you get some rest while you can. Tomorrow's going to be a long one."

"Why don't we go take care of the old women right now? I want to get this done."

"The grannies are most likely still at the cop shop giving their statements. Once they're done, the cops will take them home. Our best bet would be to hit them early in the morning when they least expect it."

Toad nodded his head in grudging recognition of the other man's assessment of their situation.

"By the way," Razor said, "you still have the parking stub for the Merc?"

"Yeah, I kept it just in case we decided to use it again." Toad scooted forward in his seat and pulled his wallet from his back pocket. He extracted the stub and held it up.

"You're going to want to dump that," Razor said. "You don't want the cops to find it on you in the event we get caught. Just another thing to tie you to the Merc."

"If we get caught? Seems you aren't too sure your plan will work." Toad tried to resist sneering into the know-it-all face staring back at him but failed.

"Is that how it seems to you?" Razor casually rolled up his sleeve. He made a big deal of checking the Rolex then shot a self-congratulatory smile at Toad. "Anyone with a brain the size of a pea would know to clean up after himself, and it's always a good idea to have a backup plan."

"Problem solved." Toad tore the stub into tiny pieces, rolled his window down, and threw the confetti-sized bits onto the asphalt.

"One down and half a dozen to go." Razor shook his head and shot a dismissive look at Toad. "I'm going to take a leak. You want something to drink?"

"No thanks." Toad threw a look of pure hatred at the other man.

Razor grinned, stepped out of the SUV, and headed for the store.

Chapter Fifty-Nine

By the time LeDuc had gotten off the phone with his nephew earlier that evening, rage had all but blown the top off his head. A weight pushed against his ribcage, as if a five-hundred-pound gorilla had mistaken him for a settee.

Maybe he should have seen a doctor when his symptoms first showed themselves. At least a doc could have given him something for the heartburn that had worsened since he met the Condit woman. Just hearing her name sent shooting pains through his chest.

BeeBee stroked his chin and stared at the wall opposite his chair. It seemed likely the geek kid had already given the FBI everything they needed to make a case against him and his acquaintances. Popping the old women and the geek kid wouldn't make any of that go away, but LeDuc would not allow them to skate. Snuffing Condit and Razor would send a message that it was a mistake to jerk him around, especially when it was done in such a way that would curdle the blood of anyone who heard about it.

Of course, the next few months would be a nightmare for anyone left standing. The FBI would search LeDuc's homes and boat, and they would get warrants for his attorney's files. They'd find enough to put LeDuc in prison for a very long time...that is, if they could put their hands on him. Then they would trace the threads back to his business associates.

The old saying that hell hath no fury like a woman scorned was way off the mark. Worse than a jilted lover, hell's fury couldn't match that of anyone in the business who not only lost a pile of money but had been made to look like a chump.

BeeBee grabbed his phone and punched in the number of a bank at which he had an account under an alias and into which he consistently deposited large sums. The Maldives would be beautiful this time of year… If he hurried, he might just have time to blow town before either the cops or his associates found out he was gone.

As the automated voice cued him to enter his password and personal identification code, he consoled himself with thoughts of beginning a new life. It would be a new chapter—like turning a page. With BeeBee's know-how, he could have a lucrative startup going from his new home in no time. Life would be good again…even better than it was before Condit showed up.

Humming a Liza Minnelli show tune, LeDuc tapped his fingernails on the table beside his chair while waiting for the automated teller to identify his account balance. When the disinterested voice returned, however, it was to inform him that his account had been closed out.

"What?" BeeBee shouted into the phone. He shut off the call and redialed. There had to be a mistake. The prerecorded voice, however, repeated itself; there was nothing left in the account.

Zero dollars. Zip. Nada.

Stunned, LeDuc punched the codes of another

account into the phone. He cursed as the automated voice told him that account had been cleaned out as well.

BeeBee pulled the wooden handle at the side of his recliner to bring it upright, and something in his chest popped. He grimaced.

He was soft. Once he started his new life on the islands, he'd join a gym.

He finally managed to lift himself out of his recliner, but his legs had turned to gelatin and he stumbled. He fell backward against the table, knocking it over and shattering a small glass bowl of hard candy. Individually wrapped squares of fruit-flavored spun sugar ticked and skittered across the floor

Crawling on hands and knees, LeDuc pulled himself to the heavy, ornate wooden bookcase against the wall. Perspiration poured down his face, stinging his eyes and blurring his vision. He grasped the bottom shelf, hoping to use it as leverage to pull himself upright. Once he managed to haul himself onto his knees, he grabbed the second shelf.

Congratulating himself on making it to the bookcase, he struggled to pull himself completely upright. His weight, however, proved too much for the freestanding bookcase. The heavy piece of furniture wobbled then fell forward.

The ten-pound copy of Webster's Dictionary dropped from the case onto the floor just beyond LeDuc's legs. In the instant before the bookcase toppled onto his chest, a small box he never saw before fell to the floor beside the dictionary.

BeeBee tried to call his two men but could only whimper. Air whooshed out of his lungs as weight from the settling bookcase and its contents made it impossible to breathe.

Feebly, LeDuc banged the back of his head against the floor hoping to attract his men's attention. No one came.

Flashes of his life shot through his mind as his brain synapses fired their final salvos. In less than a second, every purely selfish decision he'd ever made threw itself into relief on the white screen of his consciousness.

All he ever did was to take care of business… Surely, he couldn't have been expected to let people walk all over him…he'd even donated to the occasional charity.

The gray mist that had begun to cloud LeDuc's vision parted, and his dead uncle beckoned from inside a deep pit. Against his will, BeeBee was pulled inexorably toward the darkness.

LeDuc sensed his bodyguards enter the room just as his essence was leaving his body. By then, however, the five-hundred-pound gorilla combined with the weight of the bookcase had stomped his heart into mush.

Chapter Sixty

LeDuc's bodyguards had been preparing for bed when they heard what sounded like a chair being thrown across their boss's room, followed by glass shattering. They glanced at each other, the looks on their faces telegraphing their concerns over whether it would be safer to enter the boss's presence during one of his temper tantrums or wait for the storm to subside.

"Do you want to go or should I?" Gordo said to the other thug.

"You go. Last time I interrupted him he docked my pay."

The two men glanced toward the door then at each other as a loud crash was followed by a strange thumping sound.

"Whatever's going on, it must be bad," Gordo said. "I've never heard him this worked up before, and I've worked for him since I was a kid."

When several minutes passed without further sound from LeDuc's room, Gordo stood and headed for the connecting door. "Maybe he's gone to bed."

"Don't say I didn't warn you." The second man shook his head, a look of pity on his face.

Gordo had been gone only a few seconds when he strode back into the room, a look of surprise on his face. "The boss is dead," he said.

"What? Are you sure he's not just passed out or

something?"

"Oh, he's dead all right. I know a stiff when I see one." Gordo motioned to the other man. "Come on, you got to see this."

The two men hurried into LeDuc's room.

"Whoa," the second thug said. "Kind of ironic that antique bookcase he was so proud of is what killed him." He stepped over the thickest book he'd ever seen, stooped, and picked up the small wooden box beside it. "What's this?"

"Dunno," Gordo said. "Jewelry?" He pulled the box from the other man's hand and pried open the tight-fitting lid. "What the…"

"Is that cocaine?" the second man said. "And here I thought the boss hated the—"

"Nah, it's too coarse to be cocaine." Gordo tilted the box on one side and poured its contents into his hand. "Crap a maggot," he said at the same instant a chunk of what appeared to be beef jerky fell into his hand. "Whatever that thing is, it's seriously messed up." He dropped the chunk back into the box and handed it to the other thug. "Flush the white stuff and jerky then wash the box out with soap and water. Put it in your bag; we'll dump it once we're out of here. The cops will be all over this place, and I don't want to be connected to whatever the hell that was."

"Will that box-of-rocks nephew be the new boss?" the second thug said when he returned from dealing with the box.

"That was the boss's plan," Gordo said. "But he's dead, so…"

"What're we going to do?"

"You know the old man's hiding places?" Gordo

said.

"Most of them, I think. You?"

"Some," Gordo said. "Tell you what, you find whatever you can, and I'll do the same. We'll put it all on our sofa and divvy it up fifty-fifty. Deal?"

"Deal."

Within a half hour, both men were standing beside the sofa in their room and stared down at the hoard of cash and jewelry piled there.

"Dang, Gordo, we're rich."

"In lieu of severance pay." Gordo chuckled. "Good thing U-Haul doesn't have offices in Hell, or that tightwad would have taken everything with him."

After the men divided the spoils to their mutual satisfaction and stashed their portions in their duffels, Gordo reached for his phone.

"You going to call an ambulance?"

"At some point," Gordo said. "No need to rush, the old man's croaked. There's no bringing him back from what happened in there."

"Then who're you—"

A sly look crept across Gordo's face. "I figure Razor would like to know the news." He smiled. "I'd rather work for him than that sorry-ass nephew."

"Yeah, me too. I always liked Razor." Pause. "You might be starting a war, you know. Won't the nephew put up a fight?"

"He might want to," Gordo said. "He might even *try* to. But I don't know anyone other than that snorting freak friend of his who'll back him up."

The other man nodded.

"Once I'm off the phone with Razor, I'll call an ambulance," Gordo said. "The cops will show up pretty quick, so we need to get our stories straight."

"Agreed."

"Here's the way it'll go down—we were in bed when we heard what we thought was Mr. LeDuc losing his temper, throwing stuff around, things like that. We didn't think much of it because it was something he often did."

The second man nodded.

"His standing orders were for us to go into his rooms only when called, so we stayed in our own room. It wasn't until we thought we heard him call out to us that we went in and found him." Gordo looked at his watch. "We went into his room a little after midnight, not before."

The second man nodded.

"The police will show up along with the coroner," Gordo said. "The ambulance people will hook him up to a machine to make sure he's really dead then they'll haul him to the morgue for an autopsy."

"How do you know all that?"

"My cousin's a paramedic," Gordo said. "You remember when I got shot last year? My cousin patched me up…no hospital and no gunshot wound reported to the cops."

"What about all this stuff?" The second man pointed at the booty-filled duffels on the sofa.

"I figure we'll have time to haul our bags to the car, put them in the trunk, then hustle back before the cops get here." Gordo smiled. "The cops will ask a lot of questions, take our statements and all, but once they find the boss's death was an accident, we'll be free to go."

"Beautiful."

Gordo returned his attention to his phone and shushed the other man.

"Hey, Razor," Gordo said into his phone. "I know it's late, but you're going to want to hear this."

Chapter Sixty-One

By the time the call from Gordo ended, Razor had to fight to keep from pumping his fist up and down and whooping out loud. It seemed ironic that old man LeDuc had croaked from natural causes. Razor had always figured the man's nemesis Diamond would eventually find a way to get to him, but he never thought the bastard would just up and pop his clogs.

Pasting a bland expression on his face for Toad's benefit, Razor glanced at LeDuc's nephew. The good news was the boss's passing left a vacuum at the top of the food chain that made up LeDuc Enterprises, LLC. The less-than-good news was that as rumors of LeDuc's death spread, every gangster wannabe in the country would be pouring into Los Angeles hoping to pick up the pieces.

Razor shot a sideways glance at Toad and squelched his impulse to laugh out loud. That old saying about the apple never falling far from the tree was sure off the mark when it came to LeDuc's nephew. LeDuc was smart...but whatever Toad had banging around inside his skull, it sure wasn't a brain.

The fact that the jerk had not yet heard of his uncle's demise could be useful. One thing for sure, Razor had no intention of joining ranks with the boss's incompetent nephew.

With Gordo's backing, Razor would take over the

business and run it his way. Over the years he'd worked for LeDuc, he'd met a ton of powerful people—people LeDuc basically owned.

Unbeknownst to the boss, Razor had kept a record of every *favor* those people had done for LeDuc. He carefully jotted down names, dates, and dollar amounts the boss had paid in return for services rendered. All Razor had to do was inform the rich and powerful that he not only knew their grubby secrets but wouldn't hesitate to send an anonymous note to the feds, complete with documentation. Before LeDuc was in the ground, Razor would be sitting on the boss's proverbial throne and running the show.

Pretending to listen to the local weather report on the radio, Razor considered ways to do away with Toad and the grannies.

Once he arrived at a decision, he smiled inwardly, leaned the seat back, and pretended to go to sleep.

Chapter Sixty-Two

Toad had jumped when Razor's phone unexpectedly rang, its gangster movie soundtrack ringtone echoing inside the SUV.

After glancing at the screen, Razor tapped the phone and lifted it to his ear. "What's up?" His face set in a bland expression, he sat still as stone for several beats. He said, "Thanks, I'll do that." He shut down the call and stared out the windshield.

"Who was that?" Toad said.

"Just Gordo passing along a message from your uncle. He said to be sure to take plenty of photos." Razor looked at Toad, an innocent expression on his face.

The suddenly charged atmosphere inside the SUV along with a subtle shift in Razor's tone of voice made Toad's fight or flight instinct kick in. It didn't make sense for Gordo to call after midnight just to repeat an order Uncle BeeBee had already given.

"I'm going to snooze." Razor pulled his phone from its dock and began punching the screen. "I'll set the alarm for seven-thirty. That'll give us time to get coffee and take a whiz before the rental office opens." He pulled a lever at the side of his seat and reclined. "You going to sleep sitting up?"

Toad reclined his seat but only slightly. If he had to make a speedy exit, he didn't want to have to spend even an extra nano second trying to sit upright. Something about Gordo's call...if it really *was* Gordo...had set Toad's adrenaline pumping, and he had a feeling he wouldn't be getting much sleep.

"The grannies only live four or five miles from the Los Lunas landfill," Razor was saying. "Convenient, don't you think?"

Toad looked at Razor in time to see a crooked smile crease the man's face. A years-old memory of words from a fairytale popped into his head—*Oh, Grandma, what big teeth you have.*

Chapter Sixty-Three

When Kelly regained consciousness, she was lying on a soft surface. Every muscle in her body ached. Her head hurt, and her mouth was dry.

She tried to open her eyes, but they were so swollen she could only lift the lids into slits. Moving her head from side to side, she studied the room in which she found herself.

For an instant, she wondered what she was doing in a hospital, then she remembered the car crash. Like a slide show, images pulsed through her head of the final seconds before some kid plowed his car into her.

Kelly tried to move her arms but froze at the resulting pain. She tried to take a deep breath, but pain in her ribs testified that at least one might be broken.

Tubes pumped fluids into her arms and monitors beeped in cadence with her heartbeat. At least she hadn't been intubated, so she wouldn't have to hang around long enough for hospital staff to pull a tube from her lungs. Darkness outside the window beside her bed meant it was either late night or very early morning.

How long had she been there? The more important question was whether she'd been there long enough for Razor and LeDuc to learn what she did with their money. Once they found out, they would move mountains to get at her.

Kelly tilted her head back and lifted her chin to read the hands on the large clock affixed to the opposite wall. Between her swollen lids and cloudy vision, though, she couldn't make out the time.

That she was still alive was reassuring. Either LeDuc and his pals hadn't yet discovered what she'd done, or they hadn't come up with a plan to get to her. She still had time to get away.

With Razor's, LeDuc's, and the Collaborative's money safely tucked away, she could pursue her agenda...could still make her dreams come true. She would beg the nurse for pain killers, hoard them, then hobble out of the hospital and melt into the mist.

Kelly reached for the nurse call button attached to her bed.

Chapter Sixty-Four

Dix, Lil, and Val sat around the breakfast table, the expressions on their faces contemplative. Conversation was sporadic and subdued, as if the dark, early morning clouds had wandered into the kitchen and hovered along the ceiling above the three women.

Lulu lay on the floor beside the table, for once, her cone in perfect order. Seemingly sensing the mood, she remained silent and unmoving.

"I think I'll take her for a walk," Val said after an extended period of silence. "We both need the exercise."

At the mention of her name, Lulu lifted her head. Her ears perked up, and she whapped her tail on the floor.

Val took a final sip of coffee, shoved her chair back, and stood. "Thank you for breakfast, Dix. I've never had such a marvelous omelet. And that homemade sourdough toast was amazing."

"I'm not sure it's safe for you to go outside," Dix said. "There are at least two really bad actors still unaccounted for."

"We won't go far. I feel like I'm turning into a fungus, just sitting around, eating, then sitting some more." Val patted Lulu's head beneath the cone. "Besides, I have a protector." She patted the back pocket of her jeans. "I'll have my phone, too."

With Lulu happily padding along in her wake, Val headed for the front door. "We won't be gone long," she hollered over her shoulder.

The leash's metal components clinked as Val hooked it to Lulu's collar. The excited tick-tick of Lulu's toenails against the tile entryway floor was followed by the sound of the front door opening then closing.

Dix took another sip of coffee.

Lil studied the toast on her plate then looked up at her sister. "Why must you butter the toast like that?"

"Like what?"

"A single pat plopped down in the middle of the bread." Lil held up the offending slice. "That covers about a square inch but leaves the rest hard as a brick." She tapped a corner of the toast against the table.

"You're supposed to finish spreading it yourself," Dix said. "That's what your butter knife is for." She scowled at her twin. "Or maybe it's that you're too lazy. Shall I peel you a grape?"

"Cute," Lil said. "I would be delighted to finish spreading the butter, but by the time you bring the toast to the table, it's already cold." She stood and headed upstairs. "I'm going to take a shower. I need to wash that warehouse smell off."

The front door opened. Dix scooted her chair back, stood, and started toward the front door.

"That was a short walk," Dix said to the person who she assumed to be Val.

Instead of Val, however, it was SUV-man who stepped through the door.

"Hello, Granny Eyebrows." Holding a pistol leveled at Dix's midsection, the man smiled then licked his lips. He glanced around the kitchen then added, "Where's your sister?"

The sudden, loud, and unmistakable *shhhh-plop-shhhh-plop* of Dix's largest, heaviest Slinky flopping down the wooden stairway took SUV-man off guard. A puzzled look on his face, he momentarily turned toward the sound, allowing Dix the opportunity to disarm him, jerk his arm around behind his back, then drop him to the floor.

By the time the Slinky came to rest on the floor in front of the stairs, Lil was running into the kitchen with her Taser in her right hand.

"Excellent work, Sis," Dix said. "How did you know?"

"I glanced out the window and saw this creep pull into the driveway." Lil growled and pointed the Taser at the man. "Let me at him."

"Just call the police," Dix said. "He's going nowhere."

Chapter Sixty-Five

A few minutes after Kelly pressed the nurse call button, a young woman came into the hospital room and approached the bed.

"Yes?"

"Could I have something for pain?" Kelly said.

"You've already had an injection," the young woman said. "You're not scheduled for another one until…"

The nurse's voice faded into the background as Kelly's glance was drawn to the room's open doorway where a uniformed cop stood staring in at her. Her stomach sank.

So, this was how years of hard work and meticulous planning were going to end. Kelly would be brought up on kidnapping, money laundering, RICO, and who-knew-what other charges. She would be an old woman by the time she got out of prison.

Kelly sighed. Maybe she could…

"Would you call whoever's in charge?" Kelly said to the officer in the doorway. "I'd like to make a statement."

****

When Toad regained consciousness, he was lying on the cold, wet banks of the Rio Grande. His soaked clothes clung to his body, and he shivered as a breeze sent chilling gusts through the fibers. With the loud burble of flowing water in the background, a young man stooped over Toad and pressed a mask against his face. Rhythmically, the young man squeezed the attached bag, thereby forcing oxygen into Toad's lungs.

"Can you tell me what happened?" the young paramedic asked.

Toad wrinkled his brow. What *had* happened? The last thing he remembered was sipping from a cup of coffee Razor bought at a convenience store early that morning—coffee Razor had insisted Toad drink before they went to the car rental agency.

"Coffee…" Toad managed to say, his voice muffled by the mask. "Bad coffee."

"Do you remember falling into the water?" the paramedic said.

Toad shook his head once.

"Is it possible someone pushed you?"

It was only too possible.

"No," Toad lied. "I slipped and fell into the river."

As the paramedic asked more questions, Toad tried to pull up details of what had happened. He remembered fighting to keep from falling asleep, jerking awake when Razor's alarm went off, then watching Razor head into the convenience store for coffee.

After that, nothing.

"Have you taken any drugs recently," the paramedic said. "Do you take prescription drugs?"

"No." Toad sucked in a deep breath of the calming oxygen. "No drugs, no booze, and I didn't jump."

He would call his uncle as soon as he got a chance. Once he reported how Razor had poisoned him, thrown him into the muddy Rio Grande, and left him to drown, there would be no place on earth the jerk could hide.

A sense of pleasant anticipation sent warmth through Toad's body and he relaxed.

A cop approached. "Can we call anyone for you?" he said. "Do you have family nearby?"

"Just my Uncle BeeBee in Los Angeles."

"Last name?"

"LeDuc, BeeBee LeDuc."

Too late, Toad realized his mistake in mentioning his uncle's name. Even though LeDuc's business activities were mostly relegated to California, his name would be known all over the country. Toad had just red-flagged himself, and he had two outstanding warrants for his arrest. Although one was for a traffic violation, the other was for breaking and entering…enough to make the locals investigate him.

Not only would the cops have the bloody strip of denim the monster dog tore from Toad's pants that was covered in his blood, if Razor was right about the Mercury, it would be just a matter of time before the cops connected Toad to Taylor's hit.

Since murder trumped either of his outstanding California warrants, Toad would stand trial in New Mexico. There was no death penalty in California, but what about New Mexico?

Toad shook his head under the mask. He was well and truly screwed.

For real, Booger's voice rang inside Toad's head as if he were standing next to him.

****

Booger sat in his jail cell and studied the splint on his broken finger. In keeping with the counsel of his court-appointed attorney, he had refused to answer questions during his hours-long interrogation. No matter what the cops did to make him talk, he would never betray Toad.

He had decided, however, that next time they questioned him, he would be only too happy to spill what he knew about Razor and Condit. Although he didn't know all the details about their business, what he did know might earn him a few brownie points and get him less jail time. Maybe he would tell the cops about the Rolex Razor stole from him and Toad. Didn't the people who sold that high-dollar brand keep a record of anyone who bought one?

On the bright side, Booger would use the time in prison to sharpen his skills as a mechanic. He heard some prisons even offer college classes to inmates. He would take every class he could, maybe even economics and bookkeeping. By the time he got out, he would be in a good position to open his long-dreamed-of cycle repair shop.

Booger leaned back on his cot. Cradling his head on the pillow in his unbandaged hand, he crossed his legs, and placidly stared up at the ceiling.

****

Having slept only a couple of hours after LeDuc's body was hauled away, Gordo and his roommate relaxed on the boss's sofa and watched the local news on the dead man's ninety-inch, LCD television. Periodically, one of them would make an excited comment about how good life would be once Razor took over the business.

"You and me'll be on easy street," the roommate said. "New blood and a fresh perspective...just what this business needs."

"He'll make some much-needed changes, that's for—" Gordo's words died in his throat when a segment of video scrolled across the screen, accompanied by a young female reporter's voice.

Early this morning, an LA native was arrested in Albuquerque, New Mexico... The rest of the announcer's voice dropped off into white noise as images of a handcuffed man being placed into the back of a cop car flashed on the television.

"Hey," the roommate said, jumping up from his seat, "isn't that Razor?"

"Yeah," Gordo said. "It's him." He sighed, retrieved his phone from the small table beside LeDuc's sofa, then punched the screen and held the device to his ear.

"Who're you calling?" his roommate said.

Gordo held up his hand in a shushing motion.

"Hello," Gordo said into the phone. "I would like to speak to Mr. Diamond. I understand he's hiring." He paused as the person at the other end responded. "Sure, I'll hold."

Chapter Sixty-Six

Dix, Lil, and Val stood around Dillon's hospital bed, concern etched on their faces as they stared at the bandages covering portions of the young man's head and wrapped around his ribcage.

"Are you sure you're okay?" Dix pushed the young man's hair off his forehead.

"I'm fine." Dillon's smile was crooked and his voice raspy. "At least, I will be. The doc says it's just a broken nose and a couple of broken ribs."

"You fared better than Kelly Condit," Lil said. "Her face will never be the same after she smashed into the passenger's side window."

"I have a question," Lil said. "What did Henry's note about coins or tokens mean?"

"It's cryptocurrency-related terminology," Dillon said. "While tokens are limited to a specific project and can be used anywhere, bitcoins can buy tokens, but tokens can't buy—"

"Okie-dokie." Lil held her hand up to stop the flow. "I'll Google it."

Dillon chuckled then grabbed his chest. "Hurts to laugh."

"By the way," Val said. "Thank you for the thumb drives." She teared up. "One of them was a photo album, and the other was a letter from Daddy. Some of the pictures were of my mom and me, and some were of the three of us during summer vacations." Her voice grew thick. "The letter was an oral history of my life from my dad's perspective. I can't thank you enough for saving them."

Dillon blushed bright red and studied the intravenous tube running into his forearm. "I'm sorry I couldn't attend your dad's memorial yesterday."

"Please, don't apologize," Val said. "What you've done is a far better gift to Dad's memory than sitting through a eulogy." She placed a hand on Dillon's arm. "Dad would have liked you."

Dillon's answering smile was so wide his eyes nearly closed.

"I've decided to live in Dad's house, now that I have a job in Albuquerque," Val said.

"That's great news," Dix said.

"Cool," Dillon said.

"Yes, it is." Lil looked pointedly from Val to Dix and back again. "That means you can take the Bantha."

"Dad loved Lulu," Val said, her eyes never moving from Dillon's face. "I'll keep her, but you're welcome to come see her whenever you like."

"You must allow us to dog-sit whenever you're out of town," Dix said.

Lil cleared her throat. "We're going to the cafeteria. Can we bring either of you anything?"

Val and Dillon shook their heads simultaneously then resumed looking into each other's eyes.

Dix and Lil stepped out of the room and headed for the elevator.

"They're perfectly suited to each other, don't you think?" Dix said.

"I suppose so," Lil said. She stopped walking and

tugged on Dix's arm. "I have a confession to make."

"Now?" Dix said.

"Yes, now. I can't go another day without getting this off my chest."

For the next several minutes, Lil poured out the story of her machinations with Billy Oboe to keep Dix's Ex from re-entering their lives.

"Is that all?" Dix said. "I was afraid you were going to tell me Lulu dug up my kale."

Lil's mouth fell open, and she stared at her twin.

Dix chuckled. "I've known about your meeting with my ex for years. I didn't know about Mr. Oboe, but my ex came by my office before leaving town. He said he'd been by the house and that you gave him hell. I gave him the old heave-ho."

"You mean I've been needlessly carrying around a load of guilt all these—"

"And now I have something to tell *you*," Dix said, her face growing somber. "You've asked me for years why I shut down my private practice."

Lil cocked her head but remained silent.

"Do you remember the name Josh Bearden?"

"Vaguely." Lil wrinkled her forehead. "Wasn't he the guy who shot his wife and then dismembered her several years back?"

Dix winced then nodded. "He was my client, but I completely misread him. I really thought we were making progress. All the vibes he gave off during our last couple of sessions led me to believe he finally decided to get out of the toxic relationship he found so intolerable. He never showed the slightest indicators of harming his wife, although I did fear for a while that he might hurt himself."

"You misread one person out of the hundreds you helped over the years," Lil said, "so, you decided to crap-can your private practice, all because of one mentally unhinged person?"

"That wasn't the only reason, but it was the final straw. It was the right choice for me, Lil. The lessons I learned from my experiences in private practice served me well in the classroom. As a professor, my goal was to send my graduate psychology students into their own practices with an understanding that as humans they'll make mistakes. Accepting their mistakes, learning from them, and moving on is as important for the psychologist as it is for their clients."

"Physician, heal thyself." Lil looked thoughtful, then nodded. "So, have you?"

"Have I what?"

"Healed yourself?"

"Almost," Dix said. "I've come to a level of acceptance."

The two resumed walking.

"Regarding your kale," Lil said. "It was actually me that dug it up."

"Ah," Dix said. "Believe it or not, I'm glad to hear it was you."

"That stuff must have been four feet tall. The spikes on the leaves looked like shark's teeth. You could bottle whatever you've been feeding it and we would be rich."

"I was afraid Lulu had been digging in the garden."

"I think the Bantha was as afraid of your kale as I was. Once I got too close, and the thing rubbed a huge, hairy leaf against my leg, like it was tasting me. It reminded me of that movie about the plant spore that came from outer space and ate the postman."

"I thought you didn't believe in extraterrestrial life."

"I don't…I do, however, believe in genetically modified organisms." Lil grinned at her twin.

"The reason my garden does so well is because I talk to my plants, as I would to any other living thing." Dix cocked her head toward her twin. "Plants respond to other life forms."

"Whatever." Lil waved a hand dismissively then turned to her sister. "Over the past several days I've come to a couple of decisions."

"Fire away."

"Never again will I complain about the cost of your martial arts classes."

"Excellent," Dix said. "And?"

"And if gardening makes you happy, go for it." Lil smiled. "As long as you don't plant anything that starts demanding fresh animal-based protein."

"Done," Dix said.

Arm in arm, the sisters sauntered into the cafeteria.

A word about the author...

Olive Balla makes her home near Albuquerque, New Mexico with her husband Victor. When not writing, she can be found in her woodworking shop making sawdust and other fun things.

http://omballa.com

~*~

Previous Books by Olive Balla
An Arm And A Leg
Jillie